Rule Breaker

Rule Breaker

Rule Breaker

SIENNA SNOW

New York Boston

Copyright © 2016 by Sienna Snow
Excerpt from *Book Two* copyright © 2016 by Sienna Snow
Cover copyright © 2016 by Hachette Book Group, Inc.
Hachette Book Group supports the right to free expression and the value of copyright. The purpose of copyright is to encourage writers and artists to produce the creative works that enrich our culture.

The scanning, uploading, and distribution of this book without permission is a theft of the author's intellectual property. If you would like permission to use material from the book (other than for review purposes), please contact permissions@hbgusa.com. Thank you for your support of the author's rights.

Forever Yours
Hachette Book Group
1290 Avenue of the Americas
New York, NY 10104
forever-romance.com
twitter.com/foreverromance

First published as an ebook and as a print on demand: November 2016

Forever Yours is an imprint of Grand Central Publishing. The Forever Yours name and logo are trademarks of Hachette Book Group, Inc.

The publisher is not responsible for websites (or their content) that are not owned by the publisher.

The Hachette Speakers Bureau provides a wide range of authors for speaking events. To find out more, go to www.hachettespeakersbureau.com or call (866) 376-6591.

ISBNs: 978-1-4555-6874-1 (print on demand edition), 978-1-4555-6873-4 (ebook)

To Hitesh, the love of my life. Without you, I'd never have started this journey. You are everything a girl dreams of in a husband. I love you.

To Amanda Carey, for being my first-ever beta reader. Your help was invaluable. You are a true gem.

To Melissa Patel Cole, for being the best sister on the face of the planet and keeping me off the ledge when doubts crept in.

To Mom and Dad, who are never allowed to read the book—your delicate sensibilities couldn't take it. Thank you for cheering me on, even when you had no clue what I was doing.

Last but not least, to my tribe: Mia Hopkins, Ruth Vincent, Susan O'Connell, and Sharon Merrett. You have been on this crazy train with me from the beginning. Thank you so much for not jumping off.

Rule Breaker

Rule Breaker

CHAPTER ONE

Look at me, baby. I want to watch you as you come."

Opening my eyes, I stared into unending depths of green. The love gazing back at me brought tears to my eyes.

He used his thumbs to wipe away the drops and leaned down to kiss me. "You are mine, Arya, never forget that."

My body clenched around him as he slid into me. He moved with agonizing slowness, denying me the orgasm he'd been building up for hours. I lifted my hips, trying to urge him to move a little bit faster. Frustrated, I jerked on my arm restraints and struggled to free myself.

"Please," I begged, "I need to touch you. Release my wrists." The force of his thrusts increased and my body responded with tiny spasms.

Oh yes, right there.

"Not yet, not until your core ripples around me, squeezing every drop from me."

His hand moved between our bodies, toward my swollen,

aching nub. He rubbed back and forth as his pace quickened.

That's it, oh God, almost there.

The burning need inside my body increased to an unbearable level. My hips rose up and down to match every thrust.
The convulsions started.

Yes, at last.

"Arya, can you hear me?"

What?

"Arya, wake up."

Where am I?

Sweat ran down my body as my heart pounded out of control, and my body ached for an orgasm that seemed unattain-
able. I jerked my arms, expecting restraints, but found nothing.
I relaxed back onto the bed.

Only a dream.

"Are you listening? Wake up! They're talking about us on
the news." Milla's excited voice blared into my bedroom.

I rolled over, taking a quick peek at the clock. Four thirty
a.m. Wasn't it against the girl code to wake someone up too
early? Why couldn't Milla let me sleep a little bit longer?

"Did you hear me? We're big news."

"Go away, I don't care," I moaned. "I have ninety more minutes until the alarm goes off. Why are you in my penthouse
anyway? Don't you live across the hall?" Maybe if Milla left, I
could fall back asleep and finish my orgasm.

"Scoot over and listen to the report. There should be more
info right after the commercials."

Nix the extra sleep idea.

"Fine," I grumbled and shifted over, making room for my oh-so-bossy and chipper best friend.

She grabbed the remote from the bedside table and turned on the broadcast. I squinted as the blaring light from the giant TV lit up the room. Why did I put a sixty-inch plasma in my bedroom? The damn thing was too bright. As my eyes adjusted, I took in Milla's appearance. She still wore the plum Valentino suit from last night, but her hair was wet and slicked back into a bun.

"Did you even sleep? When I left, you and Carmen were busy downing shots with the rest of the team. Don't tell me you just got home."

Please have a hangover.

"Okay, I won't. After the party, I went back to Carmen's and spent the night working out last-minute details of the merger. I came home as soon as the statement went out."

Totally unfair. Even during graduate school at MIT, she drank like a sailor and still woke up at the crack of dawn for classes.

"I'm so happy that the three of us are back together. I missed her."

"You and me both. Having our resident dominant around will keep us in line."

"Isn't that the truth?"

We had been known as the three musketeers while at MIT, but I'd pushed her away when my life had fallen apart.

She was living in New York now, and returned to Boston only for the merger. I sighed. I should have reestablished the friendship we'd lost five years ago. She deserved better than my distancing myself from her because of her brother.

Wait. Did Milla say something about a statement?

"What statement?" I pinned Milla with a confused glare.

"Shush, the commercial's over. Listen."

"Breaking business news.

"It's official. MDC won the bidding war for the security technology think tank ArMil Innovations. An undisclosed sum was negotiated, with all parties remaining tight-lipped about exact figures, but analysts estimate it to be in the area of $150 billion. Our sources say negotiations were settled late last night with a celebration following.

"Many of you may recall the buzz surrounding Arya Rey when she hacked MI6's security database after a direct challenge from the chief of the Secret Intelligence Service at the Def Con Conference in Las Vegas. The brainchild she created as a result of the competition, ArMil Innovations, became the highest-valued security technology development company in the world.

"Thirty minutes ago, a joint statement was released by Milla Castra, cofounder of ArMil Innovations, and Carmen Dane, technology CEO of MDC International, through MDC representative Grant Mills.

"'We are proud to announce the joining of ArMil Innovations with MDC International. Together, our companies will harness our unique talents to develop new, innovative, and affordable technologies for all your security needs.'"

I turned my attention back to Milla. "You have been a busy girl this morning. What happened to taking a few days off to unwind and bask in our success? I think this decision requires a poll. I vote for relax. I'm going back to bed." I laid back down and pulled the covers over my head. "Make sure you switch off the television, and close the door when you leave."

Milla ignored my less than subtle hint. "Before we take our well-earned vacation, we need to meet with the new team Carmen assembled." She paused. "Ari, are you sure you're going to be okay with this? It isn't too late to delay the merger, at least until you've had a little more time to adjust. I'm worried about you."

Milla's now somber voice caught me by surprise. I tugged the covers off my head and peered at her. We might not share any blood, but she loved me, and without question, she would fight any of my demons for me.

"I'll be fine, Mil. It's been five years. I survived the darkest days of my life and came out on top. I'm not twenty-three anymore. I can handle it. Besides, he's in charge of the whole organization. He won't bother with us." If only I believed the BS flowing from my mouth.

Ever since Lex Duncan, my other best friend and adviser, suggested selling the business aspect of our company to allow me more time to focus on research, I worried about running into Maxwell Aaron Dane. With our high valuation, Milla, as CFO, only gave the top investment firms the opportunity to bid. But I never expected the highest offer to come from MDC, the conglomerate owned by Carmen and Max's family.

Rejecting any consideration of the proposition due to personal issues with MDC's CEO was not only selfish but also insane. In the end, Milla and I chose the most advantageous course for the future of the company, including the retention of all developmental controls for upcoming and current projects. Now, even if I wished to back out, it was too late. Moreover, I'd spent too much time rebuilding myself to fall again. One day, if Max and I happened to run into each other, I would wish him well and move on.

Great. Now I was lying to myself, too.

"Maybe you're right," Milla agreed. "Carmen is the head of all technology development for MDC. She's not going to let her big brother take over any aspect of the companies she oversees without a fight. Besides, she's aware of your history with Max. She's the one who hid you from him when you left South Africa. She won't let him interfere."

Why did Milla's words seem like a bad omen to me?

I stretched and glanced at the clock. Well, now that going back to bed was off the menu, better hit the treadmill. "Want to join me in the gym? It's too cold for a run outside." I pushed off the mattress and headed for my bathroom.

"No." Milla yawned. "I think I'll catch an hour or so of sleep before we have to meet at corporate. Lex wants us to arrive thirty minutes early in case there are a few surprises. He's always trying to protect his adopted baby sister."

I leaned my head out of the bathroom. "He loves me, but you, on the other hand…" I hummed aloud. "You could put us all out of our misery and jump him already. That way all the sexual tension between you two will end."

Lex and Milla had had an ongoing thing for each other since Milla was in high school, but neither possessed the balls to act upon their feelings. I loved teasing them about it.

"On that note, I'm out of here. Sleep is calling my name."

Milla jumped off the bed and left me to my morning routine before I headed to the gym.

I started my run around five a.m., giving me a few hours before my nine o'clock meeting at corporate. I gazed out toward the beautiful view of Boston's midtown, while Pink blared her "girl power" songs in the background.

I am one lucky lady.

My success seemed surreal at times. Not many twenty-eight-year-olds get to say they went for a run in the home gym of their penthouse on the fifty-fifth floor of Boston's Millennium Tower. I had gone from a physically and emotionally exhausted and financially strained PhD graduate to one of the wealthiest entrepreneurs in the world in less than five years.

"See world, women are tech wizards, too." I fist-pumped into the empty room and caught myself before I fell off the treadmill.

I gave all the credit to Lex and Milla. They supported me when I needed them the most and encouraged me to make my vision a reality. I guessed I owed Max, too. If he hadn't broken me, I wouldn't have achieved any of the things I had accomplished to date.

A few years ago, I would have given up my whole life to please him, putting aside my dreams to fit into his world. I handed him complete control only for him throw it back in my face.

Never again.

I had buried that side of myself. No man would gain that level of trust again.

I tapped the button to run faster. I wanted to sort through my thoughts before the meeting. If only exercise made life easier.

Milla insisted I needed to get laid. Maybe she was right, but I wasn't sure if my equipment worked without BOB, my battery-operated boyfriend. My dreams highlighted my non-existent sex life, and almost orgasming didn't count.

Oh hell, there I went again, back to thinking about Max. Well, I couldn't help it, since he was the sole experience I'd ever had.

Over the years, I went out with a few guys, but none of them gave me what I wanted or needed.

Dominance.

My lack of interest wasn't their fault; I picked men I could dominate, not the other way around. They were the polar opposite of Max. Once or twice, I contemplated starting a sexual relationship, but I'd ended things before we reached first base. One kiss and I lost interest.

"Arya, get off the treadmill. I've been calling you for the past fifteen minutes," Milla shouted from the doorway of the gym.

How long had I been running? I glimpsed at the wall clock. Seven fifteen a.m. Shit. I jumped off the machine and lowered the stereo. "My bad. I left my phone on the bench and with the music so loud I couldn't hear it."

"Don't worry about it. Get moving. There isn't much time."

Man, she was already dressed. Did she even go to sleep?

"What's going on? We aren't due in the office until later in the morning."

"Lex called. He had to reschedule the meeting to eight

o'clock. The MDC teams know we're all leaving town tonight, and they want to meet earlier in case extra time is needed to discuss the final logistics."

"There is no way I'll reach the office by eight o'clock. I haven't even showered yet. With the weather and traffic, I won't make it until at least eight thirty. You head over there and let Lex know I'm running late."

"I don't think so. Remember, he likes to shoot the messenger. I'm not in the mood to deal with his Irish temper."

This thing with those two was now getting on my nerves.

"Fine. Tell him that I'm stuck on a call or something. I'll get there as soon as possible. If he gives you shit, remind him that not everyone has a corporate copter on standby to pick them up for work."

"So speaks the girl with a brand new Maybach and a private jet."

I shot Milla the bird, snagged a water from the cooler, and chugged.

"Mmm," I hummed, as the chilled water slid down my throat and cooled my overheated body from the inside.

"So sad, after making a billion-dollar deal, girl gets lazy and starts running late," Milla remarked with a smirk. "Wait, you're always running late."

I rolled my eyes, rushed past her, and charged straight for my shower. I hoped I'd be only a few minutes late.

CHAPTER TWO

An hour and a half later, James, my driver, pulled onto the driveway leading to ArMil's headquarters. I took my last sip of coffee and collected my papers, stuffing them into my briefcase. The forty-five minutes it took to arrive at the office were occupied fielding numerous calls from reporters, former college friends trying to cash in on ArMil's success, and Kerry, my amazing, but seriously grumpy assistant.

"Ms. Rey, we're almost there. Which entrance should I use?" asked James.

I rolled my eyes at his "Ms. Rey." Even after spending the last four-plus years as my driver/bodyguard/therapist, he refused to call me Arya. He was more than an employee. He was family, my surrogate father in all aspects of the term. That is, if dads came in the form of scary, former Russian assassin types. He would protect me from past demons and any new ones creeping up to spook me.

Nope, not going there right now.

I shook the thought from my mind. "Take me to the main garage. It wouldn't seem very professional for the cofounder of the company to sneak through the private elevators, just to avoid Carmen's MDC employees." Butterflies floated into my stomach. I seized some antacid from my bag and popped it into my mouth.

Why am I anxious all of a sudden?

Perhaps it was the bad omen I sensed when Milla had been talking about Max.

"Everything will be fine, Ms. Rey. Remember you're one meeting away from a week's vacation in Monterey."

I relaxed a bit at the image of unwinding at home with my aunt Elana and eating all her incredible food.

The car stopped by the main lobby entrance in the garage, and an immediate wave of nausea attacked me. I closed my eyes and placed a hand on my stomach.

Breathe, Arya.

"I'll give you a few minutes before I open the door to gather yourself." The man was perceptive beyond measure.

"Thanks." I lifted my gaze and caught him watching me through the rearview mirror. "I better straighten myself up and put on my game face."

"There is nothing to straighten. You look sharp today. Take a moment, and let me know when you are ready." He opened the door and stepped out of the car.

I opened my compact to check my makeup. Large hazel eyes accented perfectly with the correct shades of shadows stared back at me. My brown hair remained tucked into a loose bun, and my olive skin appeared flawless.

Wow, the hair and makeup lessons Milla drilled into me worked. No one would guess a minimalistic half-Indian computer nerd who loved ponytails, soft linen pants, and cozy sweaters hid under there. With the right hair, makeup, and attitude, Milla had converted me into a tough-as-nails entrepreneur prepped to take over a male-dominated world.

I finished my final check and knocked on the window, telling James I was ready. The second he opened the door, a waiting Kerry handed me a phone.

"Milla has called three times. She says it's urgent, and you need to get upstairs, ASAP."

What could she be freaking out about? I was only about thirty minutes late. I peeked at my wristwatch. Oops, make that forty-five.

I grabbed the phone and dialed. "Hey Mil, what's up? I'm walking into the building." I rushed through the doors and headed to the elevator Kerry had waiting for me.

"Arya, what's the point of having a cell phone if you never keep it on?"

"I placed it on silent when I got tired of all the calls from reporters. What's the big fire?"

"Arya, you need to be prepared. There are a few developments with the merger. I can't say much more but stay calm. I have to go," Milla whispered into the phone.

Leave it to Mil to sound cryptic and then hang up.

"What's going on, Kerry?" I questioned.

"From what I understand, there were more people at the meeting than anticipated. I only saw our crew and Ms. Dane with a few of her colleagues. We expected other new team members, but they hadn't arrived. However, Ms. Dane did seem quite agitated. I'm not used to seeing her simmering."

Carmen simmering? She was the most poised woman I'd ever met. Something big was up if both Milla and Carmen were upset.

Lucky for them, the ice queen has arrived to save the day.

I hated the nickname the media had given me, but keeping my emotions out of business had helped me succeed. How else would I have survived the aftermath of South Africa without pretending I didn't feel anything?

The elevator dinged, and I rushed out. It was too late to worry now. I walked toward the conference room door and stopped. The smell I'd never forget lingered in the air: spiced cologne, crisp linen, and soap. My heart clenched. Five years of separation, and I still recognized his scent.

Oh God, he wouldn't dare.

Milla and her bad omens. My hand trembled as I clutched the strap of my bag and the other steadied my stomach. Maybe I should turn around and head to my office. I shook the possibility from my head. *Never show weakness.* I wasn't the vulnerable woman I used to be.

"Arya, are you okay? Your face is pale. Do you want me to get you anything? Water?"

Kerry's words snapped me out of my stupor. "I'm fine, Kerry, don't worry. Let me take a moment before I give up official control of my baby to someone else," I lied.

I took a deep breath, opened the door, and entered the filled conference room. The tension bombarding me was thick enough to cut. Milla's worried expression and Lex's angry one spoke volumes.

I smiled at Carmen and the few members of her team I recognized and moved toward Milla and Lex. I couldn't bring myself to look at the other end of the table. My skin prickled. His presence overpowered the room.

Get yourself together, girl.

Maybe if I ignored him, I wouldn't have to acknowledge his existence.

"I apologize for the delay. Please continue," I announced in my most professional voice.

Remember to fake it until you make it.

Lex gestured to the seat next to him. "Arya, we decided to wait for you to begin. Ms. Dane has informed us of a few changes to our original plan. Due to other project commitments she will be stepping aside, and Mr. Dane will be replacing her."

What? Without a second thought, I glanced at the other end of the table as I sat down. Emerald eyes stared back at me. Damn him and those eyes. My heart pounded as if it would explode out of my chest.

Stay calm, Arya.

Lex moved his hand to my back, trying to give me comfort.

The last time I'd gazed into that face was through tears. I was in South Africa on a service trip to transport technology to female-run communities, and Max was there working through his own private demons, including the murder of his father. Today, at thirty, he looked almost the same, just a bit harder and more enchanting.

"I don't believe that would be the best course of action given the transition plan we worked with Ms. Dane for the past two months to create. She's an integral part of our strategy and implementation," I interjected without my voice quivering.

Max smiled and held my gaze. "I'm sorry to disappoint you, Ms. Rey, but Carmen departs for Europe this afternoon. That leaves me as your only option. I'm confident you and your team can get me up to speed in no time."

I bet the cocky bastard planned this from the beginning. Why would he do this?

I ignored his challenge and turned toward Lex. "Is it possible to place the merger on hold until these new circumstances are ironed out? I want to make sure these surprise changes aren't a regular occurrence. Besides, I'm not sure Mr. Dane possesses the stamina or the time to understand the nuances of the technical aspect of this transition." Man, I sounded seriously bitchy.

Lex seemed surprised by my remarks as well. He shook his head, but before he could speak, Max interjected, bringing my attention back to him.

"Ms. Rey, as I'm sure Mr. Duncan, your head legal counsel and adviser, will inform you, there is no placing anything on hold. We signed and executed the contracts yesterday. You're stuck with me for the long term." Another smile touched his lips as he scanned my face and quirked a brow. "I promise to be your number one student and study everything you require me to learn."

My breath hitched. I'd said those exact words during our first night together many years ago.

Damn, he'd backed me into a corner. If I continued arguing, everyone would see my personal issues with him. Fine. If he wanted a crash course, he was getting one.

"Well, Mr. Dane, if we're to be stuck with you, as you've said, then welcome and get ready to catapult into the world of security-technology development. Don't expect much sleep over the next few weeks." I smirked.

Before he could respond, I delineated all the transition specifics in as much technical detail as possible.

Five hours after the meeting began, I escaped to my office for a few moments of quiet. I threw my jacket on the sofa, unpinned my bun, letting my hair cascade down, and kicked off my heels as I stepped onto my soft pink silk rug. Walking to the oversized windows with views of the city, I leaned my head against the cold glass. I'd accomplished so much in the past few years, but a few hours in Max's company turned me back into an unsure and uncertain twenty-three-year-old.

I closed my lids and attempted to hold back tears. Why hadn't I gone with my first instinct and rejected the offer?

Because you're a moron.

No matter what Lex or my legal team told me, my gut had screamed there was a catch. No company offered a deal this accommodating. Now here I was, back with the object of all my fantasies and the source of all my pain on a day-to-day basis.

I slid my hand down to my stomach as the agony of loss filled me. I opened my eyes at the sound of the wind picking up and the snow falling in sheets. Desiring a little warmth, I wrapped my arms around myself and rubbed the chill from my shoulders. At least in a few hours I'd be back in California with my aunt.

A knock sounded on my door, and I turned around. My breath hitched when I saw Max leaned against the frame inspecting me.

In five years he'd grown more handsome. Chocolate-brown hair, tanned skin, and piercing green eyes accented his impeccably chiseled face. His lean and honed six-foot-two physique filled out his tailor-made suit to perfection. Tabloid pictures didn't do him justice. His minimally spiced cologne and his natural crisp scent infused the room, making my knees weak. I bit back a moan as I remember the way he'd smile when I'd sniff his neck every morning after his shower. A time when I held nothing back from anyone.

"Ahh, there's the Arya I used to know and still crave," Max crooned as he strolled into my office. "The all-business, polished, and cold Ms. Rey doesn't suit you."

"A lot has changed in the past five years, Mr. Dane." I couldn't keep the panic out of my voice. Why was his sheer presence so unnerving?

Max quietly approached me next to the window. I continued watching him and waited for him to break the silence. His commanding and authoritative aura wrapped itself around me as I resisted the compulsion to lower my head and wait for his command. I couldn't be near him right now. Years of building myself up, and within a few hours in his company, I was ready to throw everything away.

His expression remained completely unreadable as he studied my face. Then he reached up and did something I wasn't expecting: He ran his fingers along my jaw and over my mouth.

I inhaled sharply, taking in his intoxicating scent, and forced back the desire to lick my lips. A brush of need scorched across my skin, and goose bumps appeared in its wake. His slightest touch aroused every sense in my body, and I prayed he hadn't detected my reaction. But of course, he noticed.

"You're as beautiful as ever, Arya. However, I prefer you with little or no makeup. It's obvious Milla has gotten her hands on you."

I stepped back, a little offended, though not sure by what—his words or my response to them. I calmly walked over to my desk and sat, the heat from his touch still lingering on my face.

I still wanted him. Dammit.

I picked up a report Kerry had left me and attempted indifference to his presence.

"It won't work with me." Max sauntered across the room and took the chair opposite my desk.

I leaned forward and glared. "What is that supposed to mean?"

A dark brow arched, and his mouth relaxed into a grin.

Damn that smile. It made him appear years younger and breathtaking. Memories of what those lips had done to me flooded my system. My pulse accelerated, and my already sensitive nipples strained against my blouse.

He leaned back into the chair. "The ice queen routine you've been playing. I'll admit you fooled me. During the meeting, you handled my presence with complete and cold disinterest. Your reports and diction were methodological. You epitomized the picture of a ruthless tech mogul, the same image that leaves the tabloids and business analysts confused as to how you inspire unparalleled devotion and loyalty. Then toward the end of the meeting, when you called Carmen's assistant aside and gave her a birthday present for her daughter, I recognized it as an act."

Shit. No one was supposed to see that.

"Believe what you want, Mr. Dane." I held his gaze. "We all change, some more than others. Aren't you the one who once said, 'We are the sum of all our life's experiences'? I am the ice queen, as you said, due to mine."

I pushed back from the table and moved to lean against the front of my desk. "Out of curiosity, how long have you planned on taking over Carmen's role in this merger? I find it more than a small coincidence that you're available to oversee a one hundred and fifty billion dollar deal your sister spent over six months negotiating?"

Carmen wouldn't betray me, would she?

"This plan was in the making for over five years, Arya. We have some unfinished business to resolve. If orchestrating the merger of our companies was the only way to do it, so be it. I've done nothing to undermine the future of either organization.

"So you know, Carmen never knew of my plans. She only found out a few days ago, and by then there was nothing she could do to change the direction of what I'd set in motion. She has never forgiven me for the situation in Cape Town. For a while, I thought I'd lost the trust of my sister, as I'd lost Lex's friendship. She's always loved you, even when you distanced yourself from her."

For a brief moment, I closed my eyes at his words. Trust him not to lie. He never pulled punches before, so why would he start now? An overwhelming desire to smack him coursed through me. I needed to get away before I started screaming.

"Well, if we're finished with this lovely conversation, I must ask you to leave. I'm already late for my flight. I will see you and your team in a week."

Max stood, not saying anything, and walked toward the door. I followed and waited for him to exit. He abruptly stopped and pivoted. "Say hello to your aunt for me."

"How do you know where I'm going?"

He took a strand of my hair and twirled it around his finger. "Oh Arya, I know more than you believe. If you hadn't spent the last five years hiding from me, using your pit bulls to keep me away, we would be in an entirely different situation right now."

He tried to get in touch with me? What did he mean by "pit bulls"?

"Okay, I'll bite. Where would we be?"

If he didn't stop touching me, I'd lose all of my composure. I pushed his hand away from my hair, but he caught my wrist instead. "We'd be married and making love every day with a few children in tow. I made the worst mistake of my life by letting you go. I won't make the same mistake again."

CHAPTER THREE

Ms. Rey, it's time to wake up. We are approaching your aunt Elana's house."

I wasn't aware I had fallen asleep until James called my name. I surveyed my surroundings as I gained my bearings. *Wow, what a quick sixty minutes from the airport.* I still felt groggy and needed more time to power back up after such an exhausting trip.

Nine hours after my scheduled arrival, I finally reached Monterey. Hazardous weather due to an unexpected heavy snowstorm caused severe delays for all aircraft out of Boston's Logan International. The airlines canceled most commercial flights, leaving stranded passengers everywhere.

Agreeing to a last-minute strategy meeting for a new billion-dollar security software I was developing for the government didn't help the situation. Plus, it wouldn't have looked good telling a top government official that I couldn't talk shop because I was worried about the storm and the possibility of the airport shutting down.

Lucky for me, Lex and Milla had convinced me to buy a private jet, and my flight was delayed only until ground crew de-iced the runways and reopened.

I sat up in the back of the limo and attempted to press the wrinkles out of my clothes. No use; the folds were set. Oh well, I planned to change into pajamas as soon as I arrived home anyway.

Finally, Aunt Elana's house came into view. The beautiful two-story stone and stucco house with Spanish tiles was majestic, surrounded by gardens and views of the ocean from almost every window.

Growing up, neither Aunt Elana nor I ever conceptualized a house on the beach hovering in our future, let alone a thirty-thousand-square-foot mansion on Pebble Beach's exclusive 17 Mile Drive. I bought the property for Aunt Elana after Milla and I "officially" made it big. It was the least I could do to repay everything she sacrificed for me.

I sighed and then giggled. "Almost there. I feel like a kid who can't wait to get home. Isn't it crazy how much we've accomplished in five years?"

James glanced at me through the rearview mirror with a slight grin. "It's been a privilege being on this journey with you. Plus having my own little house on the property is an added bonus."

"How else could I get you to keep up your tough adamantine appearance while having a scorching hot love affair with my aunt?"

James visibly reddened.

"I'm teasing. You and Aunt Elana deserve a little happiness, even if I don't understand all the secrecy."

"It isn't proper, Ms. Rey. We are from two different classes. Your aunt deserves so much better, but she chose me."

"Aunt El couldn't care less what others think. We didn't come from the upper crust, you know."

"I am well aware of that. Nevertheless, the situation is complicated."

I growled inside. Superfrustrating couples surrounded me. Between Lex, Milla, Aunt Elana, and James, the urge to yank out my hair would leave me bald.

"James, I'm only saying this because I love both of you. Aunt Elana doesn't care about your past. It doesn't matter whether you were a mobster in your youth or a trash collector as long as you love her."

"I have never doubted your aunt's feelings for me. I hope to one day be worthy of them. Maybe soon I will be. Why don't you put on your shoes? We will be at the front door soon and your aunt will be eager to see you."

Nice change of subject.

I hiccupped a little in anticipation of seeing Aunt Elana, the only person who ever loved me unconditionally. It never mattered that we didn't share one ounce of blood; I was her child, and that was it.

James had barely pulled into the driveway when Aunt Elana ran out the front toward us. Man, the woman never aged; she was as gorgeous as ever, with luxurious black hair and flawless honey-gold skin, accented by rich chestnut eyes.

Excited to be home, I opened the door and jumped out.

"Oh, *meree bachchee* is home. Come here, sweetheart." She spread her arms, and I couldn't help but rush into her waiting embrace. Her soft jasmine scent enveloped me, making it easy to allow a little emotion free.

"I missed you so much." I held her tightly and let a few tears fall on her shoulder.

She stepped back and gave me a concerned look. "Now what's this? It hasn't been that long since you were home. Come on. Let's get you inside. First food, then once we're alone, I want to know who I have to smack for making you sad." She gestured toward the pool house as the sound of laughter floated into the air. "I think Carmen and Milla are half drunk." We climbed the stairs into the house.

"Huh? I thought Carmen left for Europe today, and Milla wasn't arriving until tomorrow."

"I'm not sure of all the details, but Milla and Lex had another argument, and she decided to abandon him and come tonight. As for Carmen, she found someone else to take over her project. Milla and I thought it would be nice if you and Carmen got to know each other again, without the distraction of the past."

I scowled. I knew she meant well, but I was already working on mending my relationship with Carmen. I didn't need any added help.

"Don't glare at me like that, young lady." Aunt El reprimanded as she guided me toward the kitchen. "Carmen isn't to blame for what happened with Maxwell. You were the best of friends during school, and you both could use someone with similar losses."

I flinched as guilt filled me. How could I have forgotten what Carmen went through over the past three years? Her fiancé died amid a hostage situation in South Africa at the education foundation she had founded. A month later, she lost the baby she had been carrying. For more than a year, no one heard from her or saw her. When she got word of our request for bids, she was the first to approach us and worked with us to settle the deal.

I missed our friendship. Milla was the rebel Italian shipping heiress; Carmen, the poised American socialite; and me, the Indian computer nerd. The three of us balanced each other.

"How long have they been here?" I asked.

"About five hours. They caught their flights right before the storm positioned itself over Boston. Why didn't you come earlier?"

"I took a last-minute meeting and I had to clear up a few complications we encountered with the merger." I left it at that. This wasn't the time to divulge all my issues, and I hoped Milla had kept her mouth shut.

"Milla mentioned something about transition hitches, and you sorted them all out. You must be exhausted. Take a seat, *priya*, my love." She gestured toward one of the bar stools near the giant island in the kitchen. "I'll get you a strong cocktail and feed you before you pass out." She made me a plate of Indian food, not caring if I wanted to eat or not. Got to love her—a stiff drink and a large helping of food, and all was well in the world.

I woke early the next morning and headed toward the beach bungalow below the cliffs of the main house. The crisp air of the ocean and the morning solitude helped untangle my thoughts. I leaned back on my deck chair, enjoying the morning cold, bundled under a thick blanket and wrapped in my favorite sweater. Over the horizon, the seals dived for breakfast near the Point Sur Lightstation.

The animals had such a carefree life, going where they wanted and eating what they wanted, without a worry in the world. Well, besides the sharks, whales, and poachers.

On second thought, I don't have anything to complain about.

I continued to stare out at the ocean and drifted into a light doze.

"Wake up, baby, let's go for a run."

I woke from my nap and gazed into eyes the color of dark forest pools. Max slowly came into focus, bare chested, with ropes of contoured muscle trailing down his stomach and leading to a V that hid beneath his gray running shorts. He sat back a little and helped me up.

"What are you doing here?" I asked.

He gave me a knowing grin and tucked my hair back behind my ear. "After last night, I didn't think you'd be up early, but when I woke, you were already down by the beach. So I thought we'd go for a run before we leave for Boston."

He took my hands in his and examined my wrists; faint red marks ran across them. "I'm sorry. Why didn't you tell me they were tight?"

My cheeks heated and I cupped the side of his face. "They weren't tight. It was all my doing. I was pulling too hard."

His expression remained serious. "I don't like knowing I was too carried away to recognize you were hurting yourself."

"Do you think I wouldn't say stop if anything we did became too much? I enjoyed it. I love giving you control."

"I love you, Arya. I don't ever want to hurt you again." Max nuzzled my cupped hand.

"I love you, too. Come here." I tugged him toward me and captured his lips, savoring his clean, fresh taste.

His hand ran up the back of my spine and into my hair as he deepened our embrace. All sense of time evaporated as heat and lust filled my body. My mind slowly transformed to mush. He pulled my bottom lip into his mouth and leaned back. With a wicked grin, he lowered me onto the beach recliner. Oh, I knew where this led…

Milla jostled my lounger with her foot, startling me awake. "Arya, wake up. I brought you some chai," she shouted and sat on the deck chair.

Damn, another dream.

"What do you dream about that gives you such an *I totally got laid* face? Never mind. I don't want to know."

"My guess would be the annoying boy I had the pleasure of sharing the womb with." Carmen's cheery voice sounded from behind me. She ignored my scowl and stretched out on the deck chair next to me.

"Ari, I'm so sorry about what happened. I had no idea Max was going to pull this shit. He never hid that he wanted to win you back, but I didn't think he'd steamroll me to do it." She rubbed her temples, as if willing a headache away. "I am so pissed right now I could punch him."

The hurt in her voice accentuated her words. Carmen rarely showed her emotions, so I knew her anger was genuine.

"To be honest, I did have a moment where I thought you tricked me, but then I remembered all you did to keep Max away from me after our breakup, and I knew you weren't involved."

She gave me a weary smile. "Now I have to spend the next two months in Germany instead of with you girls."

"Is there any way out of it?" Milla asked as she handed me my chai.

Carmen shook her head. "The board requested I oversee the negotiations." She turned back to me. "Am I forgiven?"

"You did nothing wrong. I'm the one who should apologize for doubting you."

"Apology accepted. Now let's leave all that crap in the past and get on with our weekend. We have to make up for lost time."

"God, I love California weather. I can't believe I'm sitting on the beach in the middle of January with only a light sweater on." Carmen relaxed into her lounger and tilted her face to the sun.

Milla crawled off her chair and scooted in next to me on mine. "Why'd you bail on us last night? Aunt Elana said you were tired but then in passing, she mentioned she needed to find out why you were crying." She pulled my blanket over her and then tucked it around both of us.

"Spill it," Carmen said from under her own covers.

"Well..." How do I talk about someone's brother to her face?

Carmen read my mind. "I realize it's weird talking to me about my brother, but I'm okay with it. I understand why you distanced yourself, but I want to reconnect. You have to admit the three of us were thick as thieves before Max fucked up and ruined everything."

She had a point. I couldn't keep Carmen at arm's length when we both needed someone who understood surviving. Opening up was the first stage to reconciling our friendship, but how would I begin?

I opened my mouth, but before I could say a word, Milla spoke. "Carmen, there are things about the past you don't know. What you saw happen was the mere tip of what Arya faced."

Carmen sat up. "What do you mean?"

I took another breath, trying to figure out where to begin. I'd never talked about it. Only Milla, Lex, and Aunt Elana knew the full details.

Milla put a hand around my shoulder. "I'm going to give you my version. If Arya wants to add more, she will."

A sense of relief washed over me. I could listen to the story, but telling it was questionable.

"Is it that bad?"

I nodded.

"The day Max ended their relationship, Arya found out she was pregnant."

CHAPTER FOUR

W hat?" Carmen couldn't hide her surprise. Her bright green eyes, the exact shade as her brother's, shone with worry and confusion.

"From what Arya told me and Lex, Max never knew. He ended their relationship before she could tell him."

"Oh my God. That's why Lex and Max got into that fight. He beat the shit out of my brother. I thought it was because he broke your heart, Arya. I assumed Lex was in love with you, and you loved Max."

When had all that gone down? I glared at Milla, who feigned innocence by shrugging her shoulders.

"Lex is definitely not in love with me," I blurted out. That role belonged to the stupid girl next to me.

"I'm guessing something else happened, since I don't have a niece or nephew running around."

I closed my eyes and leaned back against the chair. I hated this part.

"Arya decided to keep her pregnancy a secret. Since Max didn't want her, she was determined to raise her girls on her own."

"Girls?" Carmen took hold of my hands, but I kept my eyes squeezed tight.

Please Milla; finish the story so I don't have to relive it in slow motion.

"She was pregnant with twins. During her sixth month, she went back to Cape Town to check on the women's initiative she started. Arya was abducted the moment Lex's plane landed. We never figured out who orchestrated the kidnapping, but we assume someone found out she was pregnant and thought to use it against her or Max. It wasn't a big secret back then that Max and Arya had been seeing each other."

"But Max never got any word of a kidnapping or ransom request," Carmen said, her voice quivering.

"They never got a chance." Milla's tone grew somber. "The kidnappers were actually hired to get rid of Arya, but they decided to cut the babies from her instead, thinking to ransom the girls."

The thought of how my girls suffered made me want to curl into a tiny little ball and disappear. Even with Milla relaying the story, the pain resurfaced, fresh and unbearable.

Carmen gasped. "I remember hearing about a pregnant volunteer who was kidnapped for her babies. But the reports said they left the volunteer for dead and killed the children by accident during the forced removal. How did they keep your name out of the stories?"

"Lex, that's who," Milla answered. "That man has connections everywhere. Being the genius grandson of a former Irish gangster has its privileges."

Carmen released my hand and sat on the end of my lawn chair. "But that doesn't make sense. Max has the same connections Lex does. When Max learned of the abduction, he tried everything to find the volunteer. He felt responsible for the kidnapping, since he hadn't provided adequate security for the project."

She covered her face with her palms and then glared at Milla. "How the hell did Lex convince the authorities you were a simple aid volunteer? Especially when they wouldn't budge on information, no matter how much money Max threw at them."

I finally felt able to speak. "Let's just say Lex has a few less than reputable resources at his disposal." I used the back of my sleeve to wipe away the tears running down my face. I hadn't cried for my girls in months, and now I'd done it twice within forty-eight hours.

Damn Max and his fucking with the emotions I'd buried. Oh no, what if Carmen tells him? "Carmen, I need you to promise me you won't say anything."

"He needs—"

"No," I interrupted. "If the time comes, I will tell him, no one else. It's taken five years, and I've barely recovered. I'm not prepared to open freshly healed wounds."

"I understand. I won't say anything," Carmen whispered and wiped away her own tears. "Maybe one day I'll get there, too." She moved closer and gathered me into a hug. A sense of relief washed over me as her warmth flowed into me. I never thought talking about the past would help ease the pain. But then again, she understood my loss better than anyone else I knew.

The sound of Aunt Elana's shoes interrupted our emotional discussion. Carmen scooted back to her seat and wearily smiled as Aunt Elana approached.

"What are you three talking about?" Her brow creased. "From the looks of it, I'd say it's something too serious for a day like this."

Aunt Elana came around my chair and sat across from me next to Carmen. She quietly searched all our faces using her *I already know what you were talking about* scan, then lifted her own cup of chai and sipped. "So what are your plans for the day? I suggest the three of you relax and enjoy the heated pool. Then, when you have transformed into prunes, come join me in the kitchen for some drinks and breakfast."

I giggled. The woman never stopped talking about feeding us, someone, anyone.

"Don't make fun of me, young lady. The three of you need meat on your bones. Men don't like stick figures. They need curves to hold on to."

"Aunt El, I'm Italian. God blessed me with more curves than should be legal." Milla pointed to me with a wicked grin. "This one, on the other hand, could use a few more pounds on her ass."

I gasped, pretending to be offended and stuck my tongue out at her. "I can't help that my Indian genes keep me from having an amazing booty like yours."

"Speak for yourself, young lady. My Indian ass is perfect the way it is." Aunt Elana touched her butt and made a sizzling sound.

I shook my head at her. I loved this woman. No one enjoyed life the way she did.

"Can I be like you when I grow up? An ageless and sexy goddess with a hot Russian gangster as my boyfriend?" Milla quirked her brows and sipped her chai.

I peeked over my aunt's shoulder and saw James's face redden.

"You watch, young lady. You have your own Irish gangster to handle. Karma's a bitch."

My eyes widened. She rarely cussed. "You said a bad word."

"Maybe you girls are rubbing off on me. Especially you, Arya. I taught you appropriate vocabulary, but you somehow learned words I've never ever used. Must be your influence." She gestured to Milla and Carmen. "Not you, Carmen. You are a very proper young lady. Mil, for an Italian aristocrat, you could put a sailor to shame.

I burst out laughing and pointed. "She's got you there, *priya*."

"Whatever. Who taught me to cuss in Hindi? You learned that from somewhere."

She had a point. My aunt would have kicked my ass if I said anything inappropriate. New worlds opened when I learned swear words in my native language.

"Now, now, girls. Behave."

"Excuse me, Mrs. Rey." We all rotated in the direction of my aunt's butler. "You have a phone call."

"Thank you, Andrew." She took the phone and walked toward the balcony overlooking the water.

"Whoever that was, she didn't want us eavesdropping. That could only mean it's Walter."

Milla pulled me back against the lounger and glared at me. "Is that asshole still harassing you?"

I shook my head. "Not since he lost his lawsuit against me." I listened intently, trying to hear even a small snippet of the conversation taking place on the phone.

On what planet does a grandfather sue his own grand-daughter for her inheritance? On Walter's planet, that's whose. I couldn't believe he thought by threatening to take my inheritance I'd walk away from my aunt, the only woman who loved me, for a cushy job in his company.

He hadn't learned from the mistakes he made with my mother. He'd disowned his only child for marrying my father and fired her from the company that he'd groomed her to run. One day soon, I planned to get back what should have been my mother's.

Aunt Elana paced back and forth and waved her hands as she spoke into the receiver.

"I wouldn't put it past him to harass her as a means of get-ting what he wants," voiced Carmen.

"Let me scoot a little closer and then we can hear better," Milla suggested.

In normal circumstances, I'd have objected, but Aunt Elana was upset. "Okay, but don't let her notice."

The three of us moved one lounger within listening distance of my aunt's side of the conversation.

"Are you out of your mind? No, you ignorant old man, I will not put her on the phone. Why won't you leave her alone?"

She smacked her hand against the wooden railing. "That girl has more brains in her little finger than you possess in your entire head. She doesn't need any help from you with her merger. You—"

Walter must have cut her off with another tirade. Aunt Elana ran her palm across her face in exasperation, pressing her fingers to her forehead.

This was not good; whenever she reacted that way, it meant she was about to lose her normal calm, level-headed demeanor. "Let me stop you right there, Walter. Never, ever, question my intelligence." She exhaled a deep breath. "I will tell you this only once. That girl is mine. You may share genetics with her, but you abandoned her. I may not have raised her to your standards, but she turned out amazing.

"Your anger forced your wife to sacrifice any open relationship she could have had with her granddaughter, and now, even in death, you won't give the poor woman peace. You can pretend Arya doesn't have any pedigree, but that girl has more class than you have ever possessed— No, I will not upset my daughter. Did you hear that? *My daughter.*"

She ended the call and slammed the receiver against the nearby table. At that moment, her gaze focused on me and tears rimmed both our eyes.

"*Main aapase pyaar karatee hoon maan.*" I love you, Mom.

Walking to me, she kissed my forehead and whispered, "*Mai bhee aap se pyaar karthee hoon.*" I love you too.

Then Aunt Elana turned to the others. "Ladies, I think I will return to the house." She blew all of us a weary kiss. "Don't stay out here too long." Her footsteps echoed as she left us alone.

"That pompous, ignorant geezer has gone too far. I feel like taking a flight back to the East Coast to kick his ass," Milla exclaimed.

Ignoring her, I moved to the spot Aunt El vacated. "I'm never going to fit in, am I? It doesn't matter how much money I have or how refined I behave, I'm always going to be that half-foreign interloper."

"Stop letting Walter's antics get to you," Carmen interjected. "Ever since I met you, you have allowed him to make you feel unworthy. Those are his issues, not yours."

Carmen spoke the truth, but it was difficult to accept that my only connection to my mother would never love me.

"Besides," Carmen continued, "you fit better into the world of the elite than either Milla or I ever could, and we were born into it. I've never seen anyone wrap even the dodgiest of society's elite around their finger as you do. Don't let that bitter man affect you like this."

"She's right, Ari. People love you, not because of your money, but because of the way you treat them."

I kept my head down, watching the surf hit against the pier. Milla's arm crept down my back and around my waist, followed by Carmen's from the other side. They both leaned their heads against my shoulders.

"We're here for you, baby girl." Carmen took my hand and squeezed it.

"This is the way it was supposed to be, the three of us against the world."

Milla's words caused my heart to clench. The guilt of abandoning Carmen weighed heavy on my conscience. "I'm sorry I pushed you away, Carm. You deserved an explanation. Because of me, you lost Milla, too. We should have been there for you."

Carmen pulled back from our embrace. "Even though it hurt, I never held you responsible. I actually placed the entire fault on Max. We barely spoke for over a year. I blamed him and his stupid ego for the loss of my two closest friends. I'm not trying to embarrass you, but I knew about the type of relationship you had with him."

"But how?" I bit my lip. I thought Milla was the only one aware of the extent my relationship with Max.

"He's my twin, Arya. We've known each other's secrets from the time we were young, including the types of kinks we practiced. That's why I was so angry with him. What he did to you broke a very sacred trust."

"I feel a little weird right now. I must have done a lousy job of keeping the nontraditional aspect of my relationship under wraps."

"Don't worry about it. Honestly, I couldn't believe my nerdy, little virgin best friend would be open to exploring kink."

I laughed and felt my cheeks burn.

Was I that naïve about sex?

"Okay girls," Milla interrupted. "Enough with the sex talk. My innocent ears can't take it."

I rolled my eyes. Milla's adventures in kink put mine to shame, and Carmen wasn't innocent, either. Under her gentle and demure exterior sat a feisty Domme who loved to take charge.

Hooray, no more serious talk.

"So what's the plan for tonight? Carmen, are you up for a trip into San Fran?" I asked.

"Sure, after these past few weeks, I could let off some steam with a night on the town. Do you know any hot guys who can join us?"

"Of course. I'll make a few calls and set it up. Be prepared. Milla and I are going to show you how we smart Cali girls party."

CHAPTER FIVE

Dressed in our sexiest clothes, Carmen, Milla, and I strolled to the entrance of Saba, the new club Milla and I had secretly invested in. Located in San Francisco's SoMa district, it had a twenty-five-and-older clientele and was perfect for club hoppers.

"Ms. Rey, Ms. Castra. It's good to see you two again." A handsome, burly bouncer approached us. He leaned down to give both of us a hug. "It's nice to know you girls remembered us little people in the world."

"There is nothing little about you, George. I don't even come close to your elbow," I joked and got a tighter squeeze in response.

"We missed you. The only time I get a glimpse of both of you is on TV or in the newspapers. The pictures in the paper don't do you any justice." He gestured toward Carmen. "Who might this be?"

"George, this is Carmen Dane. A good friend of ours. We

thought she needed a peek at what San Francisco nightlife is all about." I smiled at him. "James is parking. Be nice for me, will you?"

George snorted. "That old man can take care of himself. Don't worry, I'll send him to his usual perch at the top of the club."

I rolled my eyes. George liked to tease that James was my hawk, watching and ready to strike his prey if anyone came too close to his charge.

"Why do you have a Russian geezer like him around when you could have all this gorgeous chocolate looking after your person?" He rubbed his chest, emphasizing his brawny form.

"Because you're too pretty and a complete distraction. I wouldn't be able to keep my hands off you." I stood on tiptoes and kissed him on the cheek. At six foot eight and 280 pounds, George looked like a scary bouncer, but in reality he was all mush and a perfect teddy bear.

"Is Thomas here?"

George gestured inside. "He's waiting for you at your usual table. Go on in." He removed the red rope blocking the entrance and let us pass.

"You girls head up. I need to go check on something," Milla mumbled as she walked toward the offices of the club.

"Work, work, work. All work and no play makes Milla a boring girl," I called.

Yeah, I'm one to talk.

Milla flipped me off and kept walking.

"Arya, I had no idea you were such a flirt. George is totally in love with you," Carmen commented, as we headed to our table on the second story of the club.

I laughed. "George has eyes only for his partner of ten years. He flirts to keep everyone guessing. Besides, his lover's over there." I gestured toward Marco, the slim Latin-model-looking person managing the bar. "He would slit my throat if I tried to convert George over to the straight side of life."

"Wow, everyone working here is hot," Carmen exclaimed.

"I hope you include me in that statement." A deep voice stated from behind us.

I twirled and hugged the man carrying the sexy baritone. "Thomas. I missed you."

He picked me up in a loving, brotherly embrace. Why couldn't I have fallen in love with a person like him? He was smart, gorgeous, and sexy as hell.

"When are you coming back to Boston?"

I had met Thomas as an undergrad at Stanford. A few years ago, when he and a group of other Cali kids wanted to break into the nightlife industry, they offered me and Milla an opportunity to invest. We thought, *Why not?* and decided to take the plunge. Now, ten clubs later, we were major stakeholders in some of the top clubs in the world. Thomas managed all the venues and kept our association silent.

Milla and I already didn't fit the stereotype of the dotcom executives, and we didn't need any extra scrutiny of our personal investments while trying to broker IT deals. Besides clubs, Thomas was one of the first investors in ArMil. The man had the pulse of anything technology related and had made a fortune following his instincts.

"I was in Boston last week but had to get back sooner than I expected." He glanced up and caught Carmen staring.

Her face was slightly flushed as she clenched the clutch in her palm.

"Thomas, I'd like you to meet my friend and business partner, Carmen Dane."

Thomas took Carmen's hand in his and gave it a gentle kiss. "We've met before. It's good to see you again, Carmen. Or should I address you as Ms. Dane?"

Carmen snatched her hand back. "Carmen is fine."

Whoa, there was definitely a story there.

"How do you guys know each other?" I was so nosy.

"We met at a charity event in New York. It started out boring as hell and then transformed into a most pleasant evening. Wouldn't you agree, Ms. Dane?" he purred.

Carmen's face turned red.

Holy shit, they totally slept together. Once we're home, I'm getting the scoop on that one.

"Thomas, this is not the time or the place," Carmen snapped.

I decided to corral Carmen before her head exploded. "Hey, Carm, follow me. I want to dance before the crowd moves in. All of Thomas's clubs hire the best DJs. They're the biggest draw outside of the ambiance." I glanced over my shoulder. "Thomas, be a doll and send Milla our way once she's finished scrutinizing your books."

Thomas laughed and blew both of us a kiss.

I grasped Carmen's hand and dragged her to the dance floor. "What happened between you two?"

"It was nothing. We went out after the event. Nothing happened," she insisted.

Yeah, right, and I'm not still in love with your brother. Dammit, I'm not supposed to think about him. "You're such a liar. You totally banged him."

Carmen abruptly stopped and glared my way.

I raised my hands in surrender. "Okay. Okay. I'll let it drop."

We snagged a spot on the back of the dance floor away from the performance dancers. The music flowed, and for the first time in over three months, relaxation coursed over me.

I loved dancing and enjoyed letting the beat and rhythm fill me. I had hated all the lessons Aunt Elana forced me to take as a child: ballet, tap, urban rhythm. But now, a night out dancing provided the perfect remedy to a stressful week.

About fifteen minutes into the club mix, Milla tapped my shoulder and handed me a cocktail. Thomas with a few of our other Stanford crew followed her and joined our group. I chugged my drink, deposited my glass on a nearby tray, and continued dancing and laughing. That was until a hand crept around my waist and pulled me back against a firm chest. My heart leaped into my throat.

The hold was unyielding and possessive, and I knew without a doubt Max was behind me. Carmen cringed and then glared at her brother. I laid my hand over his, thinking to tug it away, but a shock of arousal flashed through me. His slightest touch turned me to putty. Thomas moved toward us, but I shook my head. I could handle this without causing a scene.

He covered my hand and whispered in my ear, "Relax. I just want to dance." His warm breath on my neck and the slight caress of his mouth against my ear increased the inferno blazing in my center.

"I don't think that's a good idea. I'm not ready for this," I admitted.

"One dance, for old times' sake. We always had great rhythm together."

Without giving me a chance to decide, he pulled my hand up and behind me to the back of his neck.

I closed my eyes and gave in without protest. The soft feel of his hair under my palm brought out the compulsion to thread my fingers through his dark strands and yank him closer.

My other hand still remained on his and clutched tight as we swayed to the music.

"What are you doing here, Max? Are you following me?" I whispered.

"Yes and no. Don't stiffen up on me—keep dancing and let me explain. My assistant had scheduled me for a few meetings this week in San Francisco, but when I found out Carmen skipped out on her European assignment, I arrived early to see if everything was okay. She's been acting weird for a few weeks."

I had a gut feeling the weirdness Max described revolved around the evening with Thomas. But until I had more details, I wasn't mentioning anything to anyone.

Max continued, "I planned on calling her after my appointment tomorrow. Meeting like this is a coincidence. I didn't expect to see you here. I purely wanted to check out one of the clubs my new business partners were heavily invested in." His lips grazed my neck, and the tip of his tongue made small circles behind my ear.

Without a thought, I tilted my neck, giving him better access, and moaned.

"Lucky for me, you and your entourage decided to come here as well."

What am I doing?

I moved forward, but the effects of his lips and tongue lingered.

The music sped up, and our hands reversed their grip. He spun me around, pulling me close. My belly pressed against his hip, my breasts to his firm muscular chest. I inhaled deep and stared into his smoldering eyes. Our lips were mere inches apart, and the desire to kiss him overwhelmed me. If I moved my mouth a little bit closer, I could release some of this need building inside me.

"I know you feel it, Arya," Max whispered, keeping the minuscule distance separating our lips. "From the beginning we were drawn to each other. Years and distance have only increased the pull."

I wanted to disagree, but the hitch in my breath gave me away. I licked my lips, and Max's attention slipped from my eyes to my mouth.

"Would you stop me if I kissed you right now?"

Oh, God no! I've dreamed about it for five years.

"That's not a good idea, Max. We have to keep a strict line between business and our personal lives."

"You didn't answer my question, Arya. Your eyes are dilated, and your breath is shallow. You don't need to say it. I already know the answer."

Cocky bastard.

"Max don't do this," I pleaded. Everything in my body screamed to close the distance and remember, but the consequences outweighed the benefits.

His hand crept along my side, just under the swell of my breast. My nipples tightened and strained. "Nothing will ever happen between us that you don't want."

That was what I feared.

"I'm not getting involved with you, Max. I've lived with the scars for five years. I won't add new ones. I'll never be anyone's temporary fling again."

Temporary fling. The words he called our relationship five years ago still hurt every time I remembered them.

His grip tightened on my side. "I regret everything I said that day, Arya. If I could take them back, I would. Like I told you in your office, life would be different if I hadn't been such a coward back then."

My lip trembled, so I bit it. How many years had I waited for those words?

"Why are you telling me this now? I've built a new life. One that doesn't involve you. There's no going back."

"I'm not asking to go back. I want to move forward. I'm not making the same mistakes twice. I won't ever let you go." He closed the distance between us. The first touch of his lips was both soft and intoxicating. He tasted so good. I threaded my hands around his neck and into his hair. I wanted more.

As if reading my mind, he opened his mouth, and his tongue touched mine. All coherent thought escaped, while my body drowned in a flood of need. We continued kissing until the music changed and someone passing by nudged us.

The fog finally cleared, and I stared into Max's emerald eyes. His erection pressed against my stomach, and my breath caught as I resisted rubbing against him.

I stepped back out of his hold and touched my lips. My face was flushed and mouth swollen. "Max...that...that shouldn't have happened." A tear slipped down my cheek.

Great, now I'm crying.

I walked past Thomas and my friends. Thomas stopped me. "Arya, are you okay?" He shot Max an angry glare over my shoulder.

"I'm fine. Make sure the girls get back safely. I'm leaving. Don't worry, Thomas. James will take me home." I glanced toward the observation area, and James was already gone.

I peeked behind me as I moved toward the exit. Max remained in the same spot, staring at me. I yearned to run to him and confess everything that had happened to me, but I couldn't take that risk.

I exited the club and let the cool night air hit me in the hope of calming my oversensitized nerves. James waved me over to our car. I climbed in and leaned my head back against the headrest. My phone rang, and I answered without checking the caller ID.

"Hello."

"Open your eyes, Arya, and look out the window."

Oh no, the voice.

I followed his command.

Max leaned against the outside wall of the club, watching me.

"No matter what you tell yourself, you know where you belong. Don't think I'm giving up. I know you aren't ready yet, but soon you won't be walking away."

"Max, you have no claim on me. Not anymore." I protested. Closing my eyes, I willed my body to calm.

"Keep telling yourself that. Even now, I know your skin is on fire, craving my touch. I know that with the slightest change of my voice, you react. If I told you to slide your hand down between your legs, you would, and you'd find yourself wet and aching."

I didn't need to touch myself; the dampness soaked through my underwear. I couldn't go back there again. "Max, please don't do this to me. I've built a new life for myself without you in it."

"Well, you'd better start making room for me. I plan on becoming a very permanent part of your life, and it isn't beneath me to use every opportunity to remind you of who you belong to."

"This isn't fair—"

"I'm not playing to be fair," he interrupted. "I'm playing for keeps. Consider yourself warned."

CHAPTER SIX

Monday morning arrived faster than I'd expected, but the luxury of having my own plane with a bedroom and shower on board allowed me to maximize my time in Cali. The girls had left the night before, Milla back to Boston for a four a.m. meeting with the Italian board of her family's holdings, and Carmen flying across the Atlantic to Germany.

James woke me an hour before we landed, giving me plenty of time to freshen up and change for a quick run in the park before heading into the office.

After my incident with Max at the club and my resolution to keep a professional distance between us, I'd had a rather relaxed week. Most of it was spent stuffing my face with Aunt Elana's food, reconnecting with Carmen, and retail therapy with Milla. That girl knew how to spend money, and it was very contagious, though the guilt of buying a twenty-thousand-dollar gown still lingered in my gut.

I strode onto my private elevator and turned on my phone.

I hadn't looked at it since I'd left for Monterey, and I probably had a hundred missed e-mails and messages. If I was lucky, Kerry would have cleaned the junk from my inbox before I reached the office. Then I'd only have to sort through the important ones.

My phone illuminated and I scrolled through the messages and noticed one from Max. What could he want?

I hope you had a most relaxing week. When you have a moment, I'd like to discuss a few things with you. Personal things. In private.

Oh no, that was never going to happen. Being alone with him went against everything I'd told myself in California.

I leaned back against the metal walls of the elevator. His sheer presence unnerved me. A simple brush from him and I was ready to let him dominate me. If my reaction at the club hadn't proved it, nothing would. I relished his touch, his smell, his taste.

Goose bumps prickled my arms and body. I shook the thought from my mind. No matter what my true feelings were, I had to maintain our professional relationship.

The cab stopped at my floor as I skimmed for other important messages. I exited into the hall and heard a commotion.

"Is she still the cold bitch she always was?"

I stopped midstep around the corner from my office. I recognized the voice and his words.

Jacob Brady. Jackass extraordinaire.

The morning had started off great; I even had the time to grab a cup of coffee from my favorite coffee shop. But, no, Jacob Brady had to ruin it all.

From the moment I met him six years ago, he'd been a thorn in my side. He believed old New England money should never mix with the lower class—that is, me, a half-breed Indian who earned her money instead of inheriting it. He took every opportunity to remind me of my place with my *above my station* friends, especially when it came to my relationship with Max. According to Milla and Carmen, Jacob was a prick from birth, and neither understood how Max could stand being friends with him, let alone allow him to work at MCD.

On top of his attitude toward me, there was something about him that never settled well with me. He gave me the chills, like the creepy guy parents warn their kids away from.

"I don't know who you're talking about, but if it's either of my bosses, than you better watch your step. The people of this company are completely loyal to them. Don't think they won't see through your pencil-pusher, elitist attitude."

I loved Kerry. Even if things frazzled her on occasion, no one pushed her around.

"Oh, I see. This company only hires other cold bitches."

That fucker. I wasn't going to stand for him harassing my people. I moved toward my office when a hand settled on my waist.

Max.

I glared at him over my shoulder. He placed a finger to his lips, signaling me to stay quiet.

I scowled but waited.

"Listen up, buster. I don't know who you are and I don't personally care."

"Sorry, I didn't mean to offend you. I was testing the waters to see if everyone here is as dedicated to Arya and Milla as all the columnists say."

"Why don't you stop wasting my time, and tell me what you want."

"You seem a little tense. Do your bosses overwork you?"

"Hardly. Now back to my previous question. Do you have an answer?"

"You seem like a smart girl. Direct me to Arya's office and I'll wait there. We have a few things to discuss that you may not understand."

That jackass's arrogance never ceased. Why was I waiting here with Max instead of feeding Jacob his own balls?

"Not so fast, buddy. No one enters her office if she's not there. Why don't you wait in the reception area until Arya comes in? If she wants to speak with you, she'll invite you in herself."

I had better rescue Kerry before she killed Jacob.

"Max if you don't let me go right now, you're going to turn into collateral damage after I get done with your friend over there." I motioned around Max, but he blocked my way.

"I know he's a jerk half the time, but he isn't bad once you get to know him. Let me handle this and come in after five minutes."

"Do you think I'll allow you to fight my battles?" I planned to make toast out of that self-righteous ass.

"Please Arya. Let me see if I can defuse the situation."

Please? Max never asked for permission.

"Fine, you've got five minutes, but if Kerry gets any more upset, we may have a homicide on our hands, and I will support Kerry when she claims it was self-defense."

Max grinned and ran his thumb across my lips, and immediately fireworks coursed through my body. "Duly noted."

I attempted to bite his thumb, but expecting my reaction, he pulled back and walked around the corner with a laugh.

What was wrong with me? I was behaving like a lovestruck high schooler. I was not letting Max handle this, but going in guns blazing wasn't a good idea, either. After a few minutes to calm my temper, I walked to my office and found him charming Kerry, and Jacob nowhere in sight.

"Arya." Kerry blushed as her eyes glowed with adoration. "Mr. Dane, I mean Max, was telling me about his weekend. Did you know he sails?"

Wow, five minutes with him and Kerry was ready to bear his children.

"Yes, I did. Lex and Mr. Dane were on a sailing team together while in school."

"Ari is an avid sailor as well."

Kerry jumped up with a smile. "I didn't know you sailed! Why haven't you come out with us on our yearly girls' trips?"

Oh great, Max and his big mouth.

"Kerry, don't believe him," I said. "Mr. Dane exaggerates. I learned to sail years ago but never kept up with it. Don't you remember Lex said he didn't trust me to take his yacht anywhere unless he was there to supervise? I'm not very good."

"Now who's exaggerating? Ari, if I recall correctly, you took to sailing like a fish in water. Remember how Milla and Carmen made such a big deal about popping your sailing cherry?"

Really? Did he just say that in front of Kerry?

My cheeks warmed.

"I knew you two had met before the merger." Kerry clapped with excitement, as if she had discovered the mysteries of the universe.

Max quirked his eyebrows and smiled at me. "I was around for a lot of firsts. Wouldn't you agree, Arya? I mean, Ms. Rey."

"This is great. We've all wondered about your history with the Danes."

Who are 'we'?

"Kerry, we have work to do. Plus we're occupying Mr. Dane's valuable time." I glared at Max. "Don't you have somewhere to be? Businesses to conquer?"

"I'm not busy right now. I can chat with Kerry if she likes. My next appointment isn't for another thirty minutes or so."

"Fine, you two chat while I do some actual work." I huffed and moved through my office door. Max laughed in the background.

I proceeded to my desk and found my newspaper waiting for me on top of it.

For the past ten years, my guilty pleasure had been the gossip section. A little celebrity news would get me in the mood to work all day. I sat and opened the paper, but as I scanned the headlines, my excitement went out the window. A grainy picture of me at the club in San Francisco was on the front page of the section. My head was arched back and a dark head nuzzled my neck. The caption read: "Formidable Arya Rey thaws for unknown suitor."

"I hate paparazzi," I grumbled out loud. "Can't anything make this morning better?"

"What's wrong, Arya?" Kerry asked from the door.

"Nothing." I leaned down and banged my head against the desk. "This day is shot to hell."

"Oh, come on, Arya. It can't be that bad," Max said as he strolled into my office.

Great, he was still here. I cringed and covered the article with my hands.

"Do you still read the gossip section?"

"Yep. Every Monday since I've known her," Kerry informed Max.

I must invest in a muzzle. On second thought, I'd need a dozen. She came down with a bout of verbal diarrhea around him.

"Stop hiding the article and let us see why you're so irritated." Max tugged on the paper, but I refused to move my arms.

"No, it's nothing. Both of you go away and leave me in peace."

Max snatched the newspaper out of my grasp and laughed as he read the headline. He lifted his gaze from the image and gave me the wicked grin with which I was very familiar. I bit my lip and waited for some comment.

Kerry peered over Max's shoulder. "Arya, who's the guy that's got you all hot and bothered?"

I ignored Kerry's question and continued watching Max.

"Even with the bad image quality, the reporter managed to capture how into him you are. You look hot."

"I completely agree, Kerry. The guy appears captivated by her as well."

I inhaled sharply at his words. Why wouldn't he leave me alone?

In the front office, the phone rang. Thank goodness.

"Kerry, I think the phone's ringing. Why don't you go see who it is?"

"Sure thing, boss lady." Kerry rushed out of my office, leaving Max behind.

I stood and moved toward my windows, trying to ignore Max's presence.

Please get the hint. Please get the hint.

He slowly approached me and ran his finger along my spine. I stiffened. Damn, no luck.

"You know I am."

I narrowed my eyes. "What?"

He cupped the side of my face, and my heart sped up.

"I am captivated by you. All that you were then. All that you are now. I think you feel the same about me."

I stepped out of his hold. "There's no going back. All I can offer you is a professional relationship, Mr. Dane."

He remained silent for a few moments, as he stared into my weary eyes. His own were dark with desire and intent. In a flash, he had me caged against the glass with my hands pinned above my head and his lips a hairbreadth away from mine.

"Keep telling yourself that, Ms. Rey. Remember what I told you the other night. I don't play fair. We'll both get what we want in the end."

Max released me as fast as he had captured me and left my office.

I remained pinned to the window, unable to calm my body or breathe.

Could this day get any worse?

CHAPTER SEVEN

Thank you everyone. I am happy with the progress we made today." I glanced at Max, who sat relaxed and unfazed by my glare. "Each of you has homework to complete before we begin training next week. If you have any confusion, or questions, don't hesitate to contact your ArMil counterparts. We will reconvene in the lab next week."

I pushed back from the conference table, determined to get the hell out of the room before I said something I regretted. For the past three weeks, Max had questioned every decision I'd made. I'd endured the frustration for the sake of the company, but I was at my limit. For a Harvard-educated lawyer and businessman, he acted like an idiot who didn't have the first clue about security encryption.

As fast as possible, I gathered my papers and moved toward the door. If I acted casual, no one would notice my sense of urgency.

"Ms. Rey, may I speak with you for a moment?" Max said from behind me.

Of course, he'd notice.

I paused, shifting slowly. Max's eyes bored into mine, causing me to take a deep breath. Damn that man. No escape now. I waited in silence for him to relay what he needed. But he continued to stare at me, not saying a word. His authority washed over the room; everyone stopped what they were doing and looked up. He was pushing my buttons today.

First, he acted like a complete moron every time I mentioned anything remotely technical, even things I knew he was well versed in, and then he invaded my personal space any time we were near each other. Sure, to an outsider, it appeared innocent enough, but every brush of his hand sent a surge of lust through my blood. And now this.

Why is he staring at me?

Was he waiting for me to say his favorite words? Hell would freeze over before I gave them to him.

Did he believe I was the same girl who got wet because he gave me a particular expression? Who was I kidding? My nipples ached and my clit throbbed. Damn those eyes. I yearned to squeeze my thighs together.

He peered at me as the corner of his mouth twitched slightly. He knew exactly what he was doing.

I licked my lips, and then bit them in the desperate hope he wouldn't notice my reaction. Too late. His eyebrow arched in response.

He was aware of his appeal and wasn't afraid to use it to his advantage. It was more than his appearance. It was his attitude and mannerisms; both screamed self-confident badass, nicely packaged in a tailored suit.

Milla nudged me, breaking the standoff. "Answer him," she whispered. "The others are beginning to stare."

Before I could respond, Max spoke. "Ms. Rey, I would like to meet with you in my office. I want to make sure I thoroughly understand the more complicated nuances of the next phase of implementation."

Really? Had he just said that? Clarification was for those who actually read the report. Being alone with him was a bad idea. My body was on fire, and I needed to get away from him.

Max waited for me to join him in the doorway of the conference room. I peeked at Milla for some support or at least a way to get out of this, but the traitor shrugged and smiled.

Reluctantly, I followed Max to his office. He kept his hands by his side and made no attempt to touch me. Thank goodness for small favors. But the walk to the office was torture. Neither of us spoke a word.

"Hold my calls, Marie. Ms. Rey and I have a few things to discuss, and I don't want to be disturbed." Max's personal assistant cringed and gave me the *so glad it's you and not me* face. Max must maintain a reputation for eating little computer nerds for breakfast.

He opened the door, gesturing for me to enter. Max's office housed glass on two sides with astonishing views of the Charles River. Even from the forty-fourth floor, I saw joggers running up and down the walkways while street vendors battled the blistering cold to sell their mouthwatering fare.

The door snapped closed and locked, bringing me out of my

thoughts. I whirled around and found Max leaning against the door. He had taken off his jacket and thrown it over the closest chair. My pulse throbbed out of control; his aura affected me in a way no other man's ever could.

I must get out of here as quickly as possible.

"Mr. Dane, I would appreciate getting our discussion over with." I glanced at my watch. "I'm due back in my office to finish the logistics of the next phase. I'm sure reading the report will clarify any confusion."

Max casually walked up behind me. He leaned down, his lips a fraction away from my ear. I closed my eyes, trying not to let his scent overwhelm my senses.

"Arya, don't you think we're way past formalities, especially when we're alone?"

He trailed his hand along my waist as he moved to lean against the desk in front of me. The desire to sink down to my knees and wait for his instruction surged through me.

Stop it Arya, those days are over.

"There is no 'we.' You made sure of that years ago. I agreed to the partnership for the benefit of my company, nothing more. I am no longer your sub—*yours*," I stated, trying hard not to let my voice crack.

Don't let him see you cry.

Max leaned close to my body, but without touching me. "You may not be my...what was the word you were trying to say?" He tapped a finger to his lips. "Ah, yes, *submissive*, but your body will answer only to me." His hand crept around my waist, drawing me against him, while the other slid into my hair.

My skin flushed from the heat growing in my body, and the pulsing in my clit intensified. My hardened nipples rubbed against his firm chest, making me want to cry out. Max lowered his head as he gathered me toward him. His lips brushed mine, softly at first, then seizing them, and he claimed me as his once again.

I reacted immediately, returning his kiss with all the pent-up need from years before. I wrapped my arms around his shoulders, trying to draw him closer. He broke the kiss to run his lips along my neck as a sigh escaped my mouth. He lifted me up, positioning me on the edge of his desk, not caring if his papers fell to the floor.

He nudged my skirt up around my thighs, stepping between them to rub his straining erection against my soaked underwear.

I cried out, "Please." And clutched his shoulders. I wrapped my legs around him so he rubbed harder against my oversensitive core. Max kissed me again, grasping my hands from around his shoulders and placing them on the edge of the desk.

"Don't move your hands, or I will stop." He shifted from between my legs, skimming his fingers up my arms. He slid off my suit jacket and unbuttoned my shirt to reveal my lace and satin bra. He hummed, cupped the heavy weight of one breast in his hands, and took the engorged nipple peak into his mouth.

I let out a low, deep moan and arched my chest closer.

"I love how you wear something sexy under your clothes," he murmured against my lace-covered nipple.

His mouth glided lower, down between my breast and toward the top of my skirt. I arched further and sucked in air when his tongue touched my skin. I gripped the edge of the table harder as his breath grazed the insides of my thighs. He tugged the silk barrier covering my throbbing slit to the side and blew slightly as he spread my lips with his fingers.

"Always smooth and bare. I still remember the first time I found your little secret. Something I'm glad Milla introduced you to."

I peered down and caught him watching me. My pussy clenched in anticipation.

I shouldn't be doing this. What if he sees the scars?

If I allowed this to go further, he'd trap me in his web again. This time I wouldn't survive when it ended.

"Stop thinking, Arya. Enjoy." His lips closed over my nub, drawing it gently into his mouth.

All coherent thought left my mind.

"God, I've missed the taste of you. Your flavor has haunted me for five years."

Unhurried, he sucked, licked, and tasted, driving me to the complete edge of my control and holding me there. I wanted to fist my hands into his hair, but I knew he would stop the moment they moved.

"Max, please." I was on the verge of total insanity; just a little more and I'd go over.

A desperate sensual sound escaped his mouth as he feasted on me. Then he shifted, rising back to stand in front of me. For a split second, he gazed down at me, as if I was all that mattered in the world. In the next second, the emotion was replaced by dark, hungry desire. My palms twitched, ready to run my hands over his firm, defined body. I arched my hips, wanting him deep inside me.

"Don't shift a muscle, or I won't let you come."

He unbuttoned his shirt and opened his pants, letting them fall to the floor, then pushed down his boxer briefs. His cock sprang free.

Oh God. I'd forgotten how large he was. A moment of doubt crept in, warring with the need for him to surge into me.

"We've done this before. Many times, in fact. We'll fit perfectly," he reminded me.

Pulling me toward him, he discarded the small piece of silk separating us. Anticipating my loss of balance, Max took my arms from the edge of the table, pushed my jacket and shirt completely off, and placed my palms against his shoulders.

With one arm around my waist and the other on my hip, he squeezed the head of his erection forward into my damp heat. He stretched me slowly, allowing me time to adjust.

"Baby, you're so tight." He spoke through ragged breaths and thrust deep.

A cry escaped my mouth at the invasion, and Max stilled his movement. My body felt full and in complete bliss. The pleasure-pain vibrated to my core. Five years without him inside of me, without him making my body come alive.

"I have to move now or I won't last. It's been years," he hissed.

"Okay," I replied and tugged his head toward mine. Our lips locked and with slow, short strokes, he slid in and out of me.

"Max, faster…" I cried against his mouth.

"No, I control the show." He stopped his thrusts. "Do you want to come?"

I nodded my head. My body quivered, suspended on the cusp of release.

"I want to hear the words."

"Yes, make me come."

He plunged in again, rough and intense. "Come for me, Arya. Let me feel you squeeze me tighter. I want your pleasure."

On command, volcanic heat spread through my body, lashing out and consuming me. My core convulsed as shock waves poured through my body.

Max continued his momentum, thrusting harder and harder, jolting his desk back. His hold on my thighs tightened, while his pounding became more ferocious. A hoarse cry escaped his lips as he emptied his release into me, igniting another, unanticipated, orgasm.

Wow.

I tried desperately to catch my breath and fell back against Max's desk. He followed and rested against my chest. His cock continued pulsing inside me as he softened.

"Arya, you're coming home with me. I want you with me from now on," Max said as he nuzzled my breast.

The reality of his words set in. What had I done? I shoved Max back. "This shouldn't have happened. It doesn't change anything." Still steadying my breath, I slid off the desk and straightened my skirt. Hot liquid ran down my leg.

Oh shit, we didn't use protection. And he has a reputation for having a different woman every week.

Max handed me a tissue and watched me with frustration. "Too late for regrets, Arya. You willingly gave yourself to me. Besides, we didn't use a condom. What if you become pregnant?" He buttoned his pants, shrugged on his shirt, and walked over to the window where he ran a hand through his sex-tousled hair.

"Let me make a few things clear. First off, I never gave you anything. Second, it would take a miracle for me to get pregnant, so don't worry your little head about it. Third, this won't happen again. It was a lapse of judgment."

We both knew the last part was a lie as soon as it came out of my mouth, but I continued to dress. I had to get back to my office.

What had I done?

"Max, we can't pick up where we left off. There is too much pain and too many memories between us. You're asking for your submissive back, and I'm not her. She doesn't exist anymore."

He stepped with lightning speed toward me. "I'm not asking for my submissive back. I'm asking for my lover. The woman with whom I plan to spend my life."

My breath hitched at his words, and I treaded back as he moved forward. "What's the difference? I won't ever be that girl again. I was my weakest self when you left me, questioning, doubtful, afraid, not in control of any situation. I will never allow anyone to place me in that position again."

He stalked me until my back hit the door. One hand gripped my waist and the other fisted in my hair, forcing my head back.

"Tell me, Arya, have your other lovers made you feel the power and vulnerability I do?" He nuzzled the side of my neck and a moan escaped my lips. "Can they make you wet and ready with a look? Can they make you come until you pass out?" His hand skimmed down from my waist to the hem of my skirt. His fingers trailed between my thighs to my soaked underwear. He nudged the wet material to the side and stroked me. "Do they make you beg for release? Do they play the games that make your body sing?"

My clitoris pulsed with the rhythm of his fingers.

"Max, please," I begged.

He abruptly stopped his assault on my senses and strode away from me. I leaned heavily against the door, panting, unable to regain control of my now aroused and aching body.

"Or has your taste changed to men you can dominate, who will leave you wanting?"

Anger flared inside me. "How dare you talk about my lovers? Unless you were celibate for the past five years, you have no right to question me and my decisions." I shoved my skirt down, turned, and gripped the doorknob.

"Arya," Max softly called as I opened the door. I paused. "There has been only one woman I've been with or made love to in the past six years. Everyone in the tabloids was for show. You're all I will ever want."

I closed my eyes, hoping to keep my unshed tears at bay. Without saying a word, I bolted for the elevator and then home.

CHAPTER EIGHT

"Arya, I know you're in there. Unlock the door."

I shifted from my computer toward the security monitors to see Milla standing outside my lab, tapping her foot. She jammed the button to the intercom over and over, as if that would force me to open the doors any faster.

Perhaps if I pretended no one was here, she would leave. Even after three days, I wasn't in the mood to tell her I'd succumbed to my lust and fucked Max on his office desk. And the moment I opened that door, I'd spill my guts.

"Arya, you know I have all the codes to get into your Fort Knox. Don't make me use them."

"Fine!" I shouted and opened the door.

Milla shoved past me and sat on one of the chairs in the lab. "Oh God, you're playing *Storm*."

"What's wrong with my music? I listen to Vanessa-Mae whenever I'm working on Arcane," I grumbled. "It helps me keep all the coding straight so I don't mess up the international-base security software our wonderful government is paying us to develop."

"I know you better than you think I do. You've probably played that same track fifty times. You only do that when you are stressed or thinking about Max. Lock the door, and then spill it." Milla crossed her arms while scrutinizing me.

I examined myself. I was a rumpled mess. Spending three days in the lab had taken its toll. Only breaking for a quick shower and some food meant I'd spent more time than necessary letting Max occupy my mind.

"Earth to Arya. Anyone home? Stop staring into space and start talking."

I shook the fog from my head, closed the door, and walked over to the refrigerator in the corner of the room. Grabbing two drinks, I tossed one to Milla and plopped down in my chair.

"There's nothing to spill. I've spent all my free time for the past few days working on Arcane's new features and making sure we can deliver on the time line you negotiated with General Ansgar." I opened the water and gulped down half the bottle. "Oh, and I'm a complete idiot, that's all."

"What happened? I'm positive it has to do with Max. Did he fuck you on his desk and now he thinks he's knocked you up?"

How did she do that? The girl is psychic.

"Well." I felt my cheeks burning. "That about sums it up."

"What?" Milla rotated her chair and glared at me. "I was kidding. Arya, you do know that getting involved with him again is a bad idea? If you weren't still in love with him,

I'd say go for it but…dammit, Arya, you know better."

"You're the one who pressured me to talk to him after the meeting."

"I wanted you guys to work better together, not fuck each other's brains out."

I scrunched a piece of paper and tossed it at Milla's head. "Language."

"Whatever. You say worse things than I do. I'm serious, Arya. This isn't a onetime thing. If I remember correctly, the moment Max popped your cherry you were in deep. I'm positive it won't be any different this time."

"I'm stronger now. I can handle this."

Milla raised an eyebrow and sipped her drink.

"I'm stupid. Okay, happy? I admit it. Milla, what am I going to do?" I curled my knees onto the chair and held my head in my hands. *God, now I have a headache.* "Why can't I have the kind of relationships you have? Sex with no strings outside the bedroom. Or in your case, the dungeon."

"I don't have that much experience. I've been with the same Dom for years."

"Speaking of, why is it you won't introduce him to us? Are you scared Lex will kill him?"

"Hardly," Milla said with a dry tone. "Don't change the subject. We're talking about you and Max. You said he's freaking out about knocking you up. Does he know it isn't possible?"

"No." I placed a hand over my barren stomach. "We haven't spoken since the incident in his office. He's left me tons of messages and sent me about a million texts."

"What did he say?"

"To sum it up, he's never stopped loving me, he regrets never telling me, he wants to marry me and have lots of babies with me."

Milla jumped up and paced. "Oh hell, Arya. That's intense. You don't think this buyout was all to get you back, do you?"

"You guessed it."

"Lex is going to kill him. Who puts together a multi-billion-dollar merger to get his girl back?"

"I'm not his girl," I grumbled, crossing my arms around myself and scowling at her.

"Shut up. You know what I mean. Man, he must truly love you to do this."

"I thought you were on my side."

Milla rolled her chair in front of me and sat. She took my hands. "I will always be on your side. I know you. You've kept all the hurt from the past bottled up so tight you won't let yourself risk anything anymore."

"If I hadn't helped MI6 hack a Russian mobster's computer, we wouldn't have gotten the contracts that started our company," I grumbled.

Milla cringed, releasing my hands and tucked a stray hair behind her ear. "Please don't mention Vladimir Christof. The thought of being on his shitlist for the rest of our lives gives me the creeps."

"You're not the only one, but if he didn't do anything to us eight years ago, I don't think we have anything to worry about." I leaned back in my chair. "Plus Lex is using his family connections to keep an eye on him." Even though his family was now on the straight and narrow, they kept good relationships with those who towed the legal lines.

"I guess you're right. Hey, how did we get on this subject of Christof?"

"You said I didn't take risks, and I reminded you that I do."

"I'm not talking about business. Hell, you're as crazy as they come when it involves the corporate world. Who else would agree to develop software for an insane-ass general and think nothing of it when he threatened all of our lives and livelihoods if we don't deliver?"

A tremor shook my body, reminding me that Max wasn't the only issue I was facing. Earlier in the day, around the time James brought me lunch, I received an e-mail offering to buy Arcane for a price of my choosing. What scared me the most was that no one outside of the software deal was supposed to know anything about the type of program we were creating.

Thank goodness James had been there or I'd have freaked. He kept me calm and contacted our security detail to increase surveillance and protection on both Milla and myself. There was too much at stake to leave things to chance. I'd also put out feelers on the Dark Web to see if I could locate any chatter about the software.

Maybe I should tell her about this. No. On second thought, I'll keep it to myself for now. Having Milla worry more about me wasn't something I needed to deal with right now. She was overprotective at the best of times, and with this news she'd lose her shit and we both needed to continue life as normal to prevent suspicion.

"Arya, are you listening to me?"

I refocused on Milla as she glared at me and continued her monologue on my love life.

"What I'm talking about is your personal life. The one man you gave your heart to years ago wants you back, and he will use any means necessary to achieve his goal. Maybe it's time to give him a second chance."

The thought of risking myself with Max scared me even more than who wanted to buy my software. "I'm not sure about second chances, but maybe a no-strings attached kind of affair is the key."

"You're not a no-strings kind of girl, Ari. Think this through before you agree to anything you'll regret." Milla sighed and relaxed into the back of the chair.

"Why can you do it and not me? It's worked perfectly for you."

"There're things I never told you, but let's just say it's not as simple as I've let on."

"Oh my God! You're in love with him." I couldn't believe I hadn't seen this before. Whenever she talked about her Dom, she'd had a dreamy expression in her face.

"I don't want to talk about it. We're discussing you, remember?"

Whoa, she was touchy about it. Poor Lex. The woman he loved was in love with someone else.

"What about Lex?"

"What about him?" Milla said with a bitter edge. "Lex is a big boy. He can handle my relationship."

This made no sense. She loved her Dom, and she loved Lex. Lex loved his submissive, and he loved Milla. What a mess.

"Okay, I'll let it go. I'm here when you want to talk."

Milla gave me a weary smile and winked. "Now back to the subject of you having a D/s relationship with no strings attached. Tried that, didn't work. Remember?"

I released a deep breath. "I wasn't aware of the no-strings part back then. This time I won't make the same mistake."

"But he wants the strings. Hell, he wants all of them, including the white picket fence."

"Well, he can't have them." I inhaled deep. "I won't risk my heart again."

"It's already on the line. You're still in love with him." She raised a brow, expecting me to argue.

"Mil, I can do this. If I go in knowing there's an end, I won't get hurt."

"I see heartache written all over this."

I ignored her statement. "I'm going to set the terms, and if he takes them, I'll enjoy my time while it lasts."

"Are you trying to convince me or yourself?"

"Shut up. I know what I'm doing."

"Arya, I don't think you have a clue what you're getting yourself into. Be careful what you wish for, because you might get it and then regret asking for it in the first place."

Boy, I hoped she was wrong.

"Did you change your mind?" Max asked as he entered my office the next day.

I swiveled from my computer and gauged his mood. Today he was dressed casually, trying to blend in with ArMil's relaxed atmosphere. He still stood out. In a suit or not, he carried his authority and power everywhere.

"Max, I gave you my answer when I texted you earlier. I can't marry you. It won't work, and I'm not seeking happily ever after."

His green eyes grew cold. "Then what did you call me in here to discuss?"

"I have a proposition for you." I fidgeted with my pen.

"I'm listening." He closed the door and waited for me to continue.

I had better get it out before I lose my nerve.

"I won't deny that physically, our chemistry is explosive."

Max grunted. "That's an understatement."

I rolled my eyes and continued. "But I don't want any emotional entanglements."

"A little la—"

"Let me finish. I also won't deny you're the one man who has given me what my body desires."

He strolled closer toward me. "Go on."

"So I propose we resume our sexual relationship, with no expectation of love or permanency. No strings."

A split second of anger flashed across Max's face as he stalked forward like a predator. "So let me get this straight. You're willing to be my submissive but not my wife?"

No, I want to be your wife, but you broke me once. I won't expose myself to the same danger again.

He shifted to stand behind me and waited. I refused to turn around. My heart raced out of control as his crisp, clean scent tickled my senses and the heat of his body brought forth the desires he'd ignited in his office days earlier.

"I am willing to give you my body, nothing more. Outside

of the bedroom, we'll have a professional relationship. We will remain colleagues and business partners." If I was truthful, my heart had never stopped belonging to him, but he didn't need that information. This was the only way to protect myself when the inevitable end came.

He ran his fingers over the skin on the back of my neck. I held back a moan as goose bumps appeared over my skin.

"Arya, you aren't a friends-with-benefits kind of woman. Do you understand what you're asking?"

"Yes, completely." I continued fidgeting with my pen. "I have one other stipulation. While we're together, we won't sleep with anyone else."

He stroked down my spine. "I've only been with you in the last six years. Do you think that's even an issue?"

"I want to make sure you understand the rules."

He rotated my chair, placed his hands on the arms and then leaned down. "Well, before I agree, I have a few rules of my own."

He paused and gazed into my eyes. My breath quickened, and I couldn't look away.

"The minute we're alone you belong to me. You will spend every day you're not otherwise engaged with me. You will do what I say, wear what I want, and eat what I give you. I will control everything about you."

The thought aroused me to my core. I involuntarily licked my lips. In the past, I'd have agreed to everything, but the old Arya no longer existed.

"As I said, you won't have any control of my life outside of the bedroom. You have no say in anything beyond closed doors. Things are different this time around. I'm going in with eyes wide open."

"I'm not sure you are, but why not? I agree to your proposal. But before we begin our little liaison, I believe we need to even the playing field in each other's offices." Max knelt down in front of my chair and nudged my floor-length linen skirt up.

Excitement filled me. "What are you doing?" I stuttered.

"You know exactly what. Lean back and enjoy. I've dreamed about your taste for days. I need another helping." His lips and tongue trailed up the inside of my leg.

"This isn't a good idea. Anyone could walk in. We have to keep our professional life separate from our personal," I half-heartedly protested.

Max nudged on my legs, and without resistance I opened them to his touch. A tingle shot up my thigh as his five o'clock shadow grazed my skin.

"I can smell your arousal, Arya. You can deny it all you want, but you love the idea of being caught." He gently bit the inside of my thigh, and a whimper escaped my lips as my pussy contracted.

I slid my fingers into his hair while he journeyed to my apex. He captured my hands and placed them on my armrest. "Keep them here. I control the show."

I whimpered again but kept my arms where he commanded.

He stopped and stared me in the eyes. "Did you hear what I said?"

"Yes."

"Yes, what?"

The haze cleared for a second and I narrowed my eyes. "Yes, *Max*," I answered through gritted teeth.

"Oh Arya, even though that wasn't exactly the answer I wanted from you, I will let it pass."

The hell he was getting the words he desired. I tried to squeeze my legs together, but Max held them in place at the knees.

"I think we should stop."

He leaned in and used his teeth to push my thong to the side. I held my breath waiting.

"Don't think to control me, Arya. I will follow your rules to a point. But, remember this: I'm not one of your weak men who will fall at your feet to do your bidding."

What? I stiffened. Where had that come from? What men? Who had he talked to?

"Where did you—oh, God."

Max's lips closed around my clitoris and sucked. All questions were forgotten. He lifted my legs off the chair and placed my thighs on his shoulders as he bathed my swollen sex without mercy.

I clutched the armrest and threw my head back. His mouth was incredible; using the right amount of pressure and movement, he brought me to the edge again and again. His tongue thrust into my pussy, causing my core to clench. He fucked me until I whimpered and begged, but left my orgasm out of reach.

"Please—I need—"

He tore his mouth away and replaced his tongue with his fingers.

"I know what you need, but you won't get it until you ask correctly." He pumped his digits in and out as my back arched in a feeble attempt to match his rhythm. My pussy contracted and my body screamed for release.

"Dammit, Max. We haven't started yet."

"We started the moment you walked into that conference room. Now say it or I won't let you come." His pace increased then suddenly stopped.

"No," I shouted. "Don't stop. I'm begging you." My fingers bore into the armrest, scratching the wooden surface.

"Say it, Arya. Stop being stubborn. You know how much I hate leaving you unfulfilled. But I will if you don't give me the words." His fingers drove back into me and scissored.

I clenched my jaw as my body arched in response to his torture.

This wasn't fair. I'm giving him too much power already.

"I hate you, Max."

"Nope, wrong again." He pulled out once more. My back bowed, but he used his other hand to hold me down.

Tears escaped my eyes. What had I gotten myself into? "P-p-please...s-s-sir, let me come."

He mouth settled on my clit and he gently bit as his fingers resumed their rhythm. With a loud cry, I exploded onto his tongue. Never was I so thankful for my paranoid clients and the soundproofing of my walls.

I slowly descended from my orgasm as Max carried me to the soft rug in front of my desk. He leaned back, unbuckling his belt and lowering his pants. I gripped his tie and tugged him toward me. His body lowered over mine as our mouths met. I sipped my essence from his lips, and the salty-sweet taste sent a shiver up my spine.

He pulled his tie out of my hand and yanked the silk from around his neck. He positioned my arms above my head and wound the soft material across my wrists. A thrill shot through me and my breath quickened. This was what I had craved for so long: the loss of control.

Max leaned his forehead against mine and peered into my eyes. "What would Kerry say if she walked in here and found you bound and me pounding into you?"

"She'd probably say it was about time. I don't think anything can scandalize her," I breathed out as I rubbed my body against his.

"Good. Let's see if we can make enough noise for her to investigate."

"No, I was kidding." I attempted to sit up, but my bound hands and Max's weight held me to the floor. "Dammit, Max. I wasn't serious."

"Relax. I know you, Arya. The thought of it may arouse you, but intimacy is a private affair. Why do you think I never took you to any of the public clubs? You don't share, and neither do I." Max caged me with his arms as the head of his cock nudged me. This man had me so hot I hadn't even noticed him taking off my thong.

Awareness of me being clothed, except for my underwear, and Max in a state of semi-undress, gave me a thrill I hadn't expected. Closing my eyes, I reveled in the spectacular sensation. God, I was already in way too deep.

"Open for me, Arya."

Immediately I spread my legs and he thrust his cock into me. I opened my eyes and peered into his lust-filled hungry gaze. My core spasmed at the tenderness I saw there.

"Tell me what I want to hear, Ari." A bead of sweat ran down his forehead.

I was too desperate to argue. "Please sir, I need you."

"Oh God," he moaned and pushed in to the hilt. His movements were slow at first and then increased in speed and intensity. My pussy gripped him tighter with each thrust.

"I feel you, baby. You're almost there."

I cried out as the first of my quivers ignited.

"Arya. Arya, are you in there?"

Both Max and I jerked.

Kerry's voice abruptly blared over the intercom. "Your three o'clock will be here in a few minutes. Mr. Dane's—I mean Max's secretary called to let him know he's needed back at his office ASAP."

Was there amusement in her tone? The thought of being caught both annoyed and thrilled me. I should have been annoyed that Max put me in this situation, but I couldn't help accepting the humor of my position.

Max's solid, pulsating cock still throbbed inside me, but the mood was broken by Kerry's interruptions.

"We should stop," I said as my heart slowed its rapid beating.

Max leaned his forehead against the rug. "Give me a second," he gritted out. "I wasn't expecting any disruptions."

With reluctance, he extracted himself from me and rolled to the side as he attempted to steady his breath. "Wow, this is the softest rug I've ever felt."

I giggled. Of all the things for him to notice, he picked the rug. "It's pure silk. I had it specially made for my office. I love the feel of it under my toes after a long day in heels. It's pretty soft to lay on too."

"I missed the way you laugh." Max sat up, grinned, and started to dress. "I'll have to think about adding a rug like this to our playroom."

Reality set in. We weren't a couple, no matter how much it felt like we were at the moment. He was my Dom; I was his sub.

My own fault.

"You're thinking too much again." Max's voice broke into my thoughts. "Let this run its course. In the end, we'll get what we both want."

I tried lifting up on my bound arms but fell back onto the rug. "You seem pretty confident about this."

"The one thing I am, Ms. Rey, is confident." He leaned over me and untied the knot around my wrists, then pulled me to my feet and kissed me before he finished getting dressed.

I propped myself against my desk, since my legs felt like Jell-O. Max reknotted his tie. "I'm sorry you didn't get to—umm," I said.

Max cupped the back of my head and brought my lips to his. "It's called *come*. Don't worry. I plan to get mine." He took my mouth once again. Pulling back, he bent down, picked up his briefcase, and headed for the door. He paused before turning the knob.

"I have one question for you before I go."

"Yes?" What could he want to know?

"How many men do I need to erase from your memory? You know I've been with no one since you, so I deserve to know your sexual history as well."

He had a point. Especially with him not being the male whore I assumed he was.

"I've been with one man my entire life, and until a few days ago, the last time we were together was over five years ago."

Max's face relaxed with relief. "Expect a box at your penthouse later today. I want you to wear what's inside, nothing else. I will send a car for you tonight exactly at nine. Be ready."

"I won't be home tonight. I have to go to the foundation fund-raiser. I assumed you were attending, since you're the principal sponsor."

"Damn." Max ran a hand through his dark brown hair. "I forgot. Fine. Expect my car to collect you from the venue. Wear what arrives in the box and your gown, nothing else. Since it's Friday, you'll be spending the weekend with me. I will provide everything you'll need for your stay."

"Okay." My voice hitched a little. Here we go.

"From this moment forward, you are my submissive, Arya. No more vanilla. I hope you're ready."

CHAPTER NINE

A rya?"

Carol, my housekeeper, crossed the threshold of my home office with a large gift box in her hand. "It arrived a few minutes ago with a note saying: 'To A from M.' Where do you want me to put it?"

"On the coffee table is fine."

Carol paused after placing the box on the table. "If you don't have anything else for me, I'll finish for the day and go home."

"Oh, I forgot about the boys' hockey game. Go, go." I shooed her with my hands. "I'm sorry I kept you late today."

Carol worked to support her three sons after they'd emigrated from Ireland and she'd lost her husband to cancer. The sacrifices she made for those she loved reminded me of Aunt Elana.

"Arya, you know as well as I do that I barely have to do anything here. Making a few meals for you is the least I can do for paying for my kids' school tuition in addition to my salary.

Besides, half the time you end up feeding me one of your Indian specialties."

"That's because you like spicy food. Most people run when I start cooking."

Chuckling, she moved to the office door. "Let me know when you want more test subjects. I'm sure my children will happily volunteer."

"I'll make sure to plan it for a weekend when the kids don't have a game."

"By the way, your stylist and her staff will arrive in half an hour."

Thank God, Milla insisted on hiring a beauty team for events. Otherwise, I'd have no clue how to kick up my look for galas.

"James will let them in. Don't worry about me, and go enjoy your time with your boys."

"Enjoy your weekend, and don't let Mr. Dane keep you up too late."

I gasped as she winked and shut the door.

How does she know so much about my love life? My face must have "property of Max" written all over it.

Shrugging, I strolled over to the box, untied the ribbon, and peered inside. There, tucked into the white tissue paper, was a breathtaking silk and lace basque. I traced the delicate embroidery and bit my lip.

It was happening. My stomach fluttered. For the first time in years, I was nervous. Even during negotiations for the development of Arcane, I hadn't felt this kind of anxiety.

Well, with the exception of the day ArMil merged with

MDC. Although that revolved around the same person, so it didn't count.

Picking up the lingerie, I went to my en suite, slowly stripped out of my clothes, started the shower, and stepped under the scalding spray. The heat from the water engulfed me and relaxed my tense muscles almost enough to help forget my disquiet. A beep sounded from the home automation system, indicating I had one hour left before Lex arrived to escort me to the ball.

I exited the shower, wrapped a towel around my hair, and stared at my reflection in the steam-covered mirror above the vanity. My palm slid to my stomach as I released a heavy sigh. The mist couldn't hide the jagged lines that marred my skin, twenty-four in all. Twenty three scattered across various spots around my abdomen and one long one in the center from the top of my stomach to just above my pubic bone. Each slightly raised, red, puckered mark held wishes of what might have been.

Max, me, and a future.

If I'd listened to Lex back then and stayed in Boston, I'd have a different life right now. A thickness settled into my throat, and fresh tears lingered on the horizon. Releasing another deep breath, I gathered the corset and slipped it on.

Each piece of the ensemble accentuated my assets, from my large breasts to my tiny waist. I searched the box for stockings when a small card fell to the floor. Recognizing Max's handwriting, I picked it up and read:

You can change your mind. I'd rather have you as my wife than like this.

x Max

My hand shook as I placed the note on the table. Why now? I'd loved him so much, and he rejected me. Too much remained between us for me to believe he'd stand by me. No matter what way I went into this relationship, I'd end up with a broken heart. Going in as his submissive was the one remotely possible path to protecting myself. Or so I hoped, anyway.

A knock on the door interrupted my wistfulness. A member of my beauty team poked her head into the bathroom. "Ms. Rey, we're set up in the living room. Come out whenever you're ready for us. Also, Ms. Stanfield's assistant delivered your gown."

"I'll be out in a minute."

Resigned to the inevitable, I squared my shoulders, opened my door, and let the waiting team make me presentable.

As soon as I entered the grand ballroom of Boston's Mandarin Oriental Hotel, the weight of Max's attention locked on to me from across the room. There was nothing impersonal in the way his gaze roamed my face and body. He regarded me with possessiveness. Irritation radiated from him as Lex placed his hand on my back, and it gave me a sense of confidence. Tonight I would belong to him, but right now I was my own woman.

"Ari, are you trying to cause a fistfight in the middle of this ball?" Lex asked with a hint of irritation in his Irish brogue.

I gave Lex a startled look. "What? I'm not doing anything."

"Max and I don't have any love lost between us, but I'd like to keep my shirt clean tonight. I should have ordered you to change when I picked you up. That stupid dress exposes all your assets. No wonder Max is ready to kick my ass."

I glanced down at my dress. The simple black, long-sleeved dress scooped conservatively in the front and back, but the slit on the side drew one's eyes to my bare leg. Moreover, the reason my assets were accentuated was because of Max's little gift underneath.

"The only thing showing is my leg. Hell, I'm covered all over."

"I told you before not to get involved with him again, but you went against my advice." We approached the attendant, and Lex handed him our invitation.

I feigned innocence. "What are you talking about? I don't have any relationship going on with him."

"Arya, don't lie to me." Uh-oh, the annoyed brother tone was coming out. "Milla told me you slept with him."

That was supposed to have been a secret. *I'm going to ring Milla's neck.* "For two people who can't stand each other, you sure share a lot of information."

"She's worried about you and your plan to set the rules."

Shit, Milla had told Lex the details.

"Arya, you aren't a no-commitment kind of girl. You're treading a very thin line. Does he even know about the past?"

I am sick of people saying that. If Milla can do it, why can't I?

"No, and I'm not going to tell him. It's none of his business. He abandoned that right when he left me."

From the beginning, Lex felt Max needed to know about our girls and the attack, but I had refused, and both Milla and Lex begrudgingly agreed to heed my decision.

We walked past a few business investors and smiled. Lex led me to the bar and handed me a glass of champagne.

"Of course he has a right to know. How are you going to explain the scars?"

"I'll make sure he never sees them. He prefers corsets and lingerie. I can keep them covered."

"God, I don't need to hear about all that. I think I threw up a little in my mouth."

"Seriously Lex, this is physical. Nothing more."

"Keep telling yourself that." Lex paused midstep and leaned toward me. "I don't want to argue with you here. Just know that, no matter what happens, Milla and I are here for you."

This man was amazing. He placed his personal feelings to the side and supported my decisions. I kissed Lex on the cheek. "I love you, too, big brother."

Lex grunted and walked me through the crowd. Before we entered the dining room, I glimpsed at Max over my shoulder. His scowl deepened and he raised a brow. Oh, the kiss had annoyed him. The beautiful blonde by his side noticed his frown and tried to draw his attention away. He gave her his arm and escorted her into the dining room.

I hoped that bimbo knew dinner was all she'd get tonight.

Hell, where did that come from? We've haven't started our affair and I've already become a jealous shrew.

"Arya, don't scowl at his date. It isn't polite. Remember, it's just sex," Lex whispered into my ear.

I transferred my annoyed glare in his direction. "Shut up, Lex."

He laughed and helped me into my seat.

Throughout dinner, Max watched me. He sat across the room, surrounded by people panting to gain his attention, but his concentration remained on me. Every time I looked up, his gaze met mine. Even from a distance, the hunger burning underneath was undeniable.

Why does that arouse me?

I shifted my legs and adjusted my sopping thong. My libido had been dormant for too long. Tonight we'd fuck like bunnies, and tomorrow we'd be back to normal.

I turned as someone tapped on my shoulder.

"Ms. Rey, I have a note for you."

Taking the folded paper from the attendant, I opened it and read the writing:

Stop flirting with Lex. Remember to whom you belong. The car will pick you up in half an hour.

M.

"What does it say?" Lex inquired.

"Nothing important." I stood. "Please excuse me," I said to the guests sitting around me.

I made my way out of the dining room and toward the powder room. After using the facilities, I washed my hands and opened my clutch to touch up my makeup. My hands shook as I reapplied my lipstick and stared at my reflection. In a few minutes, I'd reprise my role as a submissive. I closed my eyes and inhaled deep.

You can do this. There's nothing to worry about. This is all on your terms.

"I can see why Max is so entranced with you. I'm glad someone has finally caught his eye. But then again, you've been in his sights for a long time."

I glanced up to find Max's gorgeous date join me near the mirror. She resembled a modern-day Grace Kelly with perfect porcelain skin, blue eyes, and white-blonde hair, accentuated by a striking five-nine body.

I remained quiet, not acknowledging her statement.

"Don't worry. I don't have any interest in him. We attend these functions together to keep our families off our backs. Plus, even if I did, he doesn't view me as anything more than a friend."

I warmed and relaxed. She was in the same boat as me. "I'm Arya Rey. It's nice to meet you. I attend these functions with Lex for the same reasons."

"I'm Caitlin Stanfield."

Oh wow, she was the award-winning fashion designer I'd admired for years and whose dress I was now wearing. "I apologize for not recognizing you. I'm a bit of a computer nerd. Milla introduced me to your fashion house years ago."

"Don't worry about it. I don't socialize much myself. That is, unless Max or Jacob forces me to be Max's date."

"Jacob?" I questioned.

"My stepbrother is Jacob Brady." She must have seen my scowl because she laughed. "Please don't judge me by my siblings. I know he gives you a tough time, but he isn't as bad as you think. He's well-intentioned. Well, most of the time."

"I'll take your word for it," I mumbled.

Caitlin chuckled again. "Back to the subject of Max. Whatever your relationship with him is now, just know he's a good man. Sometimes he comes off overbearing, but he's had a lot to deal with since his father died."

"Why are you telling me this?"

"Because he's spent the last five years trying to make up for some mistake he made while in South Africa. After seeing a painting of you in his gallery, I suspected it had to do with you."

He must have done it years ago. I knew he painted to relieve stress, but I'd never thought I'd be one of his subjects.

Caitlin continued. "All I'm saying is give him a chance to show you who he is now."

"Caitlin, if he's such a great guy, why aren't you interested in him?"

She smiled and put her hand through mine, guiding me to the sofas in the lounge area. "Because he's like my brother and the thought of that is disgusting."

I laughed. "I get it. It seems a bit incestuous."

"Our parents assumed we'd end up together when we were young. Even Jacob tried his best to mold us into a couple, but it was never going to happen. I pretend for our family's sake. The idea of two well-connected families joining is good for business."

"I completely understand. Why do you think Lex and I are always seen together?"

"Yes, too bad he's already taken."

Does she know something about Lex I don't?

"I'm sure you've got men clamoring for you. You're gorgeous."

"I appreciate that, but—" her face softened all of a sudden "—I'm not interested in any relationships. You see, I gave my heart to someone years ago, and I never got it back."

Caitlin lifted her hand and tucked a stray hair behind her ear. A triskele charm hung from her wrist, in a design synonymous with the kink community. The bracelet was something a lover gave to claim his submissive.

Oh, she's in the lifestyle. I shook my head. How had I wound up in a world where nearly everyone I was close to practiced some form of BDSM? Hell, as of tonight I'd become an active member of the same circle again.

Caitlin caught me staring at her wrist and blushed as she tucked it into the long sleeve of her dress. "I'm not used to people recognizing its meaning."

"I'll keep it a secret."

"Yours is safe with me, too. I understand more than most the need for discretion."

How does she know about me? Do I have a sign on my head that states "submissive standing here"?

She answered my unsaid question: "It's in your eyes. Every time you turned in his direction, I saw it."

Milla once told me a submissive always drew her master's attention. I guess she was right. "We'll need to let my relationship with Max run its course and then see where we end up." I pulled out my cell phone from my clutch and checked the time. Max's car would arrive in less than five minutes. "I have to go, but I'd love to meet with you again. I enjoyed our chat, and thanks for the advice."

"Bye. Remember what I said about him."

We both gathered our purses and walked out of the lounge. Caitlin returned to the ballroom and I went toward the hotel entrance.

"Oh Arya," Caitlin called.

I paused.

"Tell Max I said bye."

"I will," I said as I walked out the door.

James waited for me as I exited the hotel, and he led me to Max's car.

"Do me a favor. Please tell Lex I left."

"Ms. Rey, are you sure this is a good idea? I'd prefer you didn't go anywhere without me."

I smiled. "There's nothing to worry about, James. I know you don't approve, but I am a grown-up."

"I will accept your choice," James grumbled.

He opened the door and I slipped in. Max sat in the back waiting for me. James gave him the once-over and said to me, "If you need me, give me a ring."

"That won't be necessary. She's in good hands," Max stated as he motioned for me to sit next to him.

"That is Ms. Rey's decision."

James closed the door, and I shook my head at the testosterone spraying.

"I don't think he likes me," Max commented with a hint of amusement. He handed me a glass of sparkling water.

"James thinks of himself as my surrogate father, and you don't make the cut."

"I guess we both have people in our lives that don't like the relationships we're in."

Did he have to bring up that arrogant ass, Jacob?

"I don't need a reminder of how your best bud thinks I'm a gold-digging whore. Too bad he can't say that anymore, since my portfolio is worth more than yours." I set my water in the holder and glared.

"When the hell did he say that to you? Dammit, Arya, I never thought that."

What? How could he have not known?

"Then why did you say the shit you said to me? Let me remind you of your most telling phrase. 'Arya, did you really believe you could fit into my lifestyle? We come from two different worlds.' Or did those words slip from your memory?"

"Fuck." He ran a frustrated hand through his hair. "Arya, this is not how I imagined tonight starting. I'm telling you this now, for the last time. I never let Jacob influence me. I willingly admit I was young, stupid, and scared, and you brought out emotions that left me terrified. Instead of accepting how I felt about you, I pushed you away and said horrible things. Never, I mean never, have I thought you were after my money. It never crossed my mind."

"We need to let this drop. There's no point in rehashing everything. We can't change the past, and I've already told you what I want for the future."

"Fine, we'll drop it for now." He picked up a tumbler of bourbon and downed it.

We drove the rest of the way in silence. Every so often, he peered my way but then returned to the view outside his window. I studied his profile. He'd changed in five years. Today he oozed self-confidence and determination, and he'd filled out in all the right places.

When we'd first met, he had the wounded manner of a man who'd lost his innocence. His father had been murdered, leaving him and Carmen to reassemble the pieces after a Wall Street scandal that had nearly destroyed their family's company. Lex, his best friend at the time, had forced him on an international service trip as a way to give him perspective.

I was there during the same time, for almost the same reason. After finishing my double master's and working on the MI6 project, I had lost my love of software development. Milla had thought volunteering to bring technology to remote regions of South Africa would give me a new purpose. Since there was no arguing with Milla when she had her mind set on something, I agreed to go with her and took the first flight out after graduation to Cape Town.

The minute we met in the volunteer tent, there were sparks. He astounded me. I could barely hold his gaze every time he glanced my way. Instantly, he brought out a side of me I had never thought existed. The Dom in him recognized and drew out my submissive nature. At first, I was frightened by my response, but quickly I accepted who I was and felt at home.

Over the next three months, he introduced me to all the games and kinks of a D/s relationship. To the outside world, we were a perfect case of opposites attracting: a boy from the world of privilege and a girl from the world of hard knocks who fell in love. Everything, I believed, was real until that fateful day. The day I held a positive test in my back pocket as he broke my heart.

Hearing him tell me he was scared brought slight closure, but nothing would ever seal the book on that portion of my life. Our relationship may have lasted only the few months we were in Cape Town, but the results of it had pushed me to create the future I have now.

Shaking the sadness from my thoughts, I peered out the window toward the massive gardens lining the front of Max's estate.

We drove through the entrance in continued silence. The car door opened, and Max held out his hand as we exited. My anxiety peaked.

Am I making a big mistake?

I hesitated a little and Max stopped. His eyes searched mine, his own apprehension evident in his blazing emerald gaze.

"Arya, the second you open those doors, you belong to me. Body, mind, and soul. As you said, this time you're going in with eyes wide open." His thumb traced my lips and down my neck, and a shiver prickled down my spine. "Make your choice. Enter now as my submissive or later as my bride."

CHAPTER TEN

A$re those the only choices I get?" I challenged him, staring straight into his eyes.

"Yes. There is no ending this." He paused and guided me toward the door. "For either of us. Make your decision, *mere chote pakshee*."

My little bird.

I inhaled sharply. I hadn't been called that in over five years. My heart clenched as images of the many nights we'd spent together in Cape Town appeared before my eyes.

I was positive that no matter what decision I made right now, it would lead to hurt, but I had to take a chance. At least if I went in as his submissive, my heart would remain mine.

I shuddered inside. Maybe if I kept telling myself that lie, I'd start to believe it.

Without saying a word, I moved forward. A moment of hurt crossed Max's face, but he quickly replaced it with his usual self-confidence.

He guided me through the house and into a hallway I assumed led to the private suites. "Go upstairs to the third door on the left. Wait for me. *Do not go in.*" His voice grew icy, controlled as my Dom from years ago emerged.

My core quivered.

Nodding, I climbed the stairs. I fell into a trance, barely noticing my surroundings. The house was centuries old and probably opulent, but the details remained a haze. I paused outside the room and waited.

Anticipation and need stirred deep in my belly. If his voice sent me to this place, what would happen when I entered the room?

I felt Max behind me. He plucked my hair free of its confines, allowing the pins to fall to the ground, then he gathered it on one shoulder. He leaned down and kissed the back of my neck.

Goose bumps prickled my skin and my heartbeat accelerated.

"I hate your hair up. With me, you will wear it down," he murmured into my ear. He reached around me and cracked the door open. "You know where to go when we enter, but make sure to take off your dress. I want to see if you followed my directions."

The hard contours of his body molded themselves to my back, while his intoxicating scent enveloped me. I yearned to tilt my head back and lick his neck. His straining erection nudged my behind, screaming its readiness.

I entered a dimly lit living room, illuminated by candles and a roaring fire. A small chest sat upon a low-lying table in the center of the room. A large, blue square pillow was placed on the floor next to the table. The aroma of lavender and eucalyptus filled the air. The only sounds in the room were the crackle of the fireplace and the low, sensual voice of a blues singer crooning in the background.

I casually strolled in, attempting to give the image of confidence, even though my stomach twisted with uneasy anticipation. I refused to peek over my shoulder; the slightest look would solidify my uncertainty. Moving farther into the room, I unzipped my dress, letting it fall to the floor, and then picked it up. Max inhaled a rough breath, and my confidence grew.

"Leave it."

I stilled. I left the dress where it fell and sauntered toward the pillow. The box sat calling me; the thought of its contents and the things Max planned to do with them. I bit my lip as the throbbing in my clit intensified. I rested my hand on the box and leaned on it as I knelt. I lacked the grace I possessed many years ago, but perhaps with a little practice, I'd learn to move with the fluidity of my younger years.

A low hum came from his direction.

"Open your eyes, Arya." He pushed himself away from the door and walked toward me.

My breath quickened, and I complied. I stared into his desire-filled eyes as his gaze devoured me. He'd changed from his tuxedo into a pair casual khakis and a black T-shirt. Everything about him screamed "Master of Control."

He circled me. "You're so beautiful and all mine. Every inch of you." He trailed his fingers gingerly across the front of my shoulder, barely skimming the tops of my breasts and around to my back where he paused. My skin tingled as his hand swept down my exposed spine until he met the bottom of my corset, just below my waist.

Bending down, his breath kissed my neck and spine, following in the path of his fingers. A moan escaped my mouth, and my nipples budded tight. This anticipation was killing me. I kept my eyes forward, staring at the door.

"Now let's see what we have in here." Max opened the chest with a click and took something out. He gathered my hands behind me and weaved a soft satin ribbon around my wrists and arms.

"Tonight we're going to go gently. I need to make sure you're ready for all the games we both love. Like in the past, if you say stop, we stop. No safe words needed other than those four letters. I control the scene. You control your limits. I won't challenge you beyond what I think you can take, and I will always keep you safe. Do you understand?"

I nodded my head in agreement, not wanting to give away any of my emotions. He saw too much as it was.

"I need the words."

"Yes," I stated without inflection, even though my mind was reeling for what the night would bring.

Max paused. "Yes, what?"

"Yes, Sir."

"I smell your arousal, Arya. You can try that cool, detached submissive routine all you want, but your body is begging for me."

I remained still before him. My breasts strained and trembled through the top of my corset. Five years of untapped need screamed for release.

After a while, he shifted to stand in front of me. His arousal strained in his pants, a breath away from my lips. I licked them without thought. Well aware of what he wanted, I waited for his command. He tilted my chin and peered down at me.

"Take every bit of me and don't stop until I give you permission. Do you understand?"

"Yes, Sir." I nodded my head and then cast my eyes back down at the opening of his slacks.

With slow controlled movements, Max unbuckled his belt and unzipped his pants, pulling out his cock a fraction away from my lips. He'd worn no underwear.

Saliva pooled in my mouth. A bead of precum escaped the tip, and my tongue poked out, licking the drop. A groan escaped from him, and he slid his cock past my lips, into my salivating mouth.

He tasted salty and sweet, just as I remembered. He grasped the back of my head, angled, and drove deeper into my throat, almost to the point where I would gag.

My eyes watered. He pulled out enough to let me breathe and wiped the tears running down my face.

"Swallow, Ari, and open the back of your throat. It will help you take me deeper."

I complied and the gagging stopped. He slowly worked his way in, this time giving me a gentle pace to become accustomed to his motion. The need to please him filled my core. The wetness of my arousal ran past my thong and down my thighs. My head rocked back and forth, harder with every moan I heard from him. He threaded his hands into my hair and took over. He fucked my mouth, in and out, in and out, until he grew larger.

"I'm close. Make me come, Ari." His inflexible grip clenched in my hair, sending a shot of fire and exhilaration through my scalp.

His words increased the desire flooding my pussy. I squirmed a little, trying to alleviate the need pulsating deep inside me.

"Ari…" he called as he came. He shuddered and groaned loudly as jets of cum shot to the back of my throat.

I swallowed and drank every drop he released, savoring his essence. His grip loosened from my hair and he gently withdrew from my mouth, tucking his now-soft cock back into his pants. I remained kneeling but weak from my exertion and the desire coursing through my body. My breath remained ragged, and I started to sit down.

Max steadied me and knelt in front of me, drawing me toward him and kissing me softly, sucking my lower lip into his mouth. He nuzzled the side of my face and cradled me in his arms. His fingers loosened the ties on my arms, allowing me some freedom, but he kept my wrists bound. He massaged my shoulders, making sure the circulation returned. This tender side of him was unexpected.

Is he trying to keep me off balance? My shields will break if he keeps this up.

Where was the Max of five years ago, the one who wouldn't stop his assault on the senses until he was good and ready?

I scanned his green eyes, not hiding my confusion. He gave me a knowing smile and kissed me again.

"Now your turn."

He picked me up with little effort and carried me over to the large leather sofa. He set me on my back and I waited. My hands rested at my lower back, forcing my hips slightly up.

He sat back and drank in the sight of me. "Oh Arya, you have no idea how amazing you look lying there for me."

His fingers trailed across the fullness of my bust before he lowered the cups of my corset, exposing my aching breasts. He knelt on the floor, squeezed my mounds, and took one of my pebbled nipples into his mouth. He laved attention until I cried out, then he shifted to the other, sucking and teasing his warm tongue over it. I moaned when he stood and walked away, but he returned with a small piece of ice in his mouth and resumed his ministrations.

His cold tongue flicked back and forth on my sensitized nipples and then circled the peaks. I cried out, arching my back, desperate for the exquisite agony to continue. His hand slipped down my chest, over my stomach, and between my thighs, pushing them open. His fingers grazed my black lace-covered clit as his mouth continued tormenting my swollen nipples.

I moaned, "Please." But I didn't know for what I begged.

He smiled against my nipples. "Is there something you want me to do?"

"I want your mouth on me."

He continued teasing my clit with his fingers.

"Where do you want my mouth? Remember, I can't tend to you unless you tell me what you need."

How could I have forgotten? Max loved forcing me to voice my desires, even to my embarrassment.

"I want your mouth on my pussy, please, Sir, now," I begged.

"Your wish is my command." His mouth followed the path of his hand, stopping at the bottom of the corset top, just above my mound. I stiffened, and for a split second, fear invaded my mind. If he unlaced the top, he would see the scars.

"Relax, Ari. I want to remove this sexy thong so nothing is in between my mouth and your swollen, tasty pussy." He nudged the flimsy straps of my thong down my hips but left them near my knees. His breath heated my labia, and my stomach quivered in anticipation. He used his fingers to spread my folds wide, and the stubble on his chin grazed my clit.

I cried out at the exquisite torture, and then his tongue pressed in. I lost all sense of time and place. The only thing my body could do was feel. Max's tongue pistoned in and out of me as I bucked, and he slid his fingers deep into my channel, pushing against my G-spot.

"Oh yes, that's the sound I want to hear," he murmured and continued his ministrations to my aching core.

I struggled against the ribbon holding my wrists. My fingers curled in the leather of the sofa as he rubbed my clit with his tongue and pumped deeper with his fingers. He fucked me, stretching me wide until I yearned for his cock.

"I know what you want, but not until you give me what I want. Come for me, Arya. Come."

On command, I cried out his name, as stars exploded behind my eyes. I clenched my teeth shut, trying desperately not to make too loud a sound, but to no avail. The orgasm tore through me, and I erupted in the throes of complete bliss.

As my mind still reeled from my orgasm, Max untied my

wrists and carried me to another room. My back hit the softness of a bed as my body finally came down from its spasms.

"Now we'll play our first game," Max said. He walked out of the room and reappeared with the chest. He set it on the floor at the foot of the bed and from its contents selected a silver chain with small screw clamps on each end and a black butt plug.

I swallowed down the apprehension coursing through me as a new level of awareness settled in my gut. Five years ago, I'd played about every scene imaginable, including anal, but now the thought of it frightened me.

"I know what you're focused on. I won't push you tonight. It's to help train your passage."

"Yes, Sir."

Max leaned over me and took one nipple into his mouth. I arched at the intense pleasure but then cried out as an intense pain shot through me. Max's gaze met mine as I gasped in air, and he smiled as he adjusted the jeweled clamp against my tender nipple. The dizziness cleared and left a dull sensual throb.

"One down and one to go."

I whimpered but didn't cry out as he repeated the process on the other bud, leaving my sensitive breasts aching and my core clenching from the arousal he'd heightened.

"Turn around and lay with your hands stretched out above your head and your feet tucked under you. I want that beautiful pussy and ass lifted for my viewing pleasure."

As I followed his directions, the beads hanging on the chain that connected my clamps swayed back and forth on my pinched nipples. Each movement of my body as it shifted sent a simultaneous wave of discomfort and gratification through me. My face rested against the soft silk sheets and the smell of spiced cologne and crisp linen filled my nose.

Max's scent. This wasn't the playroom, as I'd thought. It was his bedroom. No matter what walls I put up, he was determined to push past them. By bringing me into his private space, he knew I wouldn't be able to keep my emotions at a distance.

Oh, Max. How am I going to resist you?

He took my hands, grasped them firmly above my head, and tied them with straps attached to the headboard. Another spasm rippled through my sex.

"Beautiful. I've dreamed about you in this exact position." He ran his palm down my spine and stopped above my right butt cheek. "This is new. A phoenix. The symbol of life and re-birth."

He traced the mythical bird I'd had tattooed on myself years ago. I bit my lip and prayed he wouldn't ask me about it. This wasn't the time or place to discuss the ink.

"Stay like that. I'll be back in a moment."

I sighed in relief.

Wait a second. Where the hell is he going?

The door clicked shut, and complete silence filled the bedroom. Being alone meant I had time to think. This was not good.

Patience, Arya.

Something Max told me repeatedly I lacked when he first introduced me to this lifestyle.

With my body stretched out and my ass in the air, my wetness cooled as it slid down my legs. I needed to rub my thighs and relieve some of the desire pulsating in me.

Would he know if I moved?

Of course he would. I couldn't remember an instance when he hadn't noticed. Besides, the punishment wasn't worth the defiance. Max would bring me to the verge of orgasm and refuse to send me over until I begged him to let me come. I moaned aloud at the memory.

How long would he make me wait? It felt like I'd been in this damn position forever. I adjusted my head slightly to glimpse at the door.

"Didn't I say to stay still?" The crack of Max's hand coming down on my bottom shocked me into jolting forward.

Fuck! He was still in the room.

A second smack landed on the other cheek. I crunched my eyes and breathed through the contact.

"I can't hear you."

"Yes, Sir," I hissed out.

Max massaged the spots where his hand had landed. "I'm surprised you didn't move sooner. Now count. We'll begin with ten, and I'll include the first two since we are, in a sense, starting your training over."

His palm struck down in a whisper but with an undeniable sting.

"Three." I drew a shaky breath and prepared for the next strike.

The fourth hit landed to the side of my labia, sending a spasm into my core. By the time I called out ten, I was ready to surrender to the affliction of pain and bliss. Tears ran out of my eyes, but I craved more.

A bottle clicked open and then Max was rubbing a cool, medicated cloth against my burning behind. "I'm sorry, Ari. I hadn't planned on pushing you this far so soon."

My heart ached from the regret in his voice. I held my position, keeping my face pressed into the bed. "I'm fine, Sir. I'd forgotten how exhilarating it could be. I didn't expect to fall into the trance so fast."

One of Max's palms slid down my back and between my folds. "You're soaked. Did the waiting arouse you or the spanking?"

"Both."

His fingers teased my opening but never drove deeper. I lifted against him, the need he aroused overwhelming me.

He pulled back abruptly. "You come when I say. I hold the reins here, Arya."

He used the voice again. The one that sent heat firing throughout me.

"I'm sorry, Sir," I whimpered.

His hand returned to my center, but this time there was no teasing. He collected my wetness and brought it to my puckered opening. I contracted my cheeks in immediate response.

"Relax. I've already told you, I'm preparing you tonight. I'll save that sweet hole of yours for another time."

I unclenched as warmed lube soothed my muscles, and Max's finger pressed its way in. A slow burn seared my opening until my tension eased. He inched deeper and deeper. Another digit joined the first, and he drummed in and out until I cried out from the sensation. I arched my body, but my tied arms kept me from moving too much.

My core contracted, and I forced myself away from going over. Unless Max approved, I wasn't allowed to come.

"Please," I cried.

"Not yet."

He continued holding me on the cusp, and then all of the sudden, his finger withdrew and something solid slid into me. It gradually stretched me until the intense pressure was almost unbearable. Sweat broke out over my forehead, and I gritted my teeth against the clenching discomfort.

Max took the restraints off my arms and turned me over. He spread my legs apart and his mouth descended onto my swollen nub. "Now you can come."

My hand grasped his hair and I convulsed against his mouth and the plug, crying out his name.

As I cascaded down from my free fall, Max parted my wet folds and bathed the head of his cock in my dripping slit. Then he plunged forward and deep. I screamed from the overload of sensation. He braced his hands on either side of my head, and I bucked under each thrust. The pleasure was hot and fierce with each slide of Max's cock in my pussy and the plug shifting back and forth in my ass. The smell of hot, wet sex permeated the room.

Max reached between our bodies finding the chain connecting the nipple clamps. He held my gaze and yanked the clamps free. Pain engulfed me as another orgasm crashed through me.

"That's it, my love," he called as he followed me.

CHAPTER ELEVEN

I woke to the sun streaming through the windows. Shifting, I noticed the weight of a hand resting against my stomach. I jolted but calmed when I realized I still wore my bustier from the night before.

I sank back into the sheets and tilted my head, taking in Max's sleeping form. The warmed scent of linen and crisp body wash lingered on his skin. He must have gotten up to take a shower, since his hair was still damp.

I ran my fingertips along his whiskered jaw. He appeared so young and unguarded. Even with the hurt and pain between us, I still loved him.

I closed my eyes and inhaled. The least I could do was be honest with myself.

I'd kept up with all the news about him, from his tabloid exploits to his ruthless business reputation. Every time I'd read about his new flavor of the week, I wanted to punch something. Now, knowing the truth, I had to accept that a future without him was going to be difficult.

What if I can't let him go? Can I trust that this time it's real?

I shook the unhappy thoughts from my mind as rays of light highlight Max's features. His thick chocolate-brown hair and lashes was sharply contrasted against his light-gold skin. I traced his chiseled arms, shoulder, and abs and almost moaned, remembering how they felt against me. Man, that body knew how to make me scream.

My skin warmed. He'd made love to me several time throughout the night.

No, not love. He'd fucked me.

After our initial round, he woke me three times, once to remove the plug and hold me in sleep, then twice more for pure, emotion-filled, sensual sex. I refused to linger on that, or I'd be carried away by the feelings he'd brought forth.

I shifted again and enjoyed the soreness running through all the right places in my body. A light haze of tenderness grazed over my ass and a shiver prickled down my spine. Wow, the memory of last night's spanking was still arousing.

My Max had undoubtedly given me one amazingly erotic evening.

I went rigid.

Not my Max.

This was temporary. I couldn't let myself believe this was anything more than sex.

I sighed internally. Now if my brain and heart agreed.

My breath hitched as Max's hand tightened around my stomach.

I had to take a shower before he woke or I'd have to explain my scars, and I wasn't ready for that conversation. A twinge of disappointment coursed through me. Shower sex was one of my favorite activities in the morning. Oh well, I'd learn to live with the memories.

With slow, gentle movements, I scooted out from under Max's arm and sat up, swinging my legs over the side of the bed. I turned, making sure Max still slept, but caught his emerald green eyes staring at me.

"Do you know how incredibly sexy you are right now?" Max ran his hand down my spine, unlacing my corset. I held my breath and clutched the boned material. "I'm going to paint you like that one of these days."

His words rippled over me and sent a flood of wetness between my thighs.

"Where were you sneaking off to?" he said as he sat up and his eyes cleared.

I held his gaze and hoped he didn't see my anxiety. "To shower. I wanted to freshen up a bit. When did you wake up?"

Max relaxed against the headboard. "I woke a few hours ago and went to my studio to work."

"What were you painting?"

He quirked his brow, as if asking him that question was stupid. "An artist doesn't reveal too many details until the painting is complete. But if you must know, it's the same subject I've painted for the past five years."

My breath hitched. We couldn't go there.

"Why don't you make us something to eat while I get ready?" I said, trying to change the subject.

"I'd rather have you for breakfast." Max leaned toward me

and kissed the side of my neck. I involuntarily tilted my head to the side, giving him better access. His palm crept around my waist, over my hands, and to my bare breasts. He cupped the heavy globes and groaned. "I'm so glad no other man knows what an incredible body hides beneath your uptight clothing."

Max pinched my nipple, and I arched into his hand.

"You're mine, Arya."

"Yes." I gasped. "For…for as long as we're together." I couldn't let him think this was more than it was.

Max growled and yanked my head back with my hair, making my skin prickle.

"*You. Are. Mine*," he gritted out.

"Max," I hissed. "We discussed this yesterday."

He abruptly released me.

"Go take your shower." His voice was cold. "I'll meet you in the kitchen."

I rose and clutched the corset to my stomach as if it were a life vest. I took a deep breath and crossed to the bathroom door.

"Drop the lingerie. Your new clothes will be on the bed."

I said nothing and followed his command. With my back to him, he wouldn't see the scars. I walked into the bathroom and closed the door, locking it behind me. I leaned against the wood, shut my eyes, and attempted to steady my emotions.

Why, of all times, did he want more now?

I'd have given anything for him to commit to me years ago, but now I didn't have it in me to believe it would last.

I opened my eyes and caught sight of all my beauty products lined up on one side of the vanity.

Oh, Max.

He remembered. How was I going to resist him when he kept showing me I mattered?

Don't become attached. Enjoy him while this lasts, Arya.

A knock on the door snapped me out of my stupor. "Hurry up, Ari. Breakfast will be ready in a few minutes."

"Okay, I'll be down shortly," I responded and rushed to shower.

Twenty minutes later, I walked out of the bathroom to find a white, almost see-through, yoga tank and black stretch shorts laid out on the bed.

No bra or undies, I see.

I slipped my clothes on and padding down the corridor, I discovered the house displayed even more opulence and grandeur in the light of day. Antiques and rare paintings, no doubt collected over centuries, filled every hallway. The Danes were New England royalty. They'd moved to the United States from Denmark in the seventeen hundreds and stayed, becoming one of the wealthiest landowning families in the country.

My stomach growled, reminding me I hadn't eaten much last night due to my nerves. I headed toward the kitchen.

I crossed the threshold of Max's palatial kitchen and stopped midstep. He multitasked behind the stove, sautéing vegetables with one hand and flipping an omelet with the other. He wore a pair of loose-fitting jeans and nothing else, and his muscular back rippled with each movement of his arms and shoulders. The dragon tattoo on his shoulder stretched and bunched, accentuating his honed form.

I remembered the night in Cape Town when I convinced him to get it. I'd told him it symbolized wisdom, strength, and power. He'd smiled, told me he needed all of that to deal with his future, and sat down in the chair.

I lingered in the archway of the room, transfixed by his smooth and fluid motions. Damn, I loved a man who knew his way around a kitchen.

He must have sensed my presence, since he grabbed a plate and slid food onto it. "Stop standing there and take a seat. Your food is ready, and I made you some chai."

My heart skipped a beat. He remembered I loved Indian tea in the morning. Why did he pay attention now when he never did before?

"Arya, sit."

I jumped at his command and sat on a stool at the island. Max placed my breakfast in front of me, and I proceeded to inhale the food.

"Mmm, this is delicious. You always knew how to cook."

He took a seat across from me and smiled. "I love watching you eat. Last night you barely touched your plate. I'm glad you have your appetite back."

I paused, looking down. I was eating like a starved horse.

"Aren't you going to eat?"

He took a sip of his coffee. "I ate after my session in the studio."

"It feels weird to have you watch me eat."

"Fine, give me a bite. Then you won't be eating alone."

I brought the fork to his mouth and his lips folded around the peppers and egg. The same lips that devoured me last night. A sudden urge to cross my legs coursed through me.

"Happy? Now finish your food. I have plans for the rest of the day."

"Oh really? And what would they be?"

"A bit of exercise and then a visit to a special room."

Oh, the playroom.

A heaviness tightened my chest as I realized his bedroom last night was only to make me comfortable—it wasn't to break down the wall, as I'd thought.

God, I am so messed up, and we haven't even been together more than a night.

Oh, well, I'd never played in a proper playroom before, and the idea of it both scared and thrilled me.

"Don't worry, we'll take it slow. We made do when we were in Cape Town, but here I'm well prepared."

His cool voice sent a shiver up my spine, and I dropped my fork. As I reached down to pick it up, Max's fingers touched the ink exposed by my minuscule shorts. I stayed folded over and savored the feel of his light touch on my back as he traced the mystical bird.

Abruptly, he grasped my arm and tugged me back to sitting. "Here, use a different one." He plucked the dirty fork from my fingers and replaced it with a clean one from the other side of the counter.

He sat back on his stool and gestured for me to continue eating. "Tell me about your bird."

I glanced up from my plate. "It symbolizes my rebirth from the ashes," I said cautiously, not wanting to reveal too much.

Sadness flashed across his face. "Did I hurt you so much that you felt that way?"

"Don't flatter yourself. You were part of it, but other things devastated me even more."

"Will you tell me what happened?"

My breath hitched. "Revealing my secrets wasn't part of our deal. This is just physical." My voice quivered and immediately I regretted my words. No matter what I said, I knew it was more than physical.

I'm such an idiot.

His eyes went cold, and he stared at me as if he wanted to argue, but he let it go.

"Breakfast's over, Arya. Follow me."

CHAPTER TWELVE

W here are you taking me?"

Ignoring my question, Max pulled me from my seat, then led me out of the kitchen and up a set of stairs I hadn't seen earlier. They opened on the second floor but on the opposite side of Max's wing.

We paused outside two large mahogany doors. "Give me your hand. I'm going to program access to the room."

He placed my palm over a metal plate that illuminated red with the press of my skin.

Max keyed in the security code and the panel changed to green under my fingers and the door unlocked.

"From now on, this is where we'll play," he said, as I followed him inside. "There's a bedroom and dressing room to the left, and the playroom is to the right."

His harsh tone caused me to pause, but the gentle hand on my back moved me forward.

"I would give you the world and this is all you want." He released a deep sigh. "So be it. I'll take you on your terms."

He's giving me what I asked for. Then why does it feel so wrong?
"Go to the Saint Andrew's cross and kneel."

"Yes, Sir," I whispered.

Warily, I entered the room to the right and surveyed its contents. Wood the same shade as the door paneled the walls. Dark hues covered every inch of the space with the exception of the floor, which was a sharp contrast of polished ivory travertine.

My unsteady breath echoed around me, and even the slightest sound would reverberate like the crack of a whip.

One wall held cabinets and drawers that blended with the sharp masculine space. A spanking bench sat to the right, padded with plush leather and places to strap arms and legs without discomfort.

The cross stood in the center of the room. Saliva pooled in my mouth as uncertainty entered my being. Was this how I really wanted it between us? I swallowed and reached inside myself for courage to go through with my plan. I squared my shoulders, released a deep exhale, and moved to the foreboding piece of furniture.

Circling the unit, I grazed my fingers across the thick wood beams of the cross and noted the leather cuffs. My core quickened in anticipation. He'd fuck me on this soon.

A sapphire-blue pillow sat two feet in front of the cross. I sank to my knees, spread them wide in the pose I remembered Max preferred, and rested my palms against my thighs while keeping my gaze downcast.

That wasn't bad. I'd slid into the pose without stumbling.

"You look exquisite with your eyes down and your thighs spread, but I can't see the treasure in between," Max said as he positioned himself in front of me.

"Do you want me to undress, Sir?" My eyes remained lowered, but I couldn't help but notice the magnificent erection hidden under his pants. I licked my lips in hopes of tasting him again.

All of a sudden, I feared he'd expect me to take off everything. My shoulders tensed and I resigned myself to what came next: questions about the past and why I kept our daughters from him.

"Take off the shorts but leave the top on."

My spine relaxed as relief flooded my body.

Max extended his hand. "Why are you tense? This isn't much different from our nights in Cape Town. The only change is the setting."

I slid my palm over his and allowed him to help me stand. We stared at each other for a brief moment before he fisted my hair, tilted my head back, and kissed me.

Releasing me, he squatted down. "I'll do this."

He trailed his fingers over my neck and between my breasts, down my shirt-covered stomach to the edge of my shorts. With slow, gentle movements, he tugged the elastic down until the fabric collected at my feet. The cool air in the room chilled my body, causing it to prickle with goose bumps. My aching clit poked out between my swollen folds as Max's warm breath grazed the sensitized flesh. A moan escaped my lips.

"I love the smell of you," he said, licking my seam. "Stand in front of the cross. I'll strap you in."

Following his directions, I waited for him to position me, but soon realized my body was too small for the leather to hold me comfortably. My feet wouldn't touch the floor if he cuffed my arms. I hoped he knew what he was doing.

As if reading my thoughts, he responded, "Don't worry. You'll be completely suspended in a few minutes."

Okay, now how was he planning to get me on that thing?

"Come here."

I moved, and his fingers encircled my wrists. He pulled the soft cloth-lined leather cuffs from one corner of the beam and released them through a loop. The sound of the chain clanging resonated throughout the space. He brought a restraint toward me and secured my wrist with the soft, buttery straps, then repeated the process on the other side.

The binding felt loose, but the gleam in his eyes told me he'd soon cinch them tight against the wood.

"Now, your feet."

He caressed the insides of my thighs, sending a jolt of nervous desire through me as he skimmed lower to my feet. He harnessed each ankle, leaned to his left, picked up a stool, and placed it by my feet.

"Step onto it so I can tighten the chains."

I followed his instructions and waited.

"Ready?"

"Yes, Sir."

My heart leaped into my stomach at the first sound of the metal sliding through the hinge of the beam. My arms lifted above my head, attaching to the beams of the cross, with the stool being the only thing that kept me from hanging by my wrists. "Let's secure your legs." Max tightened the restraints, making sure I kept my balance until I was incapable of anything but the tiniest movements. He fastened two straps under my arms and across my chest that immediately relieved the strain on my arms.

"Now it's time to play." Max surveyed me from a few feet away. His eyes glazed with desire as a wicked grin slid across his face. "There are so many things I've dreamed of doing to that beautiful body of yours. I plan to explore as many of them as possible."

My sex throbbed at his words, and a smile touched my lips. For a man who'd expected some form of sexual gratification multiple times a day, five years of frustration was coming to a head, and all because of me.

"What's put that expression on your face?"

"Knowing that there is a high chance I'm not going to be able to walk properly after you are done with me."

He closed the space between us and ran a finger over my mouth. "I'll take care of you, even if I have to carry you."

Lowering the neck of my tank, Max positioned the material under my breasts. "Now this is how I enjoy seeing you. Your tits and pussy exposed and ready for me to do whatever I desire."

My breath quickened and my nipples pebbled. His hot gaze told me he approved of my reaction. His thumb flicked my taut bud, and I arched into his touch, but he pulled away. He surveyed me as I hung suspended before him.

"You're at my mercy," he hummed. "Do you know how gorgeous you are? Maybe sometime in the next fifty years or so I'll get used to it."

Please don't say things like that. I can't risk giving you what you want.

"Now let's adjust this. I want to feel that hot wet mouth on my cock."

He tilted the cross with a tug of a lever, and soon I found myself lying on my back with my head angled toward the floor and my mouth perfectly aligned with his rock-hard erection. A rustling caught my ears as Max removed his clothes.

I waited, and my vision settled on the mirror positioned above me on the ceiling. I exhibited complete wantonness, with my skin and face flushed, my nipples erect, and my pussy glistening. I stared back at myself with excitement and a little trepidation. Nothing could stop him from lifting my shirt and seeing my scars, and all I could do was hope he wouldn't.

"Open up, Arya. I want to fuck your mouth while I play with your body."

Tilting my head back, I spread my lips. He made a noise of pleasure, a tiny moan that went silent the moment I took him into my mouth. With wicked joy, I savored his flavor as he pumped in slow strokes from the rim of my lips to the back of my throat.

He caressed my jaw with his fingers as my tongue worked the ridge of his head, circling it every time he withdrew. I loved his clean masculine scent, and every sound he made shot a spasm straight to my aching core.

He continued at a slow pace, and my reverse position left me helpless and at his mercy. My body burned as if on fire, desperate for even a little touch.

Sensing my need, he cupped my breasts and squeezed tight,

almost too tight. I cried out around him, and his cock swelled in my mouth, followed by an increase in his rhythm.

"I'm going to come," he called. "I'm sorry, baby." With those shaky words, he jerked and came deep in my throat. Salty and sweet, his unique essence coated my tongue. I swallowed every drop he released.

His cock softened in my mouth, as did his grip on my breasts. With a gentle caress, he disengaged from my body and leaned down to kiss me.

"Now that you've relieved some of my tension," he murmured against my lips, "I'll be able to last longer than a teenage boy seeing his first naked woman."

He kissed me again and stepped to the opposite end of the cross.

"Let's start with these."

I lifted my head to peer down my body at Max, standing naked and relaxed between my spread legs, and the two objects he held in his hands. The first was in the shape of an egg, a butt plug much larger than the one he used last night. Swallowing, I couldn't take my gaze from the alarming item.

Would my body accommodate such a massive device?

"This is smaller than I am, Arya. It will prepare you."

"Max, I'm not sure that I'm ready." I couldn't hide the apprehension in my voice.

"You will be once I am done with you." He responded with a chuckle. "This." He held a silver rod with a bulbous head. The form was thin, no more than the circle of my fingers but at least ten inches long and smooth. "With the plug will have you so stimulated, you'll be begging for my cock."

I swallow the uncertainty down, and tried to remember the pleasure he gave me through all forms of anal play.

"Baby, this is for your enjoyment as much as mine."

He ran the dildo up and down my legs in a gentle caress, stopping a hairbreadth from my dripping pussy. He teased the outside of my labia, making sure not to touch my clit. I shifted my hips, trying to get him to brush the part of me that begged for his caress, but he pulled away the second I moved.

"P-p-please…" I moaned.

"In time, baby. Now let me place our toys in their temporary home." Leaning over to a set of drawers on the wall, Max selected a tube of lubricant. His erection was no longer soft from release but semierect.

Damn, he had fabulous recovery.

"Tilt your head back and close your eyes. I want you to feel but not see."

I followed his directions. But right before I shut my lids, I caught a brief image of my strapped, helpless self. I couldn't believe how incredibly sexy I looked.

Was this how Max saw me?

"In case you're tempted to peek." He slipped a silk mask over my eyes and tied it behind my head.

In immediate response, my senses fired to life, from heightened hearing and the sound of our breaths to the lingering taste of Max still on my tongue. Soft silicone stroked over my nipples and down the center of my shirt, stopping at the crease of my bare pussy. Cool liquid grazed against my puckered back entrance.

"You're so wet I don't need to use any lube, but I want to make this as pleasurable as possible."

He drew my arousal with his thumb to mix with the gel, and slipped two fingers into my rosette.

I arched in response to the invasion. "Oh."

"You like that," he crooned. His words were more a statement than a question, and I couldn't argue.

The plug slid lower, lingered at the opening of my soaked pussy, but quickly moved and pressed into the space his finger had vacated. At the same time, he slipped something cold and hard into my vagina.

I squeezed around both objects, gripping them tight inside me. I breathed through the simultaneous discomfort and ecstasy of fullness.

"Let me clean up and you relax."

Sure, that's going to happen with two large masses inside me.

I was lulled by the sound of Max's movements around the room, the water in the sink I hadn't known was there, and the smell of the candles he'd lit. Suddenly, I jumped as my body throbbed, my breath quickening and my mind fogging from the onslaught of stimulation.

The plug and the phallus were vibrating.

"Max," I called, as the pulsation of the devices increased.

"I'm here, baby." His lips grazed my forehead. "I want you so wet and out of your mind that when I take you, you'll only focus on your release."

Everything inside me tightened, and I arched up and squared my hips, needing some form of relief. The hot wetness of his tongue skimmed my clit and I went off.

I contracted around the dildo and cried out, "*Max!*"

"That's it, baby. I love the sound of my name screamed when you find your pleasure." He pumped the pulsating metal inside my pussy, back and forth, refusing to let me come down from my orgasm. "In a moment, my cock will fill your ass and there won't be a single place on your body that my cum hasn't marked as mine."

His words propelled me over the edge of another orgasm. My fists yanked against the restraints and my fingers dug into my palms. I thrashed my head back and forth as my body bucked.

"Please, Sir. I can't take any more."

He slid the plug from between my cheeks. "One more and then I'll let you rest." He pressed his slick cockhead against my stretched hole and surged forward.

We both groaned as he eased his cock deeper. The device in my pussy vibrated stronger, and I bore down until Max was in me to the hilt.

"Do you like that?" he gritted out.

"Yes, Sssir…"

He pumped himself and the vibrator inside of me, engulfing my body in sensation.

How could he make me love something that was taboo to the outside world?

I clenched my eyes, reveling in the sensation of the combined movement of Max's cock pounding my ass and the vibrating dildo in my pussy.

"Give it to me, now," Max bit out. "You're so tight, I'm about to go."

On demand, I came apart. My release washed over me in waves, sending euphoria into every pore of my body. Max called out moments later. Warm jets of liquid gushed inside me as he slowed his movements.

"Oh Ari, that was beautiful."

My breath calmed to a point but the vibrator still humming in my pussy prevented me from relaxing. I whimpered against the continuous torment.

The scent of our lovemaking enveloped both of us, and his sweat-dampened skin relaxed against my body. My heart clenched as the thought of what had really just happened washed over me. This wasn't just two people with no attachments enjoying kinky sex. It was two people in love, who were making love.

What am I going to do?

I wanted the emotions to be real, to know that we had a future, but what if I took the step and he hurt me again? Tears prickled the back of my eyes. Inhaling deep, I shoved aside the uncertainty.

A click stopped the motion of the metal cock, and my mind returned to the present.

"Where did you go? For a moment, you were lost in your thoughts." Max pulled himself and the vibrator out in one swift motion.

The sudden emptiness left me devoid of the passion I'd felt moments earlier. "I'm a bit overwhelmed by what we did and how it made me feel."

Max sighed and kissed my forehead. "One doesn't work without the other. Without emotion, it's just fucking. Whether you want to admit it or not, what happened between us was more than fucking."

I ignored the turmoil his words fueled and asked, "Why do we need this? The kink, the bondage, any of it."

A snap rang out into the room and I found myself propelled forward as the cross was repositioned to a standing position.

"It's who we are." Removing my mask, he stared into my eyes. "Your sexual desire is freed by submitting, while mine is through domination. There's no shame in that."

Max unlatched my legs and helped me stand on the stool. With quick movements, he freed my arms and gathered me in his own before I collapsed from the onslaught of weight onto my unsteady legs.

"Let me lay you down on the bed."

He carried me out of the playroom and to the bedroom. He placed me gently in the center of the bed, tucking the soft silk sheets and comforter around me.

My body relaxed into the mattress as exhaustion overtook me.

He leaned over and kissed my lips. "Rest, my love. I'll join you after I clean up." He smiled down at me. "Once you've recovered, I plan to fulfill my promise of making it so you can't walk by the end of the weekend."

CHAPTER THIRTEEN

Ugh," I groaned as I reviewed the script for Arcane. I'd spent the past forty-eight hours locked in my lab trying to figure out where the glitch in the coding hid, but I couldn't find it anywhere.

How could the program run smoothly last week and this week freeze at every opportunity?

I peeked at the envelope sitting on one of the counters in the back of the room and a shiver when down my spine.

Don't freak out, Arya. All you can do is let James and the security team do their jobs.

When I'd arrived at the lab, it was waiting for me by the door. I'd thought nothing of it until I opened the letter and found a detailed list of all the things that would happen to me and my loved ones if I didn't hand over the software.

This, combined with the e-mail from last week and the results of my research on the Dark Web, revealed a bidding war for my software; I knew I was in trouble. Now I had to figure out how to tell Milla and Lex without them losing their shit. Hell, I was losing my shit, so I couldn't expect anything less from them. I took a few deep breaths to settle my nerves. Milla would be here any moment, and I had to stay calm and act normal.

I glanced at the door as Milla punched in her access code and entered the lab. She carried a box of goodies that smelled divine.

"Hey, *bella*, are you ready to come up for air? I brought you a little pick-me-up."

I pushed back from my computer and sighed. "I guess so. I can't figure out what went wrong. One minute it worked and the next it's shit."

I opened the lid and selected my favorite morning indulgence, a fresh-baked chocolate croissant. I bit into the pastry and hummed, enjoying the flavor of bitter yet sweet dark chocolate.

"How is that possible? Do you think someone interfered with the programming?" Milla walked over to my computer and leaned over my shoulder.

"Hate to bust your bubble, Miss. I know basic coding. But if I couldn't find the error, how are you going to see it?" I said as I continued munching on my breakfast.

"You never know, I might catch something you skimmed over."

She had a point. "Go ahead. Let me know if you find anything. Did you bring any liquid sustenance?"

Milla leaned over to the coffees, handed me one, and continued reading the script. I inhaled the warm scent and drank.

"Oh, this hits the spot. Thanks. I'm glad I keep you around."

"You're so funny. At least I don't smell like two-day-old stinky socks."

"Hey, I took my shower this morning."

Milla lifted her gaze from the computer and growled. "There has to be something both of us are missing. Are you sure something is different?"

"No, I'm not sure, but my gut says yes." *And the fact that I'm receiving threats doesn't help.* "I'm going to have to go through the coding line by line to confirm. I know I sound paranoid, but Jacob is top on my list of suspects." I licked my fingers, trying to get every last bit of chocolate.

"Arya, he can't decipher computer scripting from chopsticks. He's a marketing and finance geek."

"I know," I said. "It doesn't make sense, but he made a comment during our transitions meeting about the hidden profits and merits of doing business with us that didn't settle well with me. It was like he was gloating about something. I don't know." I shook my head. "Mil, he's the only one I can think of who wants to see me fail. Plus, I'm positive he suspects Max and I are involved again. Which I'm sure pissed him off to no end."

"I'll see if Lex can find out anything. Stop sucking on your fingers and get another croissant. I brought you a dozen." Milla picked up the box and shoved it at me.

"Did you know he wanted Max for his sister?"

"Who's his sister?"

"Caitlin Stanfield, our favorite fashion designer. She's the beautiful blonde seen on Max's arm whenever he's out and about."

"I know who she is. You're probably the only one on Earth who didn't. It's hard to believe she's Jacob's sister. She's too pretty to be related to him."

I rolled my eyes. Jacob had worked as a fashion model in his younger days, and I'd never met anyone more narcissistic. "She's his stepsister and actually nice. I happened to be wearing one of her designs the night we met."

"When was this?"

"Last Friday at the fund-raiser. We spoke in the ladies' lounge while I freshened up before meeting Max."

"You're the only person I know who makes friends during a potty break."

I stuck my tongue out, wiped my hands, and went back to tinkering on my computer.

"So what are you going to do about your suspicions? Are you going to say something to Max?"

"I don't think Max will ever believe his best bud is the culprit. Hell, I even doubt it myself, but I'm going to track who's been accessing our system." I typed in new code for the tracking system and piggybacked it to Arcane. It would keep all changes to the software hidden, and the only person who could activate Arcane would be me. But first, I had to...

"Excuse me. We were in the middle of a conversation when you spaced out making love to your computer."

I cringed then shrugged my shoulders. "Sorry." I continued typing. "I'm going to attach a tracer program to all the modules of Arcane. This way any unauthorized access will send out a ping to you, Lex, and me. As an added precaution, I'll keep my work on the encrypted server I have hidden in the vault."

"Normally I'd say that was overkill, but we have a lot at stake." From the beginning, Milla was apprehensive about the deal we'd made with the Department of Defense for the development of the security program, especially since it would involve a major cost to us if we didn't deliver. But without risks, there weren't any rewards.

"Milla *jaan*, I have everything at stake. You, on the other hand, will forever be an Italian shipping heiress."

"Don't 'Milla darling' me. You have the money your grandmother left you. Whether you touch it or not, all that mullah still belongs to you."

"Mil, we have a lot of people depending on us. We can't let them down."

"Preaching to the choir, *mia sorella*." She got up and moved to the back of the room. "What's this?"

I paused my typing, peered over my shoulder, and winced. Shit, I was in trouble. "It's something I'm handling, nothing to worry about."

"I'll be the judge of that." She opened the envelope and her hand shook. "Ari, this isn't just some lame hoax. These are pictures of you, me, and Aunt Elana with a note mentioning Arcane." She waved the photos.

"Calm down, Mil. I'm not worried about it and you shouldn't be, either." I turned back to the computer and tried for focus on the screen.

That sounded convincing, right?

"I will not stay calm!" She walked over to me and turned my chair to face her.

I scowled at her and folded my arms.

"This is a direct threat for the software, Ari. Software no one outside of the board and the general's team know about. *Merda*, Arya. Please tell me you at least notified James of this."

I frowned at her. "Of course I did. I'm not stupid. Don't you thing I'd make our safety a priority after what happened to me?"

"I know you would. I'm worried, that's all." She folded her arms and paced back and forth. "What did James say?"

I exhaled a deep breath. "That he's increasing the security detail on both of us."

She tilted her head and stared at me, making me squirm in my seat.

"You're holding something back. Exactly how many of these have you gotten?"

"Well…you see…umm."

"Spit it out, Arya."

I cringed. "This is the third."

"What! And you didn't tell me or Lex?"

"Calm down. It isn't as bad as you think, and I've got it under control. James is on it."

"At least you had the sense to involve him. How could you not tell me?" Before I could answer, the sound of cars outside the lab alerted me to Max's arrival with his team. A new, unexpected anxiety filled me. I hadn't seen or spoken to him since he dropped me off at my penthouse two days before, and I wasn't sure how this new dynamic in our relationship would playout in our professional world.

Our weekend together was more than great, kinky sex. Max

and I had talked. Talked like we'd never done before. He told me more about himself in those two days than in the three months we'd been together in Cape Town. He even showed me a playful side of himself that was a stark contrast to the serious Max from long ago.

My skin prickled at the sound of Max punching in his access code.

I must maintain my composure and remember to keep my personal and business relationships separated.

"Let's close this discussion. I want it kept between us for now."

"What about Lex?" Milla snapped.

"Of course he needs to know. When I said 'us,' that included him."

"Just checking. Don't think this conversation is over. It's only tabled until I can get you alone."

I sighed and fidgeted in my chair. "I wouldn't expect anything else."

Milla snorted as she gathered her things. "By the way, good luck keeping your relationship under wraps. The whole team is going to notice the nervous energy shooting off you. Remember you're the ice queen, all business, all the time. If anyone suspects you're thawing, your cover is blown."

"Whatever. You're annoying."

Milla stuck her tongue out as Max entered with his team and a few members of mine. "Must be some discussion, if we're resorting to preschool behavior."

Both Milla and I scowled at him.

Max stared at me with his Dom eyes. Oh, hell no, we

weren't going to do that here. I rubbed my hands on my pants, trying to calm the lust that had crept in. I held Max's gaze in challenge. "Ready to work?"

Max's lips went up at one corner. "Yes, we are, and I brought reinforcements to help."

"I appreciate that." I motioned to my original team members. "You guys know what to start working on. I'll get the new members started, and then later I will work with each of you individually on your specific assignments."

The group moved to each of their terminals. Max sat at the computer next to mine, waiting for my instructions.

"That's my cue to leave. I have quarterly earnings reports to review." Milla rushed toward the lab doors.

"Chicken," I called after her, as she flipped me off.

"You're like real sisters," Max's technology administrator, Jane Erickson, observed. She was the one person he'd brought on who knew her way around anything remotely techie. From the moment we met a few weeks ago, it was like being around another kindred spirit. If it wouldn't have pissed Max off, I'd have even considered stealing her for ArMil. Maybe one day, I'd actually do it. On second thought, that would be a bad idea. She was as loyal as they come. She loved her job and told anyone who'd listen to her about it.

"We are in everything but blood. That's why we can tolerate each other."

Jane laughed. "The past few weeks have been great. I finally get to hang with other computer geeks." She turned to Max. "Don't get me wrong, boss, but being around other female nerds is refreshing."

"No offense taken. Now if the all-girl lovefest is finished, could we begin the class for us tech morons?"

"On that note, let's log on to your terminals…"

I went over the module details and directions. After everyone had finished his or her training, I worked with each new team member to confirm they understood the next steps for their part in the programing. I left Max for last, since I wasn't sure what he would try, and I wanted to keep everyone occupied and their attention away from us.

I strolled behind Max, putting my hand against the back of his chair. I leaned over and said, "Ready for your instruction, Max?"

Max tilted his head and his lips grazed my ear. "I'm always ready for you."

I inhaled sharply, as my nipples hardened from just his voice. "Not here," I whispered.

"I don't understand your meaning, Arya." He motioned to my chair and I sat without thinking.

Why did I do that?

"The voice. Don't use the voice," I said as I gritted my teeth.

"I have no idea what you're referring to, Arya."

Max's leg brushed mine, and I rolled my chair back.

"Fine, if that's how you want to play it." I reviewed Max's training exercise. "Max, I see you haven't completed the module. Was there some issue?"

"Am I reading this line of code correctly?" He pointed to the screen with one hand, while the other settled on my knee.

My whole body tightened in response and electricity shot to my pussy. I shoved his hand, but he gripped my leg harder.

I checked behind me and everyone seemed busy with their work, but for some reason, it felt like the team was intently listening to my conversation.

"Yes, those lines are basic commands that…" My voice trailed off as his palm moved higher and closer to the juncture of my thighs. I squeezed my linen-covered legs together as a moan caught in my throat.

"You were saying."

I steadied my breath and slowly detailed the specifics of his assignment. But my mind lost all concentration when his hand slid between my clenched thighs and grazed my throbbing clit through my pants.

"Did you have a good weekend, Arya?"

What?

Max's fingers rubbed up and down my nub. I arched slightly but kept my relaxed pose in my chair.

"Um, yes. It was most eventful."

"What did you do?"

I squirmed to the side as he pressed harder and circled to a vibrating rhythm.

My mouth went dry and my heartbeat echoed in my ears. I grasped the edge of the table in an attempt to hold off my orgasm.

"I—I—spent time with an old friend."

He grasped one of my hands and placed it over his granite-like cock. I stroked his length without thinking.

His tempo increased as my release washed over me. I clasped my eyes closed and muffled my cry by biting my lip. A tinge of copper filled my mouth as a whimper escaped.

"I hope you had a most pleasurable time." His words were gruff and barely audible.

Reality set in and my face heated. I was sitting in the middle of my team while Max fingered me to orgasm. I scanned the room, but the group was engrossed in their tasks. I sighed with relief. No one knew what happened.

My fingers continued to stroke Max's erection until his palm settled over mine. I snatched my hand back and jumped up.

Fuck, fuck, fuck. I had to get my body under control. Damn Max, he wasn't supposed to take anything outside of the bedroom. And I was a bigger moron for letting it happen.

"I'm going to take a short break. Continue with your projects, and if you have any questions, hold them until I return." I rushed out the lab door, racing into my office and toward my bathroom.

That man was going to send me over the edge.

At least the erection he was sporting gave me some satisfaction that I wasn't the only one affected. Lucky for me I had gained some release.

I leaned over my sink and splashed cold water over my face. I wiped my face and fixed my makeup, then checked my reflection and groaned. My cheeks were still flushed. Oh well, time to get back in the lab.

Next time he started anything in public, I'd stop it before it went too far. No there won't be a next time. After the training session, I'd let him know that any more breaking of my rules would mean the end of our affair.

I squared my shoulders, giving myself one last look. As I

walked to the door, the knob turned, and Max strolled in.

Shit, there goes my boss-lady stance.

The submissive me wanted to kneel down and wait for his command, but I had to remember that outside of the bedroom I was in charge. He stalked toward me and fisted one hand in my hair, yanking it out of its bun. His other hand crept around my waist, dragging me to him so fast I lost my footing.

"I told you, I don't like your hair up," he gritted out and kissed me.

No, he devoured me. My body melted as heat simmered in my belly and between my thighs.

"We're at work," I murmured against his lips. "We're supposed to keep this behind closed doors." But I deepened the kiss, drawing him closer to me.

His tongue felt soft and wet as it slid past my lips, demanding and exploring. I couldn't resist the feel of him. God, he smelled good and tasted even better. His mouth moved to the side of my neck.

"We're behind closed doors. Two, in fact. I locked your office, too, don't worry."

I pulled back. "Assuming much?"

He quirked an eyebrow. He spun me around and pinned me against the bathroom door, then gripped both my wrists above my head with one hand. His other went to the strings of my linen pants, and they pooled at my feet a few seconds later.

"I don't assume. I know. You won't need these." He grabbed my underwear and tore them off me.

I gasped. "Those were expensive."

He released my arms. "I'll buy you more." He lifted me and

I wrapped my legs around his waist as I locked my hips against his. He caught my lips again.

A low moan escaped my mouth, giving his tongue an opportunity to take advantage of the opening. I leveraged one hand around his neck as the other worked its way down to Max's belt buckle.

"Let me," Max said as he moved my hands out of the way and quickly opened his pants. His cock sprang free, poised at the entrance of my pussy. "God, I feel how wet you are. This is going to be hard and fast. But make sure you're quiet, since I'm pretty sure the boss frowns on this sort of activity." Then he thrust forward, burying himself to the hilt.

We both groaned. He stretched me with his thick shaft, filling me with the sweetest hunger. I closed my eyes, savoring the feeling.

"Hold tight," he muttered.

I gripped his shoulders and my mouth opened in a soundless scream as he pounded into me. All I could hear was the echo of flesh meeting flesh. His hands gripped my thighs so tight I knew I'd have bruises.

The knowledge that my team worked while I orgasmed in front of them and now were sitting only a few walls away sent another stream of arousal through me. Would they suspect what was happening?

"What're you thinking, Ari? You're wetter than you were a second ago."

I tilted my head back. "That a room full of people are waiting for us, and they have no clue what you're doing to me."

"Oh, my naughty Arya. Maybe one day you'll let me play

with you at the club, and then you'll see how erotic it can be to have others watch."

Max adjusted our angle so my pussy squeezed his cock tighter, making him moan low in his throat. "That's it. Ride me hard."

I leaned my head against the door, arching up. Max bit my nipple through my shirt, causing me to gasp as a jolt of energy surged through my body.

Oh God, here it comes.

My grip on Max's shoulders tightened, and my pussy contracted out of control. I bit my tongue to hold back my cry as wave after wave of my release washed over me. "Baby, yes. Squeeze me," Max growled. He threw his head back and I pulled him toward me, covering his mouth with mine to muffle his loud shout of release. His body pumped into my still spasming core.

We remained locked together for another few minutes, letting our hearts calm. Then Max's phone dinged. He buried his head in my hair and inhaled. He reluctantly released my hips, and I slid down onto unsteady legs.

I leaned against the door, my mind dazed and unfocused.

Wow, I was fucked mindless in my office bathroom.

"I guess we better get moving," Max said, still trying to steady his breath. "Making love against a door is a lot more difficult than it looks."

Making love. No, don't say that.

He must have read my thoughts because he lifted his head. "Stop analyzing everything. We both know that none of this would have happened if love wasn't involved."

I remained silent.

Max nudged his forehead against mine and stepped back. "You're exasperating, do you know that?" He ran his hand through his hair and dressed.

I stayed against the door watching him. He was offering me everything I'd ever wanted on a silver platter, so why was I so scared to trust it?

Because letting him in means exposing all your secrets and opening yourself up to another possible heartbreak and admitting his breaking up with you was for the best.

My heart ached at the thought. I'd never have accomplished anything to the scale I had today. I would have given up everything to fit into his world.

Max finished dressing, moved to the mirror, and used my brush to straighten his hair. He was now the clean-cut, confident businessman instead of my sexy, mussed lover.

He walked over to me and grasped the doorknob. "Take a shower and freshen up. If we walk in together with your lips swollen and the after-sex glow all over your face, everyone will know what we did."

I nodded and let him pass. The lock clicked as Max left my office.

CHAPTER FOURTEEN

"Good morning, *priya*. Did you have a good weekend?" I asked Milla as I entered the executive conference room of MDC.

"Decent, considering my best friend ditched me to work in her lab and then play subby to Max's Dom."

I flinched and scanned the room to see if anyone had overheard her. "Shut up, Mil. Don't talk about that here."

"Oh, calm down. No one can hear me. They're all preoccupied with preparations for Adrian St. James. He plans to pitch a project he wants implemented."

I sat next to Milla. "Now I'm intrigued. I can't wait to finally meet him. He's pretty hot." What an understatement. Not only did he possess unbelievable good looks, he was also an English earl with a reputation for being a genuinely good guy. Over the last ten years, he'd visited Milla many times, but I always seemed to miss him. Either I was working on a project with a deadline or I was in Cali with Aunt El.

"He's my cousin. Stop thinking about him like that."

"Whatever. Every girl dreams about marrying a royal."

"I hope you aren't still waiting for some prince charming. You're too high maintenance now with your billions. You won't even give the man who wants to marry you a chance to sweep you off your feet."

"Keep it down, dammit!" I kicked Milla's chair, rolling her to the side and jostling her coffee.

"Whatever. Some of us aren't that lucky." Milla rubbed her temples.

Uh-oh, she only does that when she stressed. I took a good look at her and noted the dark circles under her eyes. "What's wrong, *mera behna*?" I put my hand over hers.

She teared up. "Your sister here is a love-struck moron. We're both two peas in the same pod."

Shit, this was serious. Milla rarely cried. What happened with her Dom?

At that very moment, Lex walked in. He smiled at me and ignored Milla. Great, she was fighting with him, too. Now I'd spend all day playing referee.

Lex sat down, passed me a few folders, and continued to ignore Milla. "Read these."

I opened the first folder. "What is it?"

"Just read them. Mil's already been briefed."

Okay, I am in the middle of Grumpyville.

I read the first page and the log times of unauthorized access to Arcane. My breath hitched. "Lex, this is bad."

"That isn't even half as bad as what's in the next folder. Do me a favor, don't freak out in front of Max or any of his team." Lex scanned his phone and began texting.

I looked through the second folder and nearly threw up. Someone had broken into three of my labs. Thank God it wasn't the one holding Arcane. One of the walls in the room had been spray-painted with the words DIE OR GIVE US THE SECRET.

My hands shook as I put the folder on the table. The security measured I'd put in place were no longer enough. It was time to call in tighter security and alert the general.

Lex warned me when we first made the deal for the software that we'd become targets, but I thought he was paranoid. My need to prove I could handle any crazy development plan got us into this mess. "Fuck, Lex, what were they searching for?"

"We both know the answer to that," he stated drily, and he continued reading something on his phone. "From this point on, you and Milla will have around-the-clock security. I'm not taking any chances with either of you. I've called in Thomas's security company to handle it personally. He's not going to let anything happen to either of you."

"Okay, Dad." He was right, but I wasn't going to let him steamroll me.

"Finding you in a pool of blood once was more than enough for this lifetime."

My breath hitched. I struggled every day trying to block out the memories of the attack, but I kept forgetting others were involved. Lex and Milla were the ones who'd found me, and I was sure they fought with the nightmares, too.

"I'm sorry, Lex. I don't mean to be a brat."

"Don't worry about it. I know you have a lot on your mind with your new Dom and all."

"Lex!" I glanced at the others around the conference table. "What is with you two?"

"Shhh. They'll be here soon. Remember what I said about keeping this to ourselves. By the way, nice picture of your lover boy and his new main squeeze." Lex handed me his phone.

What?

A picture of Max with a gorgeous model, in an intimate almost kiss, was on the front page of a tabloid magazine. The headline read: THE PERPETUAL BACHELOR HAS FINALLY BEEN TAMED.

All the blood rushed from my head. I closed my eyes and took a deep breath.

I will not cry. I will not cry.

"Lex, couldn't you have waited until later to show her?" snapped Milla.

I frowned at Milla. "You knew?"

"Arya, it's a fabricated story. I didn't see the point of bringing it up."

I knew she was right. But why did it hurt so much?

Because I'm in love with him, and the thought of him touching anyone else makes me want to stab someone.

I shook the murderous notion from my head when the door of the conference room opened.

Max, Jacob, and Adrian St. James strolled in. They each took a spot on the opposite side of the table and waited as Max's assistant passed out clipped papers.

Max welcomed each person at the table and then gazed at me. "Ms. Rey." He inclined his head.

"Mr. Dane."

"Let me introduce you to a good friend of mine. Adrian St. James, the Marquis of Hawthorn."

Adrian walked over to our side of the table, shook everyone's hand, and then stopped in front of Mil and me.

Damn, he was one good-looking man. He resembled a living Ken doll, but with a rugged edge.

"It's such a pleasure to finally meet you, Ms. Rey." He lifted my hand to his lips.

For a second, I thought Max growled.

"Please call me Arya. We're not much into formalities here."

"Then call me Ian."

"Ian, I hope we'll have the opportunity to work together in the future."

"That's what I'm counting on." He held my gaze and my hand for a few seconds longer before he turned to Milla, greeting her with a hug and a quick chat about their family, then he shook Lex's hand warmly.

Wow, he's potent. The room heated, and unconsciously I shifted my attention toward Max, who clenched his jaw as the vein on the side of his head throbbed.

Oh, he's jealous. Good, now both of us feel the same way. I was aware how childish I was being, but I couldn't have cared less.

"I hate to interrupt the welcome party, but I think we should get down to business," said Jacob.

"I suppose he's correct." Ian returned to his seat between Max and Jacob.

Jacob sat with his arms crossed and a disingenuous smile plastered on his face.

"Please open to page one," Max instructed. "We called this meeting because Ian has a proposition you might find both challenging and enjoyable. Ian, why don't you elaborate?"

"My proposal is for the development of integration software for all of the St. James hotels. The implementation will have two benefits. First is to transport modern conveniences to properties in remote locations. Second is to use your Women's Initiative Foundation to bring technology not only to the hotels but also to the communities surrounding the lodges. This way the public benefits as well as the clients of St. James."

For the next two hours, we discussed the logistics and proposed time lines. Lex and Milla took the lead on the negotiations, since my hands were full with Arcane.

As we adjourned, Ian stopped me. "Arya, can I have a word?"

Max and Jacob peered up and both pairs of eyes bore into me.

"Sure, what can I do for you?"

"I would like to ask if you're available for dinner tomorrow night. That is, if you aren't seeing anyone."

Oh shit, how do I answer this?

Saying yes would hurt Max. He didn't deserve that, especially after how hard he tried to show me I mattered. Over the last month and a half, we started and ended nearly every day with a call or text to each other. Then a few weeks ago, he began giving me gifts. Sometimes he'd send me silly toys depicting techies in various stages of crazy, and other times he'd send me rare books on programming that weren't useful but something I had mentioned as wanting for my collection.

All of the sudden the image of the model flashed in my mind and my temper flared. He openly dated Caitlin and had shots of his latest supposed fling in the tabloids. Why should I stay home?

Fuck this. I'm going out with him. "No, I'm not seeing anyone. I'd love to join you for dinner."

"Wonderful. Milla's mentioned a few times how much you love sailing. Why don't we have an early dinner and then join Lex for an evening sail? My vessel's in port and we can see how you handle her."

"I appreciate the offer, but we'll make it a date only if you can convince Lex to let me behind the wheel of his new, *just delivered two weeks ago* baby."

Ian turned to Lex, who shrugged. "I'll give you a few minutes as captain. Remember it isn't the America's Cup. No racing."

"Spoilsport," I joked.

"So how about it, Arya?"

I smiled into Ian's amused green gaze. "Sure, it's a date. After I kick your boat's butt in Lex's racing catamaran, we can have dinner and spend the evening on my new yacht. I've had it for about a month, and this way all of us can enjoy a relaxed evening sail on the Sound."

"I look forward to it, even if we'll have company." Ian clasped my hand, kissing it once again before leaving.

I gathered my papers and prepared to rush to my office.

A second before I walked out the door, Jacob spoke. "Arya, I have a question for you."

I stopped, glancing over my shoulder. "Okay."

"I'm curious. Why don't you ever date? Is there something we don't know about you? Is it that you prefer dips in the lady pond?"

I hate this fucker.

"Jacob, shut the fuck up. That isn't appropriate," Max bit out.

"No Max, let me answer. Jacob, I've never swum in the lady pond, as you put it, but I do date. I just don't need my ego pumped or personal life invaded."

"So, Arya, are you with someone right now?" Max asked, his stare almost threatening.

"No, Max, I'm single, but I do have an active social life."

Max clutched his fists and contemplated me with both annoyance and hurt. Then his face grew angry. A line slowly cut across his forehead as he pushed his eyebrows down. "That's good to know." He got up and left, followed by Jacob.

"Arya, that was a shitty thing to say to Max. I guess you're taking cues from Milla now," Lex whispered to me as he glared at the woman in question, then walked out the door.

The conference room emptied except for Milla and me.

"Did I screw this up?" I didn't have to explain what I meant.

"No, but did you say that to convince yourself or him?"

"Myself, I guess." I banged my head against the conference table.

"Even if you don't admit it to me, why can't you acknowledge to yourself that you love him?"

"Because I need something to hold on to when this ends."

Milla rose. "You're such a dumbass. I guess we'll see each other tomorrow on the yacht?"

"Where are you off to?" I asked as I collected my papers.

"I have to meet *him* tonight and work this out."

"We're both complete and utter idiots."

"That's the understatement of the year."

CHAPTER FIFTEEN

Are you trying to kill us, Rey?" Milla shouted over the roar of the wind coming in from the Nantucket Sound.

"Man up, girlfriend. We beat them, didn't we?" Adrenaline surged throughout my body. I couldn't believe I'd raced Adrian St. James and won.

Holy shit, I beat a racing legend.

Ian waved to me from across the water as he leaned on the deck of his AC-45.

"Lex is going to slaughter you." Milla announced, while laughing. "First, you tricked him into giving you permission to take his beast of a ship, and then you nearly tipped us over three times." She tucked the stray hairs set lose from her pony-tail behind her ear. "Taking those curves like that was insane. Our crew was about to jump overboard, thinking they'd rather survive the freezing Atlantic waters than continue sailing with you."

"Whatever. You know you loved it. You're as much an

adrenaline junkie as I am." I squeezed the vessel's throttle, slowing its speed to a casual pace. My team gathered the sails and everyone cheered.

I squealed and jumped up and down. I'd won five hundred thousand dollars. Wagering against Ian was daring but hey, it was for charity. Even if I'd lost, it would have benefited my foundation.

"Why Lex believed you when you told him you'd treat his precious ship with tender loving care is beyond me. He waited three years for this thing to be built."

I ignored her as I picked up a towel from the captain's chair and wiped the dampness from my hair.

"He's never going to trust you with any of his vehicles again. Land or sea."

I cringed. Yeah, I hadn't thought that part through. Oh well.

"He knows I'd buy him a new one if I'd wrecked it."

"Fucking hell, Ari. I just smoothed things over between us, and now he's going to think I was in on this."

"Since when does Lex's anger bother you? Besides, who cares? We won."

"This boat is like his baby. And you treated it like a rag doll. You know he's going to retaliate by taking *AlySas* when you least expect it?"

"There is more security on that ship than he can imagine. I'll know if he even breathes on the boat wrong."

"I'm just warning you revenge will be sweet. And I can't wait to watch."

"Whatever. Stop worrying."

"Ms. Rey," a crew member called from behind me. "There's

a person on the radio who insists on speaking with you. I told him you'd call back once you were in dock, but he said a few things I won't repeat."

Oh hell, Lex was going to rip me a new one.

I scowled at Milla, who smiled and ran the side of her finger across her neck in a slicing motion. "I'll pull us into the dock. Go apologize to Lex, so we can celebrate our victory against my cousin. Make sure to grovel. He's a sucker for groveling."

"Thanks for the support," I mumbled.

"Anytime."

I reluctantly entered the crew cabin, took a deep breath, and answered the radio. "Hey Lex, sorry I took your baby out without permission. I promise to make it up to you."

"This isn't Lex."

And I'm in big trouble.

"Max."

"Do you have a death wish?" His voice was cold and simmering with rage.

Fuck, fuck, fuck. Mr. Control was about to bust a gasket. "Let me explain."

He cut me off. "I don't want to hear it. After Lex tears into you for stealing his ship, you'll deal with me."

Wait a second. Why was he upset? "This has nothing to do with you. I was having fun."

"Believe me when I say it has everything to do with me. Whether you admit it or not, you took what belongs to me and placed her in extreme danger, among other things."

Was he talking about me? I wasn't his property. "I don't belong to you, Max. Remember the rules?"

"Oh, I recall them in detail. You're the one who keeps breaking them."

"What rules have I broken?"

"Exclusivity."

"What are you talking about?"

"You let St. James think he had a chance with you."

I cringed. I'd forgotten that tidbit of the meeting. "Max, I was just flirting. You're the one who's still seen around town and splashed across tabloids with socialites. I don't—"

"I'm finished discussing this over the radio. We'll have our conversation in private."

The radio when dead, and Milla announced we were at dock.

Less than a few minute after I stepped onto the deck, Lex jumped aboard and strode straight for me.

"I am going to kill you." He threw me over his shoulder and glared at Milla.

She tossed her hands up in surrender. "I didn't know until a few moments before we docked that she had stolen the thing."

He growled and carried me off his ship.

Ian jumped in front of Lex and me. From the side of my eyes, I could see Max standing with his hands in his pockets, his livid emerald gaze bearing into me.

"Put her down, Lex. She didn't harm your precious boat. She handed me my ass."

Fire ran across my butt as Lex smacked me. My gaze shot to Max, who looked ready to pounce. He stalked toward us.

"Put me down, you Neanderthal. There was no way I'd have won without your precious jewel."

Lex smacked me again and a growl came from behind us.

"I'll make it up to you. I'll let you take *AlySas* out any time you want, for however long you want. I didn't break her. I put her through her paces."

"That's not the point, Ari. You could have killed everyone taking the curves the way you did. I barely held Max back when you skimmed the tip almost to the point of no return. I think I lost a few years off my life."

"Lex, we were fine. I knew what I was doing."

"Not only did you put your life in danger, but you put Milla and the crew in danger."

Oh fuck, I hadn't considered that.

"I'm sorry Lex. I wasn't thinking."

"Stop berating her and put her down. It's over." Ian wiped the water from his head.

Not quite. I still had to deal with Max.

Lex flipped me back over and held my hand while I gained my bearings. Immediately Ian engulfed me in a bear hug. "You have to marry me. With you by my side, I'll never lose another race ever again."

"Sorry, St. James. She's a girl who doesn't have time for marriage and happily ever after. Isn't that right, Arya?" Max strolled up and shook hands with Ian.

I slid out of Ian's grasp, but he tugged me back under his arm. The vein on the side of Max's face pulsed as he grounded his jaw. He was jealous, and I loved it. Well, maybe I didn't; that meant I'd deal with the consequences later.

A shiver ran along my spine, and I zipped my jacket tighter as the winter chill suddenly hit me. Max and Ian stared at each other as if ready to duel for me.

A silent message must have passed between them, because Ian released me and buttoned his own jacket.

"Let's take this aboard Arya's yacht," Lex suggested and the tension eased.

"I could use a stiff drink to ward off this freezing New England weather, and I'm sure Arya and Milla could use a warm shower after the soaking they received from their superwoman stunts. Wouldn't you agree, baby cousin?"

Milla strolled to us, scanned all three men, and raised her eyebrow in question. I shrugged.

Ian caught our silent conversation and shook his head. "Lex, man, you've got your hands full with those two."

"Don't I know it. Too bad both of them don't realize their stunts are going to get their asses tanned."

"Bite me, Lex." Milla scowled. "We belong to no one but ourselves."

"Keep telling yourselves that."

Max remained silent during the exchange, but he never took his gaze from me. I was in trouble. And the thought of the consequences aroused me. He'd never hurt me, but he'd find a way to make his point.

"Come on, Ari, let's go clean up." Milla pulled me behind her. "Guys, meet us back in the lounge in two hours. We gals are overdue for a nap."

"Hold on a sec." I stopped mid-tug. "I need to call the captain and give him our route."

"Already taken care of."

"Shouldn't I be the one to tell the captain our destination, since the ship belongs to me? You're so freaking bossy." I grumbled.

"Pipe down. I knew where you'd take us. Plus, you had your hands full with three Doms."

Ian is a Dom? Figures.

Milla's statement had me glancing back at the men in question, and Max's eyes locked with mine, causing me to stumble. He was deep in conversation, but his focus remained on me.

"What's wrong with you? It isn't like you to trip over your own feet." Milla followed the direction of my gaze. "Oh shit, he's pissed. Glad it's you and not me."

I rushed away from the group and up the stairs of the vessel.

Milla pulled my arm as she raced behind me. "Apologize. How would you feel if he pulled the same shit you did?"

I hated that she was right. I'd behaved poorly and hurt him. "I'll think of some way to make it up to him."

"Okay, now let's change the subject. Carmen's already aboard and she sent me a text telling me she needed a Thomas-free weekend. When the fuck did that happen?"

I smiled. I shouldn't be happy that I wasn't the only one with a jacked love life, but knowing Milla and Carmen shared my misery made life more bearable.

I walked through the lounge entrance and directly to the bar. I poured myself and Milla a glass of water, handed her the drink, and sat on the cream sectional.

"I'll let Carmen fill in all the juicy details. What I can tell you is that, they had a fling a few months ago in New York, and it developed into something more after they met again in Cali. That is why we haven't seen more of her since she got back from Germany three weeks ago."

Milla choked. "Carmen? No way. She's a Domme, not a sub. And Thomas is a Dom all the way."

"I know. Maybe they're switches. Speaking of the devil, here she is."

Carmen strolled into the lounge and glared at me as she plopped down on the sofa. "What the hell did you do to my brother? He's in a complete piss-poor mood."

There went my not being the subject of discussion. "What makes you think it has anything to do with me?" I crossed my arms over my chest.

"My brother's the master of control. The single exception is when you're involved."

"I find that hard to believe. Even with me, there's little he doesn't control."

"Are you blind?" Carmen growled.

Startled, I sat up from my relaxed lounge. "Blind to what?"

"Arya, he let you set the rules of this crazy relationship you're in. This no-strings, *keep it a secret from the world* thing is counter to what's ingrained in him. He needs to make the decisions, set the pace, and take care of you. But you only give him that in private. Hiding what you have is tearing him apart. He loves you and all you do is act like a brat."

She knew about the rules?

I ran a hand across my face. I was exhausted from all the lectures. I snatched my towel. "Fine, I get it. I know he's your brother, and you have this need to protect him, but what you don't realize is I'm trying to protect myself, too. I would have given anything to be with him, and he destroyed me. I won't allow that again."

"I think it's time you forgave him. He was young and stupid and dealing with more than any twenty-five-year-old should ever be handed."

I cocked my head to the side and placed my hand on my hip. "Like what?"

"He wants to be the one to tell you. I love my brother and he deserves to be happy. You do, too. Besides, you're the one holding a whopper of a secret that he should know. Do you even realize what it's like to keep this from him? You're using your loss as a weapon against him."

Whirling to Milla, I said, "You told her?"

"Of course I did. We never finished our conversation at Aunt El's, and I wanted her to understand."

I released a heavy breath. "Fine, you're right, but I don't need advice on my relationship." My voice quivered on the last word.

"Shut up for a minute and listen. I agree with Carmen. It's time to stop playing this stupid game. You both love each other, and neither of you is cut out for the no-strings thing. There's only so much a man can take before he gives up."

Tears rimmed my eyes. I needed to be alone. I held back an emotional hiccup and turned without a word toward the stairs.

"Where are you going?" Milla asked.

I glared at both women. "To take a shower and cool down. I've had enough scolding from the two of you."

CHAPTER SIXTEEN

Thirty minutes later, after a lengthy, hot shower and a heart-wrenching cry, I leaned on my cabin's balcony, staring into the crisp breeze of the Sound. The captain had set sail moments after I'd left my two annoying best friends in the lounge.

An icy breeze hit my face, and I shuddered, wrapping my robe tighter around me. Thank goodness for the heat lamps on the deck. It kept the wintry chill from destroying the experience of a March sail.

If I was honest with myself, the girls had a point. Max and I both deserved to be happy, but could it be together? My lips trembled and I blew out a deep breath. How many tears did I still have locked inside me?

I grasped the rails and peered into the distance. The cabin door clicked, jerking me from my contemplation.

Great, Milla and Carmen are back for another heart-to-heart.

"The point of having my own yacht is to give me some peace and quiet," I called out to the occupant of the room. "I'm not in the mood for another lecture."

"Good. Because I'm not in the mood to talk."

I whirled to find Max leaning against the glass balcony doors with two sets of handcuffs dangling from his hands. He'd changed and now wore a pair of casual khakis and a ribbed T-shirt that accentuated his sculpted shoulders and arms.

My mouth went dry, and I bit my lip. My Dom stood before me, and he simmered with rage. He stalked toward me and held out his hand, and I, without thought, placed mine in his.

He kept his gaze steady and smiled. "Are you ready to accept your punishment for behaving poorly?"

I swallowed, and then nodded.

"I didn't hear you."

"Yes."

"Yes, what?"

"Yes, Sir," I whispered.

The snap of the first cuff jarred me from my haze. I jerked my wrist and found it locked to the balcony railing.

"What—"

"Shhh," Max placed a finger against my lips. "Be a good girl and follow directions." He took my other hand and attached it to the metal.

Laughter echoed from above us. It didn't matter that we were on a two-hundred-foot yacht. If someone wanted, he or she would be able to see the balcony of the owner's suite from the lounge upstairs. Privacy was questionable.

"Sir, the others will hear our conversation."

He cocked his head to the side, but remained silent. The realization hit me. He wanted everyone to hear.

Why did that both scare and arouse me?

"Now let me see if my property is still in mint condition."

He cupped my neck, tilting it to the side as he grazed his five o'clock whiskers against my cheek. "You smell incredible. It's haunted me for years. Not your soap or your lotion, but you. Sweet and intoxicating."

His own natural, crisp scent engulfed me, sending a shot straight to my core. He'd barely touched me, and my pussy soaked my thong.

His palm slid down my throat to the opening of my robe. "Are you bare under here or is there a surprise?"

I regarded him through desire-clouded eyes. "Why don't you find out?"

"My pleasure." He yanked open my robe, leaving it hanging on my arms, and inhaled sharply. The frigid breeze prickled my skin, but the lust-filled survey of my body heated me and had me wanting to sink to my knees.

I stood in front of him in a white, form-fitting Chantilly-lace garter slip connected to thigh-high stockings. Strappy bands crisscrossed over the front as it accentuated my full breasts, which spilled over the tops of the cups. The lace formed a braided pattern down my torso and ended an inch above my matching G-string.

"Did you wear this for me?" His voice gruff and filled with need.

"Yes."

He traced the zigzag design of the material. "Any particular reason?"

"To apologize for upsetting you." I moaned aloud as his face brushed my nipple and his fingers pinched the other.

"Why would I be upset?"

"For taking Lex's racing yacht." I gasped as he squeezed harder. My core quickened and I exhaled a shallow breath.

"Wrong." He bit my aching bud through the lace-covered cups. "Try again."

I cried out, arching toward him. "For flirting with Ian."

The pressure on both nipples increased to an unendurable level and then eased. "Halfway there. Why else?" His mouth shifted to the other breast, teasing the tip with light licks.

"For taking dangerous chances with the ship?"

"There is that. Why else?"

I went through all the stupid mistakes I'd made over the past twenty-four hours. I had no clue what other things I could have done wrong. "I don't know."

He stopped, clutched my hair, and forced my head back, holding it still. His angry green eyes bore into me. "Let me explain," he said through clenched teeth.

I swallowed and shook.

"You denied seeing anyone, you denied our relationship, and you denied that I mattered. On top of everything else, you let another Dom touch you and believe he had a chance with you."

He released me. I panted, trying to steady my nerves and heartbeat. He ran a frustrated hand down his face and rested his head against the cabin door. "I've never met a more baffling woman. In a matter of years, you went from the perfect submissive to a walking contradiction: dominant in the outside world and a complete submissive in private. I don't know which way is up with you."

He released a disheartened laugh. "The joke's on me. No matter what roadblocks you place in front of me, I can't get enough of you. Sometimes I wonder why I'm putting myself through this."

His hands shook as he attempted to regain his composure.

My stomach knotted and a heaviness settled on my chest. By trying to protect myself, I hurt him. It wasn't supposed to be like this. I had to make this right.

"Max, I'm sorry. I shouldn't have done that."

"Have you not realized that you're a Dominant's Garden of Eden? You captivated Ian from the first moment he met you. It was the same for me in South Africa. You were mine the moment our eyes locked. The thought of another man replacing me is unbearable."

He's going to leave me again.

Carmen and Milla were right—my stupid vow to protect myself caused more harm than I could imagine. Slowly, I knelt with my arms pulled behind me. "Please forgive me."

Max peered over his shoulder and sighed. "You're my world, baby. I'll do anything for you." He moved closer, crouching in front of me. "I'm trying to follow the rules you set, but this denying we exist is pushing me to my limits. I'm not sure how much more I can take."

I kept my gaze to the ground and held back my tears. He was right. I was pushing him too far. If this ended right now, I'd understand, even though I wasn't ready.

I held back a hiccup. "Are we over?"

"*No!* Dammit. That isn't what I want," he shouted. "You're fucking infuriating."

I flinched but kept my head down.

Max began pacing in front of me. "I can only hope one day you'll figure it out." He sounded resigned.

Figure what out?

I glanced up and caught his gaze.

"Stand up."

My core clenched at his command. The sudden change in mood sent a flash of adrenaline through my body. On shaky feet, I rose without breaking eye contact.

"Spread your legs." He placed one foot between mine and tipped my chin up, studying me with cool, distant appraisal.

I bit my lip, uncertain of what to expect.

"Keep those feet apart."

He held my gaze as his hand trailed down my stomach and tore my thong from my body. I gasped but kept still. He traced the seam of my swollen lips and over my engorged clitoris and then slowly circled the entrance of my pussy.

"God, you're soaked. I can't wait to plunge into you."

I studied the straining cock hidden by his khakis. Max followed the direction of my attention and shook his head. "Not yet. How about this?" His fingers thrust in. "Will this do?"

"Sir!" I screamed, losing my balance.

He caged my limp form with his arm, grinding my pussy against him. The wind increased and I tipped my head back, the sensations of raw need coursing deep in my belly. He hammered at a relentless pace, almost violently, just the way I loved it.

Oh yes, right there.

I went from thinking we were over to a panting mess. Sweat trailed down my body, and my skin burned with unfulfilled demand.

My pussy quivered and contracted. "P-please...harder. I'm almost over," I begged

All of a sudden, he moved away. I cried out in protest, but he ignored me. Licking his fingers, he walked over to the deck chair, picked it up, and placed it between my spread legs. My center throbbed and screamed for relief. He was torturing me.

He relaxed in the seat and centered it between my exposed thighs.

"Now, I plan to enjoy my dessert before dinner. When I'm done, you will have no doubt to whom this body belongs. Do you understand?"

His mouth lifted toward me.

"Yes, Sir." I arched as my bound hands hauled me back against the freezing cold metal. My heart raced faster and faster as sensations tingled all over my body.

My eyes closed as his tongue licked the lines of my sensitive folds. He lifted me, nudged my knees apart, and placed them over his shoulders, exposing me completely to his view.

Wetness covered my aching flesh. He blew on my pulsing nub and drew it into his mouth, sucking and flicking.

My nails dug into the railing as my orgasm rose once again. My core quickened and my clit throbbed.

"Are you about to come?" Max murmured as he continued to lave my center.

"Y-y-yesss, Sir."

"Good." He stopped once again.

"No, please don't do this." My legs trembled. All I wanted was to curl up and cry.

He swung my thighs off his shoulders, positioned my ass on his knees, and sat back in the chair. He wiped my essence from his mouth with his shirt and watched me with hooded eyes, his rapid breath the only sign of how affected he actually was.

"I hate you!" I spat.

"No, you don't. You love me. And one day I'll get you to admit it."

My heart hitched. A tear ran down my face. "Release me, Sir."

"No. Not until you admit a few things and we're both satisfied."

If he wanted to satisfy me, he should have let me come.

He reached down, unbuttoned his pants, and grasped his raging cock. My vision blurred for a moment, and saliva filled my mouth. He eyed me as he stroked his length from the root to the tip.

I squirmed as my pussy leaked onto his cotton covered knees.

"See something you want?"

"Maybe, Sir." I licked my lips and swallowed.

"The way you're soaking my pants, I'd say it's more than a maybe." He squeezed his shaft again and moved his hand up and down. "Do you want this inside you? Pounding you until you pass out?"

I whimpered.

Max shifted and angled me toward his cock. He rimmed my opening with his fat, pulsing head.

Oh God, finally.

"Who do you belong to, Arya?"

I could deny it no longer. "Yoouuu," I moaned. I'd belonged to him, from the very beginning.

He pushed in another fraction, but held me suspended over him. "Who owns this body?"

"You do."

He slid in another inch and then stopped, inhaling deep in an attempt to steady his breath. I tried positioning my knees, but his arms wouldn't let me budge, especially with my own still clasped to the railing behind me.

He must have read my mind, because he reached behind me and unlocked my wrists. I immediately put them against the back of his chair, leaned in, and slipped farther down.

Max growled and tightened his hold on my hips. Sweat trailed down the side of his face.

It hit me that this was punishing himself as much as me. Why did I gain a small sense of satisfaction at his discomfort?

"Are you ever going to put yourself in danger like that again?"

"No, I promise." I'd learned my lesson. Winning a stupid race wasn't worth risking anyone's life.

"Good." He slammed me down all the way to the hilt.

We both shouted out in pleasure. I instinctively rode him, hard and fast, my orgasm looming over the horizon.

"Do you want to come?"

"*Yes!*" I shouted. I plowed down onto his giant cock.

As I lifted, Max held me suspended once more.

"No, don't stop it."

"Who do you belong to?"

"Please let me come."

He released my hips and let me continue my ride. I tipped my head back as I reveled in the invading, punishing pace. I was spiraling on the verge of an intense, all-consuming orgasm.

"If someone asks if you're seeing anyone, what will you say?"

"I'll say yes, I belong to someone."

"Who?"

"You, Sir."

"What's my name?" he demanded.

"Maxwell Dane. I belong to Max."

His thumb moved over my inflamed clit. "Who does Max belong to?"

"Me. Arya!" I yelled so loud I knew everyone upstairs heard me.

"Come with me, my love." We both shattered together.

I lay across him as our erratic breathing normalized. My face nuzzled his sweat-slicked neck. His cock still pulsed inside me and my tender, pounded flesh continued to quiver.

"I'm sorry," I whispered.

He threaded his fingers into my hair. "I know. I wish you'd let me in. Why are you determined to keep me at arm's length? What are you hiding?"

I need you, and you are going to break my heart again.

He sighed. "Do you think if you pretend what we have doesn't exist, that it will disappear?"

I scowled. He smacked my ass and lifted me off him. As he slid out of me, I was left feeling empty. He tucked himself back into his khakis and rose. I shrugged my robe over my shoulders and tied my belt.

"Come," he held out his hand. "You have guests waiting for you and I need a shower."

I placed my palm in his. As he led me inside, his phone beeped and he pulled it out of his pocket.

How did I not feel that when we were making love?

He read his message and glared at me. "I'm going to ask you this once and it better be the truth."

I stepped back and tightened my robe around me. What the hell did the message say?

"What happened at your labs?"

Oh shit. If Lex told him, he was so dead.

"Don't look surprised. You're mine and I will know if you're in danger."

"Who told you?"

"Does it matter?"

I hated it when he answered my question with a question. I grimaced at my hands as I twisted them together.

"Did it cross your mind to tell me that three of your labs were destroyed and that your life was threatened?"

"I'm handling it. It's probably nothing." Max was blowing this out of proportion.

He isn't, Arya. You're scared and just don't want him to know.

"Handling it!" He clenched my shoulders. "There are over a dozen pictures with death threats written over your face. Not Milla or Lex, you."

"Are you having me investigated? Dammit, Max. I've taken care of myself for five years and dealt with more than you can imagine. This is minor in comparison."

"What secrets are you holding that are worth your life?" His eyes blazed with hurt and concern. "Am I not important enough to tell?"

The fight left my body. "I knew you'd worry, and Lex had already implemented precautions." I leaned my head against his. "I didn't have it in me to deal with two overprotective males."

"Too bad. I'll talk to Lex about what he's done to increase security around both you and Milla. I know you think James is the Terminator incarnate, but he can't be with you at all times. Your aunt needs guarding, as well."

I pushed out of Max's grip. "You're pissing me off now. I said I'm handling it. I'm not stupid." I paced back and forth. "I told you before and I'm reminding you again: I won't let you take over my life."

"If that's how you want it, fine. *Come here.*"

I stopped pacing at his change in tone. In a flash, my body reacted to his Dom voice and quivered.

"I said come here, Arya."

My heart sped up. On shaky feet, I approached him and waited, keeping my gaze lowered.

"Look at me."

I stared into smoldering green irises.

"Take off your robe."

I untied the silk and let it fall to the ground. I wore nothing but my camisole, with my pussy exposed and my legs in gartered stockings.

"Turn around and put your hands on the back of the sofa." He trailed his hand over the back of my spine and I shuddered.

"I'm going to fuck you and you won't come until I give you permission."

I whimpered and took the position. A zipper echoed against the roar of the ocean.

"I'm going to take you hard and fast. I won't need to prepare you since you're still wet from my cum. Now bend over."

I swallowed and mentally prepared for the onslaught.

The crest of his cock skimmed down the folds of my ass, glided toward my puckered hole, and then slid lower to my newly awakened pussy. He slammed in and I jostled forward onto the couch.

"Uhh." My nails dug into the fabric as I lost leverage.

His palm gripped my hip and the other was buried in my hair. "Do you like my cock? Do like how it fucks you?" He pummeled me, his breath ragged and labored. "Do you like that my cock is the only one that can satisfy you? Is this what you need from me?"

"Yesss…Sir."

"Does fucking without emotion satisfy your desires?"

"What?" I glanced over my shoulder confused, but he forced my head back.

His pace increased, and tears rimmed my eyes. He held my hair in an agonizing grip as he pounded me. My mind clouded, pleasure and pain taking over.

"Come now," he commanded and I followed.

Bliss surged through my body, rocking me completely forward onto the couch.

"Max!" I screamed and he tugged my head back, kissing me. He continued fucking me until he called out his own release and collapsed on my back. My breath hadn't steadied when, without warning, he withdrew from me and dressed. Not saying a word, he strode to the cabin doors.

Huh? What happened? This wasn't like him.

"Where are you going?"

"I'm leaving."

"But why?"

"This is what you requested. A Dom to use you and your body, give you pleasure, then leave. Well, now you have it."

My lips trembled and shame filled me. I'd cheapened what we shared into something cold and meaningless.

"Be careful what you wish for, Arya. You might get it." He slammed the door as he left.

CHAPTER SEVENTEEN

I entered the lounge on the deck and everyone stopped talking. Milla and Carmen lingered by the bar and grinned. Lex and Ian sat near the dining area playing cards.

"Why are you guys staring at me?"

"No reason," Lex called. "Hope you had a nice rest."

I narrowed my eyes as Ian winked and grinned. I shrugged my shoulders and moved toward the bar.

"You're late for dinner. We've been waiting on you." Carmen approached me with a drink. "Also, you were very vociferous in dealing with a personal matter of yours."

My cheeks heated. I'd shouted at the top of my lungs that I belonged to Max. I bit my lip and glanced at Lex and Ian, who'd resumed their game.

"Why the hell did I buy a ship with the fucking lounge near the owner's suite?" I muttered.

"Speaking of fucking." Carmen cocked her head at welts on my wrists and raised an eyebrow. "Handcuffs?"

I instinctively rubbed them and shrugged. Now, I was confident everyone in the lounge heard everything we'd said. "It was rude of you to listen." I mumbled.

"We could hear your orgasm on the other end of the yacht."

I frowned and glared at her.

Laughing, Carmen sipped her drink. "I hope all the rough monkey sex you and my grumpy-ass brother had has put him in a better mood. I don't think I can deal with any more meetings where he spends most of the time chewing our heads off."

At that moment, Max entered the room. He regarded me with both aggravation and ambivalence. He shook his head as he glanced at my wrist then dismissed me and turned to Ian, who approached him. They shook hands and strolled out to the balcony.

"I guess that answers my question. I'm not sure if things are worse or better with you two."

"Definitely worse. Every time I think we're taking one step forward, I do something that sends us back ten." I covered my eyes with my hands.

"You and me both. Here, drink this."

I grabbed the cocktail and swallowed it down in a few gulps. The sharp vermouth burned down my throat and heated my belly. "Thanks, I needed that."

"You're welcome."

"Mil is right. Maybe I'm not cut out for this no-strings thing."

"I heard my name. What am I missing?" Milla approached us and looped her arms between Carmen's and mine.

"Only that the all-knowing sage Milla of the island of Castra's predictions are coming true. Among them being: Arya sucks at affairs, makes stupid choices in them, and by trying to protect herself she hurts the man she's with."

Milla sighed. "Well, ladies, the three of us are a match made in fucked-up-relationship hell."

"That's the understatement of the year," I mumbled. "Girls, I'm sorry about before. I'll think about what you said, okay?"

"We're here for you, even when you don't want to listen." Milla leaned her head against mine. "I've waited for this reunion. I'm glad the musketeers are back in action."

"Me too," Carmen and I said in unison and giggled.

"Ms. Rey, dinner is served," my chef announced from the archway of the dining room.

I gestured for him to inform the men outside, and the girls and I took our seats at the table. Somehow, a seat on each side of me was empty, and my culprit best friends gloated at their treachery. They were going to seize Lex, and I'd have no choice but to deal with two irritated Doms.

"I'll get both of you back one day."

"You have me shaking, Rey," Milla mocked.

"Castra and Dane, just watch out. Your days are numbered." I pointed an imaginary gun in their direction and pulled the trigger.

Both women raised their hands in surrender and laughed. I couldn't help but follow suit. Even in graduate school, they knew how to transition a tense situation into something light-hearted.

"Did I hear you threaten your partner and my sister?" Max strolled in and took the seat to my right.

Oh, now he's talking to me. The tension I'd released reappeared tenfold.

"Yes. They deserved it."

Ian took the seat on my other side as Lex sat across from me, between the girls, and gave me a *sorry I didn't get here fast enough* shrug.

Max lightly traced the lines around my wrist and sighed. "Why didn't you tell me they were hurting you?"

"Would it have mattered?"

"Of course it does," he hissed. "Anything that happens to you affects me. When will you understand?"

Before I could respond, the wait staff served our first course.

Dinner proceeded in a casual, not quite relaxed manner. Max and I continued ignoring each other, and he occupied his time discussing events with the group. I kept my mouth shut, since it had been what got me into this situation in the first place.

"A penny for your thoughts," Ian asked, pulling me from my melancholy.

"Oh, I was just enjoying your debate with Lex about European and American politics. It's fascinating to hear your take on the state of the economy."

"Since my side job is a seat in the House of Lords, I'd say it's my duty to stay abreast of the comings and goings in the world. A political sparring match with Lex keeps me on my toes."

"Touché, Lord St. James," I replied with a smile.

"So are you ready for the UN Women's Conference this week and the launch of your education foundation? Milla mentioned that you've spent the majority of your free time with last-minute preparations."

I took a sip of my wine. "Almost. Only because Lex and Mil have taken a lot of the grunt work off my shoulders. Now all I have to do is write and practice my speech."

"Is it true that the three of you thought of the charity while at MIT?"

"Somewhat," Milla interjected. "The original idea started after we attended a speech by the then First Lady at the UN Women's Conference." She pointed toward me. "But Ms. Overachiever decided to start a small education co-op after meeting this boy in Cape Town who was passionate about the same issues."

What was she doing? She mentioned that on purpose. I leered in Milla's direction and kept quiet. She shrugged her shoulders and smiled.

"You don't seem like a lady who's swayed easily."

If Ian only knew. I sensed Max watching me, but I refused to look at him.

"Exactly how old is your original co-op?" Max asked, startling me into glancing his way.

"A little under five years," I answered.

I finished my glass and allowed the smooth merlot to numb my senses. Maybe a little more wine would help this dinner progress faster. I gestured for a refill, and immediately the server obliged.

"I can't wait to see Arya onstage in a few days." Milla bubbled with excitement. "Too bad you won't be there, Carmen. We could make it a fun girls' weekend in Miami."

"That's all I need—a group of grown women reliving their college days," Lex mumbled, as Ian laughed.

"I wish I could, but my grumpy brother insists I hold down the fort while he's in Japan negotiating some contracts."

What? This was news to me. What happened to spending every weekend with him?

"When will you be back?" Lex asked.

"In a week, maybe two." He sipped his wine and regarded me with cool apathy.

"You're not going to be at the conference?" I couldn't disguise the surprise in my voice. "I thought you were going to attend the Carson Ball."

I hadn't planned on going to the invitation-only event, even with Milla nagging me that mingling with the country's business elite would help with future projects. But, when Max had suggested we go together as friends, I agreed to be his date. Now, I'd have to go alone.

"Since it's necessary for company purposes to attend, I'll fly in for the ball but will leave immediately after. I'm not needed for anything else."

"Oh."

"Disappointed?"

I sensed a headache coming on and pinched the bridge of my nose.

Max leaned toward me. "Put down the wine. You've had at least three glasses and if you include the cocktail Carmen gave you earlier, you are way past your limit. Drink some water," he whispered.

I set my wine down and picked up the water glass before

I grasped I'd followed his directions. No point in being stubborn when I needed the hydration.

"Max, I have a question for you," Milla said as she finished her bite.

"Sure, shoot."

"What's going on with you and the pin-up girl from Page Six?"

My glass stopped midway to my mouth, and everyone's eyes shifted toward me. Why focus on me? I wasn't the one she'd asked. But I wanted to hear his answer as well, so I remained quiet, waiting for Max to reply.

"Going to the event was a last-minute decision, and when my first choice in dates refused to be seen with me, I took a friend." He cast a glare at me and resumed eating.

I bit my lip and stared at my food. When he'd called to invite me last week, I was in the middle of a software update. I could have taken a break, but I'd reminded him of the rules instead, and he didn't insist further. Now remembering the intimate image captured by the photograph, I regretted blowing him off. Hell, I regretted many things. *Oh shit, my wine's gotten to me.* My lower lip trembled, so I bit it.

"I'm sure your lady had her reasons," Ian interjected.

"Maybe one day she'll decide to enlighten me."

"Women are a curious breed. Wouldn't you agree, Mil?" Lex turned to Milla with a smile.

"Shut up, Lex."

I took a deep breath and decided to steer the conversation to safer waters before things got worse for Milla and me. "So Ian, are you seeing anyone?"

"No one special right now. I'd hoped you'd be interested in becoming my partner in crime." He touched the welts on my forearm, leaned in, and shot a smirk at Max. "But I believe you are very much entangled with someone else."

Damn, didn't work. "I'm sorry if I gave you an impression otherwise."

"Don't worry about it. Harmless flirting keeps the spirits up. Wouldn't you agree, Max?"

"Depends."

"On what?"

"On whether the girl in question understood who she flirted with. My guess is she didn't have a clue."

I glanced at my three best friends across from me, who seemed to enjoy the discussion happening at my expense. Milla even made the motions of eating popcorn from a bowl, until Lex nudged her elbow.

"Maybe she's instinctively drawn to the strong, commanding type."

"Or maybe she likes to play with fire."

I swallowed and resisted the inclination to slide under the table.

"I could never be upset with someone who held such an innocent aura about her."

"Wait and see how you react when it happens to you."

I was in the middle of a Ping-Pong match with me serving as the ball. No wonder my head pounded.

"Ms. Rey," the butler called from the doorway to the dining room. "You have an urgent call that requires your attention."

Thank goodness for interruptions. Another moment and I'd have lost my mind.

"Excuse me, everyone." I pushed back from my chair and the men stood. "Please enjoy the rest of your evening."

"Aren't you coming back?" Ian asked.

"No, I think I'll call it a night. I'm exhausted from the excitement of beating you, St. James."

"Good night, sweet lady." He took my hand and kissed my knuckles.

Out of the corner of my eye, I noticed Max's scowl, but he didn't say anything.

"Later, *bella*. Don't work too hard while we enjoy your extensive and expensive bar selections."

I sent Milla a weary smile and left.

After the call from conference security about last-minute logistics, I'd decided to crash for the night, hoping a good night's sleep would calm my nerves. Around three in the morning, I roamed onto the sun deck at the back of the yacht with a cup of tea. For two hours, I'd tried to relax and sleep, but every time I drifted off, I'd wake to thoughts of how I'd left things with Max.

I set my cup on a nearby table and relaxed on the outdoor couch with my feet tucked under me. Clutching my robe tighter, I gazed into the night.

"I see you couldn't sleep as well." Ian strolled up and sat near me. "He loves you, you know."

"You don't understand our history."

"Yet I do. I was the one who found him in a dingy bar in

Cape Town, drunk off his ass and beaten to a pulp. That night, he not only lost the woman he loved, he ruined his relationship with his best friend."

"What?" I sat up. "If you knew about us, why did you pretend to be interested in me?"

"I wasn't pretending. From our first handshake, the natural submissive in you called to me. But I didn't realize who you were until right after the race."

I remembered the expression that passed between him and Max that had confused me.

"Max, Lex, and I have been friends since we were young. Who do you think introduced them to the lifestyle?" Ian chuckled.

"So you're the earl whose club he wanted me to visit in Cape Town?" I cocked my head to the side and smiled. "Do you know how much stuff he stole from your club to help initiate me into your world?"

"I wouldn't consider it stealing, since he owned a third of the place."

Wow, even at twenty-five he had his hands in many pots. Max's versatility never stopped surprising me.

"This is crazy. I'm surrounded my Doms, Dommes, and subs. Even my favorite designer is one."

"That's because people of our persuasion are drawn to each other."

That made sense. The wind increased, and I shivered. "Can I ask you something personal, since you're the resident expert?"

Ian's eyes crinkled and he took a sip of his drink. "Sure."

"How do you keep emotion separated when you know the relationship has a time limit?"

"You don't. A true D/s relationship involves real affection. Otherwise, it's cold sex. When it ends, you separate knowing you cared for each other. In your case, I think he's in it for the duration. You'll have to decide if you feel the same."

I closed my eyes and ran my palm over my face. "How do I trust it?"

"That isn't something I can decide. Loving each other means exposing all your secrets and accepting your partner's in return."

One day I'll tell Max. Hopefully.

"How did you become so wise?"

Ian's face fell and he peered toward the dark waters. "I made the same mistake I see you making. Caitlin was young and scared and pushed me away. When she wanted me back, I refused to forgive her, and now we both have to live without each other."

Caitlin. Her words echoed in my head: *I gave my heart to someone years ago, and I never got it back.*

My own sank. Was this my future? I had to make things right with Max. I stood. "Thanks for talking with me, Ian."

He continued gazing out into the distance. "No problem. Go talk to him—though you may have to wait until morning."

I moved into the stairwell that led to the sleeping cabins and paused outside Max's suite. Light glowed from underneath the door. It was now or never. I exhaled, squared my shoulders, and opened the door.

As I entered the room, I found Max in bed reading. He

lounged shirtless against the headboard. I licked my lips and waited for him to look up.

He kept his concentration on the book and spoke. "Is there something I can help you with?"

"Yes." I dropped my robe, crawled onto the bed, and tugged the book from his hand. I straddled his hips and trailed my hands up his muscled arms.

"Wha—"

I placed my finger against his lips before he spoke another word. He gazed at me with such unsaid emotions, I wanted to cry. Dropping my hand, I covered his mouth with mine. I poured everything I felt into the kiss. His hands fisted in my hair as he took control of the embrace. We savored each other's taste while I rubbed my wet heat against his growing erection.

Before he fully took over, I trailed my lips down his neck, over his chest, flicking his nipple. He sucked in and I moved to the other.

I peeked up and he regarded me with hooded eyes filled with yearning. Could I believe what I saw, or was I fooling myself?

I grasped the edge of his pants, and freed his hard, pulsing erection. Taking hold of him, I squeezed tightly and then ran my hand up and down his length, trailing the throbbing vein underneath with my tongue. I licked the drops of precum spilling from his tip and closed my eyes, basking in his unique taste.

"Ari, take me in all the way," he moaned.

I smiled and engulfed him with my mouth.

"Oh, fuck," he hissed and arched his hips.

Wetness pooled between my legs, causing me to squirm. I pumped his thick root with long strokes and sucked. Hollowing my cheeks, I increased the tempo. I worshiped him. He was mine. My hand moved to stroke the sensitive pad underneath his balls.

"Stop, baby. I'm going to come," he panted.

Good—that's what I want you to do. I continued my careful ministrations until his cock swelled. *Yes, that's it, baby.*

But before I could relish in his masculine flavor, he extracted me from his pulsing cock and rolled me underneath him. "I decide when I come, and that will be with you convulsing around me."

He slammed into me as my mind whirled and my breath shot out of me. I gripped his shoulders and delighted in his hard-and-fast assault.

He clasped my wrists above my head, locking them in an unbreakable hold.

"Please let me touch you."

"No. I've already allowed you too much control." He stilled and rested his head against mine with his eyes scrunched closed. "Besides, I'm barely holding on as it is."

Pleasure blossomed inside me; his disciplined domination hung by a thread. A moan escaped his mouth as I tightened my core muscles.

"Stop that, I know what you're doing."

I gazed at his closed lids and smiled, feigning innocence as I flexed again.

"We'll see about that," he growled as he surged forward.

"Yes," I screamed and my pussy rejoiced. He hammered his

way in and out of me at a ferocious pace. I arched to meet each thrust, desperate for my release.

"Come now," he demanded, and my body answered.

My flesh trembled around his beating cock, squeezing him to his own explosion.

"Arya," he called as he pumped jets of semen into me.

Then Max rolled to the side, gathering me over his chest while keeping his still erect shaft inside of me.

I exhaled in an attempt to catch my breath. I loved this man. He'd hold a place in me forever. I closed my eyes as my exhaustion washed over me.

"So was this an apology fuck?"

I stiffened. This was a stupid idea. What was I thinking? I was supposed to talk to him. Sucking him off or fucking him wasn't going to solve our problems.

I held back the tears that rimmed my eyes. If I left now, I'd make it back to my room before my emotions let loose.

Resigned, I slid out of his hold and moved to the edge of the bed. But Max tugged me back against him. His arm crept around my waist, and he cradled my head against his shoulder.

"You're not going anywhere. If you need to cry, then cry, but I won't let you hide behind the walls you've erected to keep us apart."

I remained silent and stiff against him. Then after what seemed like hours, I relaxed and let Max's warmth surround me.

"Go to sleep, baby. We've got a long week ahead of us."

CHAPTER EIGHTEEN

Y ou stupid bitch, don't make me kill you."

I shook as the knife at my throat pierced my skin. Pain shot down my neck and tears blurred my vision. "Please, don't hurt my babies."

Oh God, where were Lex and Milla? Please don't let anything have happened to them.

"You should have thought of that before you kicked me. I told you to come quietly, but no, you decided to play hero. Get in the car, or you'll die right now."

I stumbled, falling to my knees. I peered up at my assailant, but the bright sun blinded me. A tanned hand grabbed my head, jerking it back. Out of the side of my eyes, I saw a car turn a corner.

"*Help! Someone help!*" I screamed, but no one stopped.

"Greg, shut that bitch up. We don't want any attention."

Oh God, I'm going to die.

He continued pulling me by my hair and dragging me into

the car. Pain fired through my scalp and body. My head hit the side door, and spots appeared in my vision. A trickle of blood trailed down my nose, mixing with my tears.

I curled into the far corner of the car, holding my breath and praying.

The one called Greg leered at me as he took his seat next to me. "Drive, fucker. Her security will come searching if we don't get out of here." He wiped his face. "I hate this country. It's so fucking humid. If it wasn't for the money, I'd say fuck this job."

"Six mil is more than enough to compensate us for our troubles."

"No kidding. She's a looker, don't you think, Dave? Too bad we can't keep her." He reached over and groped my breast.

I flinched and slapped his hand away. No, I'd rather die than have this bastard touch me. I tried kicking him again, but he caught my foot and climbed on top of me.

"I like a fighter. Too bad you've got this fat stomach, or I'd show you a really good time."

A wave of nausea permeated my body. I was pinned underneath Greg, and the pressure on my swollen belly tore through me.

"Please, get off me. My babies—"

"You better start worrying about yourself and not those dead babies."

What? Don't kill my babies.

"No, don't hurt them. They don't deserve this. Please, I can pay you whatever you want."

"Did you hear that, Dave? She wants to negotiate. All of these high-class whores think they can buy us with their lover's money. Where's your lover now?"

Max! I need you.

"Please—"

"Shut her up. I can't drive with all her sniffling."

"I'm in charge here. Let me handle it."

"Our orders were to get rid of the kids before we got rid of her. They'll kill us if we don't follow through."

"Keep your panties on, asshole, and drive. These kids are valuable. If they're offering six mil for them dead, what do you think they're worth alive?"

"No!" The first stab of a knife ripped through my stomach.

Stop, Please, Someone help me!

"*Arya!*"

My body shook and shuddered.

"*Arya.* Wake up, baby."

"Max!" I cried, as he dragged me up from the depths of my nightmare.

"I'm here, baby." Max cradled me in his arms.

Sweat covered my body, and the night air prickled my skin. I burrowed into his arms, soaking in his warmth. "Please don't leave me."

He kissed the top of my head. "I'm not going anywhere."

I released a loud sob and poured my tears and pain out. He held me as I bawled without control, crooning and rocking me. After what felt like days, I stopped crying and whimpered into his chest.

"I'm here. I've got you."

I breathed in his comforting scent and allowed my heart to calm.

It had been six weeks. This was the longest I'd gone without dreaming of the terror. Why tonight? I shivered as a chill ran down my spine. It was because I thought I'd lost him; because I was alone again.

"Want to tell me about it?"

I hiccuped and shook my head. "No. I…I…can't talk about it. It was too real."

Sighing, he reclined back into the bed with me cocooned against him. He slid his palm against my stomach and held me tight.

"One day, will you tell me?" he whispered into my ear.

"Yes, soon."

"You promise?"

"Yes."

We remained quiet, listening to the cascade of the waves outside. This man brought me peace. It wasn't his fault what happened to me, and I couldn't punish him for it. I wanted to be happy with him.

"Is there any way you can come to the conference?"

"No, I'm sorry. My meetings are set in stone. Until dinner, I had no idea you even wanted me there."

My heart sank. "That's okay. I guess I'll see you at the Carson Ball."

Max rolled and leaned over me. Brushing my hair back, we peered into each other's eyes. "Will you be my date for the ball and spend the weekend with me in Miami?"

I hesitated but then thought better of it. It was time I met him halfway. "Yes, I'd love to spend the weekend with you." Smiling, I grasped his hair and drew him forward, capturing his lips. "Make love to me, Sir."

"With pleasure."

Forty-eight hours later, I stood on the observation deck of the Mandarin Oriental Miami and gazed out at the beautiful turquoise ocean. The warm, late-morning breeze felt soft and inviting.

Today I would announce the official international launch of my foundation at the United Nations Women's Conference. Even after giving hundreds of speeches over the past few years, butterflies swam in my stomach.

This was the most important speech I'd ever give. Thank God, both Milla and Lex would be in the audience. Seeing familiar faces would help me stay focused. If only Max was coming, but that was my fault. I shouldn't have made him feel like I didn't need him. Me and my brilliant plan to keep everything separated.

I closed my eyes and I blew out a deep breath.

You can't hold the past against him anymore. You have to talk to him, Arya. Let him know you want it to be real, not something hidden.

If I did what my heart wanted me to, I'd have to tell him about our girls. Then I'd have to admit I did something just as bad as he did by leaving me. Would he forgive me? Would he still want me, knowing those lost babies were the only ones we'd have?

Well, I wouldn't know unless I risked talking to him. I

nodded to myself. The next time I saw him, I'd tell him everything.

"Excuse me."

"Yes." I opened my eyes and glanced to my side. A petite Indian lady and her twins walked over. The girls, no more than nine, gazed at me. My heart hitched. They were lovely. Like my own would have been, if they'd survived.

"Are you Arya Rey?"

From the corner, I saw James and a few of my security detail walking toward us, ready to intercept the family. I gestured for them to stay back and answered the question.

"I am."

"My name is Minu. My girls"—she gestured next to her—"Lima and Riya, insisted on coming to meet you."

I smiled at them and shook their hands. "How are you three ladies today?"

"See, I told you, Mom. She's just like us." Both girls spoke in unison.

I couldn't help but grin bigger at the glare their mother gave them.

The mom turned back to me. "We're sorry to disturb you, but my girls recognized you and wanted to meet you in person."

"You weren't disturbing me. I was going over a speech I'm giving at a conference this evening."

"What conference?" One of the twins blurted out.

"I'm here for the UN Women's Conference. Have you heard of it?"

"We talked about it in school. Our teacher said the purpose

was to bring attention to areas of the world where women aren't treated well."

"That's part of it, but the other part is to show women that knowledge is power. Did you know that teaching a woman in a developing nation basic skills like sewing could help her support her family and keep them out of poverty?"

"Really?" The twins spoke again together.

I laughed at the wonder on the girls' faces. Their interest warmed my heart. "Yes, that's why I run the foundation through ArMil."

"Ms. Rey, we don't mean to take up your time. I know you're busy. My girls admire everything you've accomplished. And the fact that you're Indian means so much to them."

The mother's words humbled me. I'd never thought of myself as a role model, but to many young girls I was someone to aspire to be like.

Instead of focusing on the past, I should have focused on the present.

"Please don't worry about my time. Meeting you and your girls was exactly what I needed. Would you three ladies care to join me for some dessert?" I gestured to the bakery café across the street from the hotel observation deck.

The twins giggled and jumped around. The mom hesitated but agreed. "Sure. As you can see, my girls are over the moon."

"We can show her the city as well," they said in unison.

Lima and Riya were better than any tour guide I could imagine. Their enthusiasm was contagious, and by the end of the afternoon, I had learned everything possible about Miami and the girls. From their favorite subject at school to their perfect choice for superstar boyfriend. The girls even brought James out of hiding with their desire to meet a "real-life spy man," as they called him.

The four of us walked back to the hotel a few hours before I left for the conference. "Thank you, Minu, Lima, and Riya. I thoroughly enjoyed myself. Next time you're in Boston, let me know. Here's my office number." I handed Minu my business card. "Let my assistant Kerry know who you are, and she'll help me arrange my schedule to come hang out with you."

James held open the door. "Ms. Rey, I don't mean to rush you, but Ms. Castra texted to inform me that we need to get you to the center sooner than expected."

"James, we still have two hours. What could be so important to get there early?"

"The Secret Service needs to clear anyone who'll be within close proximity to the First Lady. That would include you."

My stomach jumped into a somersault. There went all the good vibes and relaxation of the day. No more tourist time for me; back to reality and the reason I was in Miami.

Less than two hours later, after a detailed security inspection by the Secret Service, I walked onto the stage where the rest of the conference presenters gathered. I'd practiced my speech and the calming meditation cues Milla had taught me, but my panic wouldn't settle. The ringing in my ears grew louder and my anxiety peaked.

Breathe, Arya. Take slow, deep breaths.

I scanned the audience, and found Milla and Lex sitting in the crowd. Milla blew me a kiss and mouthed, *Good luck.*

My cheering squad never failed me. I hadn't heard most of the First Lady's speech, but I recognized my name and refocused on her introduction.

"Arya Rey represents what every young women can achieve. From humble beginnings, she used knowledge as the key to success. Even in a world where the other, less inviting sex drove technology. Don't tell my husband I said that." The crowd laughed. "She allowed her work to speak for itself and pushed past all the naysayers. Today she is one of the most successful women in the world. Her business accomplishments are overshadowed only by her desire to help other women use knowledge and education to overcome strife and create opportunities for a better life. Please welcome our keynote speaker, Arya Nema Rey."

I exhaled and moved to the podium. I shook the First Lady's hand, faced the audience, and let the words I'd practiced flow free. A light sparked in many young faces as I spoke about using my brain to overcome all the hurdles life threw my way. Many of the girls came from the same type of homes I had. Some with even less. I told a story about how a mother kept her family out of poverty by learning to sew and explained how knowledge most of us think of as inconsequential could make a difference in so many lives.

As I approached the announcement of the foundation's launch, my eyes caught bright emerald ones watching me from the back of the room.

Max. He came.

He smiled and all of a sudden, the apprehension and uneasiness from earlier vanished.

"Before I conclude my speech, I have an announcement to make. Today, Milla Castra and I are officially launching the Women's Initiative Foundation with the commitment of one billion dollars over the next five years through the AlySas Fund.

"I named the fund after two beautiful girls who were never allowed the chance to spread their wings. In their memory, we will focus on providing education and opportunity for any woman interested in bettering her life. Thank you—and remember, things can be taken away, but knowledge remains with you for life."

The crowd erupted in applause and cheers. I released a sigh and proceeded to the end of the stage, shaking hands with the other presenters as I moved toward James, who waited to usher me back to our car. I glanced behind me, but Max was gone. At least I had gotten a glimpse of him.

I walked out the conference hall, signed a few autographs, and posed for pictures.

"Ms. Rey, he left a few seconds after you concluded your speech," James whispered while escorting me past the swarm of reporters.

"I'm in way over my head, James," I announced as I climbed into a waiting car.

"We both knew that from the moment you two were reunited. Now all either of you can do is ride this train out."

My only problem remained attempting to figure out where I would end up.

CHAPTER NINETEEN

The phone rang for the third time as I was putting the final touches on my hair and makeup. "Hey, Mil," I said.

"I called you earlier. Why didn't you answer?"

"Because I wanted to shut down technology and enjoy a scorching bath, Mom." I clipped the last of my curls into place and pushed the speaker button. "Talk to me while I finish getting ready."

"What happened to the glam squad?"

"I cancelled."

"What? Are you crazy?"

I glanced at Max's suitcase and duffel bag in the closet and my heart skipped a beat.

When he asked me to be his date and spend the weekend with him, I didn't think he'd be able to rearrange his schedule. I expected him to come in for the ball and then jet off to Japan the moment it ended. Then when I saw him in the audience during my speech, I realized he was there for me, not out of obligation, but because I mattered to him.

Arya, it's time to let him know he's important to you too. No more secrets.

"It would look suspicious if they noticed any of Max's thing in the suite. No one knows Max and I are here together."

"Ari…"

"I know, Mil. I'm working on it. I actually plan to talk to him about it tonight. By the way, how'd I do during the speech?"

"Nice change of subject. You did well for someone who was going to vomit on the First Lady."

"Thanks for the vote of confidence."

"Lex and I joked about what the headlines would read. Our favorite was: DISTINGUISHED ARYA REY TOSSES HER COOKIES ON THE PRESIDENT'S WIFE AFTER ANXIETY ATTACK."

"You both suck, making fun of me when you know how I feel about speeches."

"Seriously, you did great. Especially during the second half, you seemed calmer. Your face went all soft and relaxed. If I were a guessing gal, I'd say you caught a glimpse of your sexy Dom."

"Umm…maybe." No point in denying the obvious.

"In a sense, I'm glad you did. Don't get me wrong, your speech was great, but initially you were the controlled Arya Rey of the news reports. Then after you saw him, you were the approachable and lovable Arya that our company knows. I think it gave the announcement more meaning and credibility."

"I'm glad my need for Max worked in our favor."

Shit, I said that aloud. Oh well, no denying the truth. Hey, I'm making progress.

Milla didn't respond. That meant she didn't like what I'd said.

"What?" I exclaimed and clasped my earring on my ears.

"Have you fallen back in love with him?"

This time I didn't reply. I unhooked my dress and slid it on.

"Well?"

Damn Milla for picking up on everything. "Yes. No, that's not true. I never stopped loving him. Why do you think no guy I went out with interested me?"

"Eventually he's going to catch on. Most likely sooner rather than later."

I crossed my arms and glared at the phone. What was I doing? She couldn't see my scowl.

"Has he seen the scars?"

I closed my eyes and sat back down. "No."

"Arya."

"I know." I pressed my fingers against my temples. *Great, now I have a headache.* "I've thought of telling him nonstop, but in the end I never go through with it."

"He's going to figure out you're hiding something," Milla countered.

"I wouldn't be surprised if he hasn't already. I'm never fully undressed in front of him. Hell, I lock the damn door to shower."

"Ari, you have to talk to him. He wanted to marry you before you came up with your stupid plan for a no-strings-attached relationship."

"I kept his children from him. I'm scared that I'll lose him when he finds out."

"What if you don't?"

I closed my eyes for a moment, taking a deep breathe.

Tonight. I'll tell him tonight.

"Mil, I need to go. Max will be here any minute."

At that moment, the bell to the suite's elevator rang and the sound of footsteps echoed in the living area. I jumped up and slipped on my shoes.

Please wait in the other room.

"Saved by the bell. Go enjoy yourself tonight, while those of us who weren't invited stay home to work."

"Whatever you say, boss," I laughed. "Love you. I'll see you back at home in two days."

"Love you too, *bella*."

I ended the call, took a deep breath, and went to meet Max.

I opened the door and found him waiting by the couch. Dressed in a perfectly tailored tuxedo, he was every woman's fantasy. The cut of the jacket accentuated his broad shoulders and his lean, muscled frame. I licked my lips. This gorgeous man was mine.

He approached me and ran a finger down the side of my face, along my cheek, and over my neck. His hungry gaze devoured me. "You take my breath away." He lifted my hand and kissed it.

I looked great and felt confident. My floor length, navy-silk dress hugged my body in a lover's embrace. Silver beading lined the high neck and trailed the fringe of the open back that was just shy of revealing. My waist-length hair gave the illusion of cover, but as I moved, it would hint at the secret underneath.

"Thank you. Your friend Caitlin designed it especially for me."

Max smiled. "So my secret is exposed. When did you find out?"

"The night of the fund-raiser." I grinned back. "We became friends while visiting the ladies' room."

He skimmed his hands along my arms, sending goose bumps throughout my body.

"So what do you think?" I twirled and smiled at Max over my shoulder.

His eyes darkened. His hunger shot through me like a bullet. He liked the back. "Turn for me again, Arya."

Oh, the voice.

I followed his command. He gathered my hair to the side and ran his finger from my neck all the way to where the beading started above the lower dip of my waist. My core throbbed from his possessive touch.

"Did you wear your hair down for me?"

"Possibly."

"When we return, you will go straight into the bedroom. Do not take anything off except your shoes. You will wait for me at the foot of the bed. I have plans for that beautiful, naked back."

I nodded my agreement.

"I didn't hear you."

"Yes, Sir." My voice came out wispy.

He placed his hand on my lower back, motioning me toward the door. "We better get going." He paused before we exited. "Just so you know."

I looked up.

"Tonight will be the last time you will ever wear that dress. I don't like others seeing what belongs to me without permission."

My breath hitched, as excitement tingled through me.

Looks like our conversation will have to wait until the morning.

We arrived at the Carson mansion thirty minutes after leaving the hotel. The trip was short but filled with lighthearted banter. The serious conversation I'd had with Milla was all but shoved to the back of my mind.

When James opened the door to the limousine, a new anxiety that I hadn't known existed jumped into my gut. I slid my palm over my stomach and exhaled slowly. As the face of the company, this was a regular part of my role. And I'd encountered most of the people who'd be attending the ball at various occasions over the years. So why was I feeling this way? The only difference tonight was having Mr. Most Eligible Bachelor as my date.

Max's gentle touch on my arm guided me out of the car. I stepped out, brushed the folds of my dress, and paused for a few pictures.

Max's hand moved to the small of my back and he bent, grazed my ear, and whispered, "Relax. This will be a piece of cake, completely painless. I promise."

His warm breath sent a blaze straight to my core, and my

cheeks heated. "The last time you said that to me, I came home deflowered," I responded breathlessly.

"Keep thinking of that night and what I'm going to do to you once we get back to the hotel. That way the evening will go by faster."

Oh, yeah. Thinking of what awaited me was going to keep the night from dragging on.

We climbed the steps of the mansion and entered the ballroom. Though considered a small, intimate affair with around a hundred attendees, some of the wealthiest and most influential people in the world filled the event. An invitation to the Carson Ball meant official acceptance into the elite circles of society. Many business deals, political careers, and socialite marriages had been arranged during the ball. Tonight, I'd work the corporate relations end of the spectrum.

The minute we crossed the threshold of the ballroom, dozens of eyes turned our way. Max's hand remained on me, helping me stay calm.

"Time to work the room, my beautiful date."

"No, stay with me for a few more seconds. I feel like I'm in a room of vultures preparing to strike."

"A very perceptive observation. I have no doubt that many would enjoy taking a piece out of you."

"You're not helping."

"Now if our relationship were in the open, I could stay by your side all night, and no one would think anything of it. But since you insist on separating our public and private lives, I must attend to my own business matters." Max smiled and walked away.

I deserved that.

"Arya. I'm glad you're here."

Carmen walked up with Thomas. They looked fabulous together. Like a pair of models who graced the cover of a fashion magazine.

"Carmen, Thomas. You look great." I hugged both of them and slanted Thomas a glare. "When did this officially happen?" I gestured to the two of them.

"Don't jump to conclusions. We're getting to know each other," Carmen answered.

Yeah, right. The possessive vibe radiating from Thomas screamed something else altogether.

"So you're here with Max?"

"Yes, and please keep your comments to yourselves."

Such a sly girl, trying to deflect the attention.

Thomas smirked. "You make a striking couple. The gorgeous Arya Rey and the equally dashing Maxwell Dane. Every eye was on you as soon as you entered the room."

"Shut up, Thomas." Carmen nudged him. "You sound like a social columnist."

Unoffended, he chuckled and put his arms around both our waists. "Let me introduce you to a few of my mother's people."

If I hadn't known Thomas better, I would have thought that statement was odd, but Thomas grew up with similar issues as I did. His mother was an all-American socialite who fell in love with a lowly Mexican rancher. Their marriage was a scandal in New York society, especially when Thomas's mother renounced her inheritance to live as a working rancher's wife.

We approached an elderly couple drinking champagne. "Thomas, my boy, it's good to see you again."

Thomas released me and shook the gentleman's hand. His arm remained around Carmen; however, he ignored the man's wife.

"Hello, Uncle Matthew. You already know Carmen, but I'd like to introduce you to Arya Rey. We attended Stanford together many years ago, and she's one of my closest friends. Arya, this is my uncle, Matthew Hathaway. He's the current CEO of Hathaway International."

"It's a pleasure to finally meet you, sir." I extended my hand, but he gathered me into a full embrace.

"Oh, none of that. Thomas has spoken highly of you for years. Hasn't he, Darla?"

I turned to Mr. Hathaway's wife.

"It's nice to meet you as well." I held out my hand, but she ignored it.

Well, I guess she doesn't like me. What did I do to her?

"Yes, we've heard all about you. Having friends in high places can be very beneficial to one's success. Similar to the way your father worked by marrying your mother."

I yanked my hand back. Now I remembered her name. Her brother had been groomed to marry my mother before she'd met my father.

"Ignore Aunt Darla. She hasn't taken her sedative today. It makes her a little unrefined."

"I see that your money hasn't taken into account your lack of pedigree." She directed the sneer at Thomas, who acted as if he hadn't heard her speak.

Damn, this woman was a viper.

"But Mrs. Hathaway, aren't you the author of a societal etiquette book that states never insult or belittle those you may not like, but who hold considerable power over you?" Carmen interjected.

"And what power would this girl hold over me?"

Carmen. I don't think telling her is going to help her like me. On second thought, she doesn't like me anyway—go ahead and tell her.

"Stock, of course. Arya and Thomas each control over 35 percent of Lighthouse International, the conglomerate that owns your company." Carmen sipped her wine and smiled, leaning her head against Thomas's shoulder.

I loved her.

"Well, I never. Carmen Dane, you have become completely mannerless associating yourself with these two. Money doesn't lead to class."

"Neither does birth," muttered Thomas.

I smiled internally at the remark. "Mr. Hathaway, it was a pleasure meeting you. I hope we'll see each other at the board meeting next month. I would love to have lunch next time you're in Boston."

"I look forward to it. I must say you're as beautiful as your mother was and as intelligent as well."

"Thank you."

Darla gasped, but quickly composed herself when everyone glanced her way.

I may not have her pedigree, but I understood appropriate behavior. Why not leave on a proper note. "Mrs. Hathaway—"

But before I could finish, she cut me off by greeting another attendee. I took a page from Thomas's book and pretended I hadn't noticed the slight. It was time to escape this woman before I voiced what I really thought.

"Hello Matthew, Darla." Max inclined his head as he came up behind me and put his hand against my lower back. "I see you've met Arya. She's a refreshing addition to this year's ball."

"I couldn't agree more," voiced Mr. Hathaway.

"If you'll please excuse us, I must steal my date for other introductions." Max led me away. "You looked ready to kill that old bat."

"She's dreadful. Poor Thomas, he has to spend time with her. At least, I got away from my bigoted family members." I pinched the bridge of my nose. "Hopefully, this night will improve."

At that moment, another elderly man approached us. "Oh shit," I muttered.

"No such luck," Max whispered and took my hand in his. "Don't worry. I'll protect you."

"Please don't let me do anything violent."

"Why not? Everyone would think he deserved it." He lifted my hand for a kiss.

"Arya, I see you've been invited this year. You might have attended sooner if you hadn't rejected your family."

I stared giving no outward reaction. Max squeezed my hand for support.

"Hello to you, too, Walter. I see things haven't changed much since you sued me for my inheritance."

Before Walter retorted, Max spoke. "How are you doing,

Mr. Blackburn? I heard about the new yacht you built. Con-
gratulations on its first successful race."

"Thank you, Dane. How have you been doing? Maybe you
can teach this girl a thing or two about sailing."

"I'm surprised you don't know, being her grandfather. Arya
is an avid sailor. She took on Adrian St. James recently and
won."

Amazing how Max viewed the sailing incident differently
now, when a few days ago he was livid.

"Is that so? Must be some of her mother's Blackburn genes
coming out. Her Indian half wouldn't know the difference between a rowboat and a sailing vessel."

My fingers dug into Max's arm. The nerve of that asshole
talking about me as if I'm some dimwit and then insulting my
father.

Max gently but firmly pried my hand off his arm and
wrapped his around my waist. "I believe her unparalleled
intelligence and breathtaking beauty are the result of the
unique combination of her genes. I wouldn't have it any other
way."

I scanned Max's face as warmth filled my heart. Did he
really see me this way? God, I'd wasted so much time keeping
him at arm's length.

"I take it you two are together."

"Why do you—"

"Isn't it obvious?" Max interjected.

Walter's face scrunched up as if he didn't believe us. "Well,
if it's true, I'd say you couldn't do better than a Dane. If I
were you, I'd hold on to him with both hands. Not many in

our circle would take you on, especially with your lack of up-bringing."

Motherfucker. I understood insulting me, but directing his venom at Aunt Elana crossed the line. "You're the—"

"I'm the one who needs to convince Arya that I'm worthy of her. Maybe one day she'll believe me and agree to spend the rest of her life with me."

My heart leaped as I kept my eyes on Walter, who seemed as surprised as I was about Max's declaration.

"Now that we've had this lovely family reunion, I believe it's time I courted some prospective investors." I nudged Max's arm, but he wouldn't budge. I knew where his mind had gone.

Please don't say it, Max. I wanted it splashed across the newspapers when Walter found out. I wanted him to learn about his company the way I learned he was suing me, in public, on the news.

"Don't expect anything from my direction. The reason our money has grown is through sound investments, not high-risk gambling."

"Mr. Blackburn, Arya seeking financing from you wouldn't make sense. RPI, the company that infused one hundred million into Blackburn Industries, is solely owned by her."

Walter's face colored to a deep shade of red. "That's preposterous. RPI is a privately held equity firm. There isn't one owner."

Well the cat's out of the bag. This isn't as exciting as I thought it would be.

I tilted my head toward Walter and smiled. "Sorry to burst your pompous bubble, but I do own the company. It stands for Rey Private Investments. It would have been prudent for you to investigate the background of the company from whom you were requesting assistance. You courted RPI. I let the company CEO broker the terms. As of five o'clock this evening, I own 51 percent of my mother's company. The percentage she would have inherited had she not been disowned."

I sighed inside and my shoulders sagged a little. Telling Walter the results of my plans for his company hadn't brought the pleasure I'd assumed it would. I'd quietly played this chess match for the past three years, and now it felt like I was the bad guy. Milla was right when she told me I wasn't cut out to be a true corporate raider. My conscience tended to get the best of me.

"I'm sorry, Mr. Blackburn, to cut this off, but I need to introduce Arya to a few people." Max ushered me away.

"You did that on purpose. Why would you want him to know what I—" I stopped midstride, jerking Max. "Wait a second. How the hell did you know what I'd planned?"

"Arya, I've spent the last five years keeping up with everything you're involved in. I happened to come across an investment company that owned various businesses that were heavily involved with either you, Milla, or Lex. It doesn't take a rocket scientist to figure out the rest."

"Apparently not." I thought back to Walter. "Max?"

He peered down at me. "Yes?"

"How do you do the corporate raider stuff all the time? Telling Blackburn what I'd done didn't feel as great as I'd expected."

"When you're born into it, you don't think about the consequences beyond profit and stocks. Keeping your moral center is very hard. Why do you think the people around you are loyal?"

His words lifted some of the guilt I carried. "Max, thank you for staying by my side."

"You are most welcome. You can make it up to me when we get back to the hotel."

"If I must," I teased.

"Let's go meet Senator Carson. He's the burly, silver-haired gentleman over there." Max gestured to a distinguished-looking man standing in a crowd of other politicians. "He's requested an introduction. Apparently, he's been a fan of yours for a while."

"Why not? I've had a less than stellar evening. It would be nice to meet someone who is happy to see me."

CHAPTER TWENTY

Y ou have your instructions when you go up," Max said to me when he dropped me off three hours later at our hotel. "I'll be up shortly. Take the main entrance to the elevators. This way people will see you arrive alone. I'll take the private one through the garage."

I gritted my teeth, trying to hold my tongue, and exited the limousine. Keeping things quiet was my idea. I hoped after tonight that would be a thing of the past.

"Arya, did you hear what I said?" Max asked in the tone that had me pausing and my core clenching.

I paused, staring at the doors of the hotel and answered him. "Yes, Sir. I will follow your instructions."

James approached me within seconds and followed me into the hotel. I rushed toward the elevators, but multiple times people stopped me for pictures and autographs. Any other day I'd have been happy to meet fans, but at this moment all I wanted was to reach my suite and calm my nerves before Max arrived.

"You could have gone with him," James said in his quiet but firm manner.

"We can't. Our relationship isn't public knowledge."

James entered the security code in the elevator allowing access to my suite. "Ms. Rey, no matter how much you deny it, you know the truth. Don't behave like this stupid old man and waste time pretending you don't love each other when you do."

He missed being with Aunt Elana in California, even if he never voiced it. Maybe I should have someone else handle my security, I thought, so he would have time with my aunt.

"James, do you want to go home to be with her?"

"No, Ms. Rey. Elana would never have me, knowing I'd left you here when there is an open threat against you." He clasped my hand, squeezed, and released it.

"I love you too, Papa Bear."

James grunted in response. The elevator dinged, and James made a quick sweep of the area and then my suite. He gestured for me to enter. "Good night, Ms. Rey."

"Good night, James. I'll see you in the morning."

He closed the door and left me in silence.

I contemplated the private elevator doors that would soon open, and my skin prickled with anticipation. Time to get moving.

I removed my shoes and left them near the sofa. As I entered the bedroom, I noticed that all of Max's things were unpacked and sitting next to mine. A lump formed in my throat. For the next three nights, we were sharing this space as a couple.

I took in a sharp breath. My comment about getting in too deep was now a complete understatement. I'd admitted on the yacht that we were together even if it wasn't public knowledge. Now I had to tell him I wanted more than what we shared in private, that I was ready to give him what he wanted when we started this whole thing.

All I can do is hope that he still wants me he learns about the past.

Shaking the thought from my head, I approached the foot of the bed and reached behind me to open the hidden zipper of my dress. At that moment, the elevator arrived, and Max strode in. I glanced over my shoulder as he prowled directly toward me. My breath hitched.

He grasped the shoulders of my dress and tore the expensive material in two. "I told you tonight would be the last time you'd wear this dress."

I trembled and licked my lips. Instead of feeling upset, his show of aggression aroused me. Max tugged my head back for a deep kiss. The taste of aged cognac filled my mouth, and lust coursed straight to my core.

Max stepped back. The emotions glazed in his eyes made my lips tremble. "Climb onto the bed and lie on your stomach."

I followed his instructions and waited.

"Close your eyes and relax. Tonight is all about your pleasure," his sexy voice crooned next to my ear.

Sure, that would happen after ripping the dress from my body. At least the one-piece bustier covered my breasts and stomach. What would he do next?

He settled down beside me and slipped a blindfold over my eyes. My senses jumped to full alert. The bed shifted, the bedside drawer opened, and then Max started placing objects on the table.

What was he getting out? Had he brought toys from the playroom?

"I see the wheels churning. Remember, curiosity killed the cat."

I blew out a breath and strove to relax my mind and enjoy. After a few more minutes, Max traced the back of my corset. Cool metal touched the dip of my spine, and then all of the sudden, my back was completely exposed. "We won't need this tonight. It would only get in the way of what I have planned."

I shifted, but then stilled. On my stomach, he wouldn't see the scars. Once he'd finished with our game, I'd find a way to cover myself.

Tomorrow. I promise I'll tell him tomorrow.

"Calm yourself, Ari. I want you to melt into the sheets and become my canvas. I know the night started out less than desirably, but I'm planning for it to end right."

He was going to paint me. I knew it.

"Are you ready?"

"Yes, Sir."

"No. Tonight I'm Max and you're Arya. Two people who want to enjoy each other. Do you understand?"

Never before had he wanted me to call him by his name. It was as if he sensed I was ready to move past the wall I created between us.

I swallowed the lump in my throat and answered, "Yes, Max."

"Good. Now hold very still."

I held my breath and then gasped at his first touch. Soft wisps of something glided along my neck and down my spine, sending goose bumps over my skin. I squirmed with the tickling sensation.

"You weren't expecting a feather, were you?"

So that was what it was.

The sensual feel of the downy barbs both surprised and delighted me. My nipples hardened, and the wetness pooling between my legs increased.

"A feather's gentle caress can quickly awaken the delicate sensors lying under the skin. I want every part of your body awake for the grand finale." He guided the plume over the curve of my bottom and down the slopes of my knees and calves.

"Max," I moaned, and my body shuddered.

"You'll like what comes next even more."

Max stopped his gentle strokes. A clasp echoed and the essence of eucalyptus, rosemary, and lavender filled the air. The scent of my favorite body oil. His hands settled over my shoulders as he massaged the lingering tension away.

"How did you know what I use?"

Max kissed the back of my head. "I notice everything about you and keep it locked away for future reference."

"Thank you," I said. But for what, I wasn't sure. Maybe it was for noticing unexpected things about me or for continuing to show me tenderness and love even though I kept pushing him away.

"You're welcome," he said as he kneaded down my spine.

Max manipulated every tense muscle in my back until I was nearly comatose. He moved lower over my butt and down my thighs, ending at my toes. I was in complete heaven. After what felt like hours, he stopped his ministration and slid off the bed. This time, I heard the sound of glass clinking.

"So tell me, Arya. Is there anything you wanted to know about me that I haven't told you?"

His question surprised me. Max never freely gave information about himself. I'd always wanted to know about his father but in the past, a giant DO NOT GO THERE sign had been plastered all over that conversation. Would he object now?

Sensing my hesitation, he said, "Ask. I'll tell you anything."

"Really?"

He sighed. "I guess I deserve that. I didn't give you the trust you sought five years ago, but I'm willing to now."

I lifted up, attempting to take off my mask and verify that he was serious.

Max pushed me gently down. "You're going to ruin my canvas if you tense up. Relax."

As I settled, my stomach filled with apprehension. "Tell me what happened with your dad. I know the media version, but I feel like it wasn't the truth."

I waited for him to refuse, but he didn't. "It was common knowledge my father loved my mother very deeply. Their romance was unheard of in the society in which I grew up. Marriages were about connections and business. My parents showed everyone that love was another reason.

"I had an incredible childhood. Carmen and I had everything, financially and emotionally. My mother was the center of our family, and my father was the best dad imaginable."

I knew a *but* was coming.

"When my mother was killed in a car crash, something broke inside my father. He changed overnight and left Carmen and me alone to fend for ourselves. Yes, he provided financially, but the man we loved and adored disappeared and was replaced with a cold, money-driven impostor."

I listened to the hiss of a match flaring to life and then the scent of lavender and vanilla surrounded me. The aroma reminded me of my first experience with wax play while in South Africa. My stomach tensed.

"What're you doing?"

"Lighting a few candles to enhance the mood." Max climbed back onto the bed and resumed massaging my feet.

"So, finish your story. I want to understand the man I met in Cape Town."

"As I said, my father wasn't the same. His need for money propelled him to make some bad deals. And then rumors surfaced about a federal investigation into his affairs. The day warrants were issued for him and his fellow conspirators, he planned on taking the coward's way out."

"But he was murdered. Why doesn't anyone know he planned suicide?"

"Before my father could go through with his plan, a woman he defrauded of over thirty million dollars took her anger out on him. He'd used her infatuation with him as a way into her finances, and he helped himself to her inheritance."

"Oh God, that poor woman. At least you weren't the one who found him."

"I'd rather have found him than discover what he'd planned for later that evening. On his bed were a shotgun, pills, his will, and a typed letter. He couldn't even be bothered to handwrite his last words."

"How'd you keep the authorities from discovering the planned suicide?"

"Lex. I called his father, and within twenty minutes a team of people arrived to search the house for anything that would hint of something other than a case of a lover scorned."

Max's fingers tensed on the lower crease of my bottom and he leaned his head into the dip at the base of my spine. "What hurt the most was that he thought he was doing us a favor. In his suicide note, he apologized for forcing us to grow up, but by educating us, we now had the tools to fix his mess and save the company."

My heart ached for both Max and Carmen. They'd abandoned the futures they'd planned for the sake of the company. Now the lost and cynical twenty-five-year-old I'd met made sense.

My poor Max. "Is that why you walked away from us?" I held my breath, regretting asking him the question.

Max slid up my body and kissed the back of my neck. "In all honesty, yes. I was afraid of what I felt for you and thought if I let you go, I wouldn't risk becoming like my father."

A tear slipped past my eyes. "I'm sorry, Max."

"Shhh, I'm the one who should be sorry. I let you go, but I won't make the same mistake again." His words squeezed my heart, but trusting the feelings scared me.

Max slapped my ass, jarring me out of my melancholy. "No more serious talk. It's time for art class to begin."

"Are you going to paint me?"

"You'll find out soon enough." Max moved something from the side table and straddled my lower back.

My curiosity was piqued.

"Ready?"

"Yesss…" Intense heat flared down my shoulders and spine before I finished my response. "Fuck!" I called out, arching up.

Shit. He meant canvas for wax, not paint.

Max forced me down. "Breathe through it and stay still."

"Max, I'm not sure I can do this." Why hadn't I remembered the pain?

"Yes, you can. You loved it in the past, and you'll love it again." He blew on the soft wax, and as the liquid fire solidified, it left a tingle of pleasure in its wake. He rubbed my uncoated skin. "Now that the initial shock is over, we can really play."

My stomach leaped at his words, my body eagerly awaiting the white-hot burn. Max gently grazed his fingers down my side and followed them with a trail of wax. This time, the heated bite left a sensual sting urging me to rub my thighs together against the arousal I felt.

"Don't move an inch. We still have a ways to go."

Oh, God.

I waited for each splash, never knowing where he'd pour. The anticipation became addictive. The shock and pleasure of each tip of the candle had my muscles melting. He covered every bit of my back from the soles of my feet to my shoulders and arms. Under the heated touch, I surrendered to the intoxicating spell Max wove.

"Stay with me for a little bit longer, love. I'm almost done."

I fell out of the trance. The weight of the wax laid heavily on my body, pushing me into the soft bed.

"Now to make sure my masterpiece is preserved."

The next thing I knew, sharp metal grazed my skin, and I jumped in surprise. Was that a knife?

"It's okay, relax. I'm scoring the thinner areas to help with removal. The massage oil on your body will clean you up quickly. I won't hurt you."

I believed him and relaxed back into the mattress. He extracted each piece of wax from my skin with meticulous precision. Some areas slid off with little effort, others with a suction pop.

A few moments later, the bed dipped and the room glowed as Max slid the eye mask off my head. My vision cleared and focused enough to find him sitting on the side of the bed.

His brilliant eyes gazed at me with deep unsaid emotion. I tucked my feet underneath me and he took my outstretched hand.

"Let's go to bed, baby," he whispered as he slipped both of us under the covers and gathered me close.

I snuggled into his arms, but waited for the smallest sign he wanted to make love.

"Don't you want to—"

He silenced me with a kiss. "No, I need to hold you tonight."

I closed my eyes and accepted his comfort.

I woke to an empty bed and the sound of Max talking in the living room of the suite. I stretched and smiled. The tension from the ball was all but erased. Who knew a little wax play could work wonders for stressed muscles?

I lifted my head and peeked at the clock on the bedside table.

Two thirty a.m.

Who was Max calling at this time of night? Most likely someone in Europe or Asia.

Next to the clock sat a rectangle object I hadn't seen earlier in the evening. It resembled a large book.

I grasped the object. It was the wax design Max had scraped from my back with the knife. The purple wax held the golden design of a sleeping phoenix resting on a dragon's back.

Wow.

Underneath the drawing were the words: *My Arya.*

He'd taken our discussion about being a phoenix to heart and created this beautiful piece of art. The dragon had the same shape and design as the tattoo on his right shoulder.

I traced the outline of the reptile.

I rolled to my side and placed the wax back on the table. Then I moved off the bed toward the closet. I tensed at my nudity, but relaxed just as fast. After the wax we'd both fallen asleep in the dark.

I studied my shredded dress, and shook my head. In seconds, a twenty-thousand-dollar gown had been transformed to rags. I should send him a bill for the cost.

I rummaged through the closet until I found my camisole and robe. I slipped both on as I entered the living room.

Max watched me cross the threshold, and his eyes ate me up. He wore nothing but his pajama bottoms. They hung low on his hips, accentuating his amazing abs and athletic body.

I knew I'd better stop staring, or I would jump him while he was discussing business.

I sauntered toward the balcony door, glancing back one last time. Max lifted a brow and gestured at the tent forming in the front of his pants. I gave him a smile and stepped into the warm Miami night.

The salty breeze rising from the sea tickled my face as I sat on the deck chair. I gazed out toward the dark ocean. Lightning struck in the far distance, hinting at an impending storm, but the thought of sitting under a tepid shower pleased me.

What would it be like to make love with Max out here on the balcony? I closed my eyes and imagined his fingers trailing from my cheek, over my lips, and down my neck.

A sigh escaped my mouth. If only privacy wasn't an issue.

"What's put that blissful expression on your face?" Max perched on the end of the chair.

"You." I kept my eyes closed and licked my lips.

The wood beneath me creaked and then Max's lips touched mine. First, his kiss was feather soft, but soon he coaxed my mouth open and deepened the embrace.

Just like I had imagined. Perfect.

Max took hold of my wrists, pulled me underneath him,

and continued feasting. My clit throbbed, and my pussy flooded with arousal.

His hand moved between my thighs to my naked pussy. "You left off one piece of clothing."

"Any objection?" I murmured against his lips.

He let go of my hands and propelled my hips toward his cotton-covered erection. My eyes opened and I stared into blazing green. Slowly, he untied the knot on my robe and worked the silk belt out. "You're so wet, I can feel it through my pants."

My cheeks heated. The desire on his face and his words increased the need searing through me. I grazed my palm over his shirtless chest to the tattoo that ran from the back of his neck to the top of his shoulder. "Are you the dragon to my phoenix?"

"From the first moment we met." He gathered my hands. "Hold them together." Then he tied the silk belt around my wrists with a bow. "You're mine, Arya."

I climbed onto his lap. "Yours," I murmured and brought my bound arms around his neck.

Max picked me up, and I wrapped my legs around his waist as he carried me through the balcony doors to the bedroom.

"I'm going to make love to you now, Phoenix," he said, laying me down onto the bed.

I heard the challenge in his voice. We'd never used scene names before, and it surprised me that he wanted to use them now. But there was no point in fighting something that felt right.

I leaned up. "Yes, make love to me, my dragon."

And he did.

CHAPTER TWENTY-ONE

The following morning I came out of the shower to find Max packed and ready to leave.

"Where're you going? I thought our plan was to spend the weekend exploring Key West."

Max took hold of my robe's collar and drew me toward him. "If I didn't know better, I'd think you were disappointed. I still get the feeling you want to keep our relationship quiet."

I wasn't sure how to respond. I'd woken with the plan to tell Max everything. After what we shared last night, I couldn't deny I wanted more from this relationship. "I—"

Max kissed me, cutting off my words. "Don't say anything you don't mean."

I stepped back from him, holding my robe closed but keeping quiet. I couldn't talk to him about the past like this. Fuck. I finally built up the courage to tell him and now he was leaving.

"There's an emergency with an acquisition overseas. I'll fly out to Japan today and then be in China for at least a week."

I bit my lip, trying desperately to keep it from trembling. I hated feeling this way.

He walked over to his bags, picked up his briefcase, and glanced at his watch. "I have to get to the airport. I ordered breakfast. It's waiting for you in the dining area. You can always call me if you need me."

"Don't worry, I'll be okay," I said, my voice quivering. God, what was wrong with me? I'd become that senseless, needy girl again.

"It may be morning before I can call you."

"You don't need to do that. We can talk whenever you get a chance."

Hurt passed in his eyes and a stab of guilt went through me. *No, I didn't mean it like that. Say something Arya.*

But Max got there first. "After last night, I thought we were past this stupid game we've been playing." He cupped the back of his neck and blew out a rough breath. "Fine. If that's how you want it, I won't call."

Max touched the button for the elevator. He turned back one last time before stepping in, and as the door closed, he said, "I love you Arya. I'll see you in a few weeks."

Tears burned the back of my eyes as I thought of what we'd shared the night before and how stupid I was to let him think I didn't care. We'd spent the night as a couple in love, not as a Dom with his submissive acting out a scene.

I sat on the bed that still smelled of the vanilla and lavender wax and curled my knees into my chest.

* * *

I crawled onto Milla's couch, tucking my feet under me. I grabbed the remote and a blanket. After a hellacious week of meetings, planning, and programming, a fun girls' night in would do the trick for both of us. I hadn't heard from Max, and Milla was on the outs with both her Dom and Lex. What a fine pair we made.

"Make sure to bring the wine," I called out.

"Like I'd forget. I have two more bottles ready once we finish this one." Milla walked in with a tray loaded with popcorn, brownies, cake, four shots of Amarula, two glasses, and a bottle of wine.

"God bless you." I plucked a brownie from the tray and popped it into my mouth. The rich chocolate taste hit the spot.

"It feels like forever since we've had time to be girls and hang out." Milla set the food on the coffee table and reclined on the cushion next to me.

"You're right. Plus with our nonexistent love lives, we've got each other for company."

"Who needs stupid boys, anyway?" She handed me a shot and lifted her glass in a toast.

"Amen to that. Here's to best friends." We both drank down the smooth, creamy liquid and giggled.

"Hey, you never told me how the Carson Ball went. Did Max introduce you to any big investors? By the way, the pictures of you two in the magazines were awesome. Too bad you won't openly date him."

"I'm going to ignore that comment and answer your question. Overall, the ball was fun, and the evening ended well." My mind drifted to the wax play and the incredible sex that came later.

"With the spaced-out look on your face, I'd say it ended better than well. But I'm asking about the actual ball."

"It was fun, with a few exceptions. Walter being one of them and then right before we left, Jacob arrived."

"Oh shit." She bobbed on the sofa and clutched her wineglass. "Tell me you caused a scene."

"As much as I know how you'd love that, I was the pillar of the cold, unemotional ice queen. I handled Jacob as I usually do. But there was something he said that rubbed me the wrong way. So much that I called James to have someone keep an eye on him." I paused.

I really hoped I wasn't being paranoid, but with the threats I'd rather have been cautious than risk anything happening.

"Don't leave me hanging. Tell me what he said."

"He mentioned how he doesn't understand how people like working for me when I keep all my software locked up like I am developing something for the government."

"No way. Are you sure you heard him correctly?"

I frowned at her, "I know what I heard. He made it sound like a joke, but I got the drift."

"I still think he is clueless when it comes to tech stuff. I give you that it is weird that he keeps hanging around our development team, but he doesn't have a clue what they are talking about half of the time." Milla shifted on the sofa to get more comfortable. "Go ahead, if it makes you feel better, have him investigated."

"Like I need your permission," I grumbled and sipped my wine.

"Whatever. Now tell me what Walter did to piss you off."

"You know his typical tirade: I have a legacy to uphold despite my tainted genes, et cetera, et cetera."

"How I wished you'd decked him."

"That's all we need. I can see the headline now: ARMIL CEO PUNCHES EIGHTY-FIVE-YEAR-OLD GRANDFATHER. Do you think the investors would approve?" I raised my wine and drank deep.

"What did Max do?"

"Well, Max revealed that I'm the owner of RPI."

"What? That's so awesome." Milla jumped up and down on the couch. "I bet Walter nearly had a heart attack."

I smiled. "That was definitely one of the more interesting parts of the evening, except telling Walter wasn't as much fun as I thought it'd be."

"Admit it. You're a softy."

"Whatever," I grumbled.

"Anything else happen?"

"Walter said I could never do better than someone like Max, therefore I'd better not screw it up. Then Max made it sound like we were courting and he was trying to convince me he was worthy of my love."

"Arya. That's exactly what he's doing. You need to talk to him about the past."

"I know, Mil. Let it go. It's not my fault he left Miami before I could tell him."

"Fine." She took another sip of wine. "What else happened? I know you're leaving something out."

The girl knew me well. "After my lovely encounter with Walter, I met Senator Carson. Apparently he and Walter go way back, and not for the better. He was a genuinely nice guy."

"Wait, isn't Senator Carson the man who likes no one? He has a reputation for insulting anyone he thinks is an idiot, whether they deserve it or not."

I laughed. "For some reason, he loves me. He has a lot of pull with the Washington Technology Committee, which is researching intellectual property protection. With him on our side, it'll not only make getting our budgets approved easier, but our lives as well."

Milla jumped on me and squeezed me tight. "Not your life, mine. Thank you, thank you, thank you."

"You're welcome, now get off me. Enough business talk—I want this girls' weekend to begin. From this point on, no more conversations about work or men."

"Deal. Now where's the controller?"

I pulled it out from underneath the pillows on the couch and dangled it in front of her. Milla yanked the remote from my hands. "Let's watch a little entertainment news before the movie, shall we."

"Sure. You know how much I love watching other celebrities' lives."

"That's as long as you aren't part of them," Milla responded.

"Shut up and start the show. Besides, I'm not a real celebrity. No one cares about my personal life. I'm just a nerd who made a big sale."

"Maybe if you keep telling yourself that, you'll start believing it's the truth."

I threw a handful of popcorn at Milla's head.

"Hey." She dodged. "Here we go."

Now to breaking news. Look what the ultraprivate do in their down time. Kinky. Kinky.

"Oh fuck!" Milla exclaimed.

"Oh, double fuck!"

A video of me on the balcony of the Mandarin Oriental Miami was on the screen. My hands were tied with black silk and around Max's neck; his dragon tattoo was completely visible on his naked back. We kissed as I wrapped my legs around his waist and he carried me inside our room.

"Yes, ladies and gentlemen, that is our beloved billionaire Arya Rey and her rumored mystery man. You remember that picture from months back? The one from the club?"

The commentator spoke to his cohost, who shook his hand as if something burned him.

"That was hot, but this picture is sizzling. Well, the rumors appear to be true. One way to tame the ice queen is to tie her up. And from the looks of it, she loves it."

"Shut it off. I don't want to see anymore." I buried my head under the pillows on the sofa.

Milla happily clapped her hands. "This is awesome. I can't wait to tell Lex. That's what you get for all the time you laughed at my expense."

I poked my head out from behind the pillow. "You think this is funny? You wait. It will be you again, soon enough."

"At least now you don't have to pretend Lex is your plus one. No one would mistake our blond boy for your dark-haired mystery lover." Milla lifted the pillow from over me. "You know you'd be laughing if it were me."

"You suck, but you're right." Sitting up, I groaned, "Great, now everyone will invade my private life even more. Shit, Max is going to find out and I wanted to talk to him before the public learned about our relationship."

"At least he's in Japan or China or someplace in Asia and won't hear about it until later." Milla said, in her *it's not a big deal* voice.

That was such a lie. Max stayed connected to anything and everything. If there were rumors, he knew about them before the rest of the world found out.

"I never knew Max had such a hot body under that suit. Damn girl. Damn. With a build like that, I bet his package is top-notch."

I glared at Milla. "Stop thinking about my man's goods. You have your own monster-cock Dom to deal with."

"Drink your wine and let's watch a movie. We can't do anything about the paparazzi, so why bother?"

"Ugh."

Three weeks of intense training had taken their toll. I sat behind my desk and rested my forehead on my arms. My head pounded from the late nights, but the new team members were amazing. They worked hard to get up to speed and never complained, even Max. Each one had other responsibilities, but they proved they were on board with all the effort needed to work on Arcane.

My conscience nudged me for the way I'd treated Max today. He'd wanted to learn every nuance of the system, so I'd given him a crash course, with module after module of training and then a few hours of programing. Now guilt filled me. I shouldn't have been so hard on him, especially with him having a job outside of this project and being out of the country for the majority of the month.

If I was honest with myself, I went after him because he'd made me miss him. Not one call while he was away or even a message. I sighed. I knew I deserved it. I shouldn't have let him leave the way he did. I'd hoped for at least some reaction to the articles about us in the gossip magazines, but I got nothing.

"Arya, you were a bit rough on Max today. Don't you think you should go easier on him?" Lex asked as he entered my office and sat in the chair across from my desk.

I lifted my head and frowned. Trust Lex to champion for someone he felt was wronged. "No, I don't. It's time he learned that he can't always be in charge. If he wants to be part of the development process, he has to become comfortable with every stage of implementation."

"But you made him study and write code for hours today. He even canceled other meetings to make sure he understood everything you were teaching. He's been away for three weeks."

My shoulders slumped and I rubbed my temples. "I know.

I shouldn't have been bitchy. I don't know what's wrong with me. Maybe I'm going through withdrawal."

"Oh God, don't talk to me about that. You have Milla for those kinds of conversations."

"Well, it's not as much fun when the discussions are one-sided. I think she's tired of talking about her problems. When she does talk, she rarely gives many details about her sex life."

"I'm glad she has some discretion, even with you."

"Why would you care? Never mind, I don't want to know. Answer me one question. How do you keep your sex life separate from work? How do you keep emotions out of it?"

"Who says my emotions aren't involved? Just because I keep it quiet doesn't mean she isn't important to me. She's the one who wants to keep it a secret." Lex ran his hand through his hair and then pinched the bridge of his nose. "Why are we discussing me? Didn't I tell you that you wouldn't be able to keep your emotions out of your relationship with him? Milla told me about the conversation you had after the conference. At least you finally admitted you're still in love with him."

"Yes, yes, you're so smart. Shut up." I hid my head in my arms again. "Why are you and Milla discussing things we've talked about?"

"We may fight all the time, but she is the person, besides you, I'm closest to. We do talk on occasion."

"Sorry, I'm exhausted and feeling guilty for how I've hustled Max into learning everything about the system."

"Don't get mad at me when I tell you this."

Uh-oh.

"If you were my sub and you tried topping me in public, I'd find a way to punish you in private."

"Good thing I'm not your sub," I retorted.

"Arya?" Kerry's voice called over the intercom. "There's a delivery via special courier for you. Should I bring it in?"

"Sure, come in. Lex is keeping me company."

Kerry walked into the office and handed me a box with an envelope attached. I set it on the table, lifted the lid, and peeked inside.

Quickly, I shut the box and peered at both Kerry and Lex, who waited for me to tell them what was inside.

"Well?"

"Well what? It's something for me. Don't you two have better things to do than sit here being nosy?"

"Kerry, I believe we aren't wanted. Let's go and let Grumpy work," Lex said. He led Kerry out of my office, shutting the door.

Once I securely closed the door, I lifted the lid again. Inside sat a bamboo paddle with a leather-covered handle. Butterflies jumped inside my stomach, and Lex's words echoed in my head.

I knew without a doubt that Max sent the package. Was he telling me I should expect a punishment for pushing him in the lab? Of course he was. The thought of him using the paddle on me sent a rush of excitement to my core.

Closing the lid, I pulled the envelope off the box and read the card.

Since you like to play games, we're going to push your limits. You will have your first club experience tonight. Your outfit will be waiting in our playroom. Go straight there after work. I will meet you there.

M.

P.S.
Bring the paddle.

CHAPTER TWENTY-TWO

At nine that night, I finished dressing in Max's playroom. I tilted my head and surveyed myself in the mirror. A disconcerting combination of fear and excitement coursed through me. I'd never worn anything so revealing in public.

The black, lace-up leather corset barely covered my chest or my ass. A satin garter was connected to the corset and attached to black stockings that emphasized my legs. The only thing preventing a complete view of my goods was a barely-there G-string.

"You're breathtaking."

I caught Max's gaze as he walked into the dressing area of the playroom. He stopped behind me and then lifted a diamond necklace.

My breath hitched, and his eyes stayed on mine.

"I had this designed for you. You will wear it tonight and from now on. No one outside of our lifestyle will know what it means."

I stared at the necklace and a tremor went down my spine. The platinum-and-diamond chain looked like something any other woman would wear. But the triskele at the fastener revealed its true meaning.

"Tonight, anyone who sees you will know you're taken and unavailable. Do you understand? Do you accept the collar?"

I bit my lip, nodded, and then whispered, "Yes."

Tears clouded my eyes, but I held them back. I knew what it meant. By taking this, there was no more hiding what we were to each other.

Lifting my hair, Max clasped the necklace around my neck. After he'd finished, his hands lingered and traced down my back.

"Are you nervous?"

"Yes," I whispered.

"There's nothing to worry about. I want you to experience something you've never opened yourself up to before. I know how private you are. You'll wear this." He lifted a black mask with two cat's-eye holes. "Everyone will know who I am, since I'm one of the owners of the club, but unless you want them to, no one will recognize anything about you except that you belong to me."

"Okay."

"One more thing. Where's the paddle?"

I glanced over to the bench where I'd set the box. "Are you going to punish me now or later?"

Max grasped my hair and his lips grazed my neck. "It will have to wait for later. Much later, after we've had a discussion about how you tried to top me in retaliation for something I didn't know I did."

"Max, I'm sorry."

His hand moved over my throat, cupping my jaw. "I know you, Arya. You probably didn't even realize how you were behaving. If you needed me, why not tell me instead of trying to get a reaction out of me?"

You left before I could tell you.

Max's grip tightened slightly as he answered my unasked question. "I felt your hunger the minute I entered the lab. Because I made sure I followed your exact rules for keeping our personal and professional lives separate. You broke your own guidelines when you brought your frustrations into the public forum."

I placed my hand over his. "Max—"

"Address me as Sir," he interrupted.

"Sir, I'm sorry."

Max abruptly released me and went toward the changing area. "Finish dressing. We'll leave in ten."

I remained standing in front of the mirror, staring at my reflection. I traced the platinum chain against my collarbone. My hand shook as my fingers grazed the three diamonds in the center of the necklace. I couldn't believe I'd given myself to him without any fight, negotiation, or anything. We were no longer just Dominant and submissive in private.

"Stop thinking. We have a long night ahead of us," Max said as he reentered the dressing room.

He walked up behind me and slid his hands around my waist. He'd changed into leather pants and wore no shirt. His heavily muscled shoulders shifted as he opened a coat for me to put on.

I licked my lips and my gaze met his. His intense green eyes were focused completely on me.

I officially belonged to him.

He buttoned my coat and collected his own. "Let's go. When we get to the club, keep your eyes on me. That is, unless I tell you to watch a scene. You may or may not recognize some of the members, but outside of the venue, we don't discuss or acknowledge anything we witness."

I nodded but remained quiet.

"I didn't hear you."

I looked up. "Yes, Sir."

Max smiled and took my hand. "From this point on, you will call me Sir, not Max. I am your master and you will do as I command. Agreed?"

I blew out an unsteady breath. "Agreed."

Max led me through the house and to the waiting car. For the most part, we drove in silence. Nervous energy had me fidgeting, unable to sit still. I took deep breaths to keep Max from detecting on my anxiety, but of course, he noticed. He'd occasionally place his hand over my thigh and squeeze, but he never spoke a word to me. Forty minutes later, we arrived at a group of gated warehouses in Boston's South End.

A security guard approached our car and verified our credentials before allowing us through the gate. The car stopped in front of a nondescript metal door, and two attendants rushed out with umbrellas.

"Wow, do they do that for everyone?" I asked Max, trying to break the silence.

"Yes" was all he said.

Great. Thanks for the small talk.

Max's driver, Aaron, opened the door, and my anxiety sky-rocketed. My stomach churned, and I prayed I wouldn't throw up.

We stepped out into the rain and Max guided me forward.

Stopping abruptly, he turned to face me. "Arya, breathe. Everything we do will be kept private." He traced a finger down my cheek. "You're mine to take care of, and I'd never force you to do anything that would make you unhappy."

He draped his arm around me as we entered what I could only describe as a jazz club lounge. The decor was lush and intimate. Deep hues of green and blue with a hint of gold draped the walls. Rich mahogany woodwork lined the corners and ceiling. Two sets of stairs stood on either side of an opulent bar that carried every top-shelf liquor imaginable. Strategically positioned sofas, armchairs, and tables created individual seating areas.

Where were the playrooms?

An attendant approached us and took our coats while another handed us each a glass of wine. I drank mine in a few gulps, not tasting any of the expensive liquid, and placed my glass on a nearby table.

"This isn't what I expected."

"We're in the social area of the club. Here, everything's very civilized. It's more like a community gathering area for dinner, conversation, and relaxation. The play areas are upstairs. We permit alcohol in this space only and no more than one glass. Scenes are conducted with clear minds." Max finished his drink and set it on a nearby tray. "Shall we?"

He lifted his elbow and I grasped it as if needing a lifeline. The wine I'd indulged in hadn't relaxed me the way I'd hoped.

Standing on wobbly legs, I followed Max up a flight of stairs. As we went, people greeted Max and surveyed me with curiosity. Many of the women were dressed similarly to me, but the men varied from tight leather pants and vests to three-piece suits.

We climbed the staircase and entered another lounge that was three times the size of the one below. In the center, ten different rooms positioned in a circle. Wall-sized windows separated each space from the lounge. Groups of people lingered around each scene.

I grabbed Max's arm for balance. "Wow, the floor is moving."

"We wanted our scenes enjoyed by all the patrons. The rotating floor creates a unique environment where those who prefer to sit in the lounge area can still experience the performances in each room."

"Do you plan for us to perform?"

"No, Arya. I may love parading you around, but I will never let anyone enjoy our private moments. Everything we do is for me and you only."

I sighed in relief, and Max chuckled.

The first room we approached held a couple engaged in a bit of wax play. The submissive was a shirtless male laid across a table with his hands bound above his head and his feet clasped to the wooden legs. His straining cock pressed against the cotton material of his shorts, and precum dampened the center of the fabric. His Domme slowly poured golden wax across each nipple and blew. The sub moaned aloud but kept still, not flinching a single muscle.

I licked my lips, remembering the night of wax I'd spent with Max.

"Maybe next time, I'll do the same thing to you. Would you like that?"

"Yes," I said with a breathless whisper.

"Come, there are more scenes to observe."

Each room contained various acts of pleasure, from spanking, orgasm denial, knife play, and ménage scenes to full-on fucking. Each of the acts built upon the other, and by the time we arrived at the last area, I was a panting mess.

This space held a beautiful, masked brunette anchored to a Saint Andrew's cross with her equally handsome and masked Dom wielding a long-tailed bullwhip. He was naked above the waist, and his sub was clad in a black leather bikini and leather thigh-high boots. I couldn't take my eyes off them. With each strike of the whip, the submissive arched toward her lover. She begged, but her Dom told her to be patient and kissed her before he stepped back for another strike.

He struck between her breasts and down her abdomen. She shifted her hips up and took each blow with pleasure. The final strike grazed the juncture of her thighs, and she screamed out her release as the Dom covered her mouth with his, swallowing her cry.

"They're beautiful. Why do they want to share this with everyone?"

Max's finger trailed down my neck. "Because here they can express their love and desire for each other without judgment. As you said, they're beautiful. The vanilla world wouldn't appreciate the raw emotion they hold for each other."

"They resemble Milla and Lex so much I almost wish it was them."

Max chuckled and kissed my neck.

All of the sudden, the couple stopped their embrace and redirected their attention toward me. Others who were watching the scene followed suit.

"Why are they staring at us?" I whispered.

His hand rested possessively on my naked lower back. "Because of who you are to me."

I shifted my gaze from the couple to his face. "What do you mean?"

"I've never scened or been with any submissive at the club. Plus the case that held this collar is empty, and the missing jewelry is around your neck."

My hand went to my throat. "How long have you had this?"

"Over five years. I had it made almost as soon as I left you at the camp. I kept it in the case, hoping one day it would belong to you."

"But why create a club like this if you've never participated?"

"Before Lex and I had our falling out, we planned this place. I thought even though I didn't have you in my life, I could still have a club for others to enjoy without the interference of the outside world." Max cupped the side of my face and drew me toward him. His lips lightly touched mine. "Now that you belong to me, I can finally play here." He deepened the kiss and any other questions running through my head disappeared. God, I loved his mouth.

A throat cleared behind us, breaking the trance I had fallen under. Max glanced up. A shadow of irritation crossed his face before he masked it.

The man spoke with a heavy Russian accent. "Maxwell, good to see you. Now who is this lovely creature? She must have many unique talents to pull you off the market."

I held back the desire to smack the condescending man. I followed Max's instructions by keeping my eyes on him.

"Hello, Christof. Yes, she's very special."

Holy shit—Vladimir Christof. Why would he come here? Rumor had it he was an over-the-top sadist. A place like this didn't cater to the urges he had.

The hairs on the back of my neck prickled. If he knew I stood masked before him, he probably wouldn't think I was special.

I knew the Russian industrialist and suspected arms dealer hated Lex, Milla, and me, no matter what I'd told Milla about him losing interest in us.

A lump formed in my stomach. What if he was involved in the threats against us?

No, I shook the thought from my mind. Christof wasn't known for threats; if he wanted someone dead he took care of it without warning.

"I see you trained her well. What does she go by?"

"Mine." Max clenched his jaw. "You're a guest here, but your reputation for poaching is well-known. Please be mindful of club regulations."

"I meant no offense. I found the news of your taking a submissive very intriguing and wanted to introduce myself. She is quite lovely. Indian, I presume?"

"Yes."

"You do gravitate toward the exotic. It's amazing that beautiful and sexually adventurous women come from such a conservative culture."

I hated this man. If he weren't dangerous, I would have punched him that second.

"Some of us are luckier than others." Max kept his face stoic, not giving away his irritation.

"It's nice to know you have finally replaced your lady love from years ago. Must be very interesting to have this stunning woman in your life when you work with your ex daily."

Both Max and I stiffened. "You know a lot about my affairs, Christof," he said carefully.

"I make it my business to study as much about my rivals as possible. Imagine my surprise when your name appeared in my research into the ever-elusive Ms. Rey. Too bad you broke her heart and changed her into the emotionless being she is today."

"Let's keep this friendly and leave personal issues out of your experience here at the club."

"Oh, I plan to. Jacob has invited me to join him in a scene with a beautiful blonde he favors. Too bad you aren't into sharing. This goddess is the epitome of a proper submissive." He ran his finger down the back of my arm.

It took all my willpower to stay still. His touch made my skin crawl.

"Not once has she taken her eyes off you to glance my way."

"Yes, I'm a very fortunate man who never, ever shares. Enjoy your evening."

Max led me past Christof and into a dark area where he

pushed me against the wall. He took my mouth in a desperate demand, stopping for a mere second before devouring me again. "Watching him touch you made me want to kill him. You are mine, Arya. Do you understand?"

"Yes," I voiced breathlessly.

"Please tell me the rumors aren't true, and you weren't involved in his lost arms deal." He leaned his forehead against mine.

"I didn't know we were targeting anyone when we designed the program. Working with MI6 as a graduate school intern was a dream come true. I never thought they'd use it in an actual operation."

"Ari, you have too many secrets. Every time I turn around, I discover another one."

Boy, he didn't know the half of it. I closed my eyes, letting him hold me.

"Maybe one day you'll stop keeping me at arm's length."

My lips trembled. "I promise. Max, why is Jacob sceneing with Christof?"

"I don't know, but I plan to find out. Jacob's association with him puts everyone at the company under scrutiny."

Max released me and pressed his thumb against a plate on the wall. A green light appeared and the wall opened, revealing another room. Max guided me in and I gawked in amazement. Each wall of the decagon-shaped room was glass and looked into one of the public playrooms. In the center of the room, monitors displayed camera angles from every point of the facility.

"Can they see us?"

"No, this is one-way glass. We're in my private office. Only a handful of people know about its existence."

I spotted a spanking bench sitting in the center of the room but thought nothing of it. The couple performing with the bullwhip and the Saint Andrew's cross drew my attention. I touched the glass of the room and fell into their scene.

The Dom used the handle of the whip to trace a line over the sub's breast, down her abdomen and then between her legs. The sub moaned and thrashed against her restraints.

My breath hitched.

He stopped and walked over to the observation windows. With a touch of a button, the glass clouded over to black, blocking out the public viewing area. He returned to his submissive, kissed her, and whispered something in her ear that caused a tear to run down her face.

She mouthed the words *I love you*. And her Dom resumed his ministration with the bullwhip.

"Do we look like that when we're together?"

"Yes. We feel about each other the same way they do."

I continued observing the couple.

"Does watching them arouse you?" Max whispered into my ear as his palm crept around me.

I gasped. I was so lost in the scene, I hadn't sensed Max lingering behind me.

"I asked you a question."

I didn't respond. My fingers remained on the one-way glass and my gaze fixed on the couple. I licked my lips.

"Arya, are you listening?"

"Yes, Sir."

"What are you saying yes to?"

"You asked if they arouse me. Yes, Sir. They do."

"Let me see." Max's fingers slid from my waist to my G-string. He used one hand to move the silk to the side and the other to explore my folds.

"Mmmm, you're drenched." He rubbed my clit as he spread my juices then pushed two digits into me.

"Ahhh."

"Do you like that?"

"Yesss," I moaned.

He pulled out and brought his fingers to my mouth. "Suck."

I followed his command and my own essence exploded in my mouth, which sent another rush of wetness down my pussy.

"Did you enjoy tasting yourself?"

"Yes, Sir."

"Good, now come here, but keep your eyes on them."

I moved in a trance, a voyeur to the couple's intimacy. They stared intently at each other, their love for one another blazing with each strike of the whip. Desire pulsed throughout the room, evident by the sub's moans and her Dom's straining erection.

I ached to touch myself. I shifted my hands but they were bound by two leather straps attached to the sides of the spanking bench. Startled, I jerked my arms but it only pitched me forward against the bench.

Oh hell. I hadn't noticed Max maneuvering me or tying me down.

"Sir?" I asked.

"It's time for your punishment."

CHAPTER TWENTY-THREE

My heart leaped into my throat, as Max pressed his leather-covered, rock-solid cock against my back and positioned me so my knees rested on the sides of the bench. He angled my ass high into the air and my face downward.

The paddle sat within arm's reach to my side.

When had he brought that in here?

"For every question you don't answer truthfully, you will receive a strike." Max slid my G-string down, leaving it hanging around my knees. "Did you lie when you said you didn't want me to call or communicate with you outside of the playroom?"

"No, I—"

Smack.

The sting shot through me. My butt cheek burned, tingling more than hurt.

"Do you push me away because you're afraid you'll become attached?"

How do I admit I'd never stopped being attached? "No, Sir. I—"

Smack.

I cried out. My core spasmed and my pussy wept. Dizziness filled my mind.

"Are you sorry for pushing me today?" Max rubbed my sore cheeks.

"Maybe."

Smack.

I hissed.

"Yes or no?"

"No, Sir."

Smack.

"I told the truth," I called out.

"No, you didn't. You wouldn't have apologized earlier if you hadn't regretted it." Max took the handle of the paddle and traced the seam of my lips, stopping a heartbeat away from my clit. "Are you falling in love with me again?"

"No, Sir." *I never stopped loving you.*

Smack.

"Why won't you admit it?"

"I can't." Tears ran down my face. My orgasm loomed and my ass pulsed with fire.

Smack.

Wetness ran down my thighs. How was it possible to be aroused and cry at the same time?

"Do you need me?"

Of course, I do. But how do I know you won't leave me once you learn about the girls?

I didn't respond and waited for the next strike, but nothing came.

I glanced behind me to see the paddle laying on the side table and Max walking away. He sighed in frustration and then ran his hand through his hair. He moved to the bar near his desk, poured himself a drink, then downed the contents.

He came back to me, crouching down to make us eye level. "For every lie you've spoken you will receive two strikes. Now tell me how many?"

I remained silent. Max walked behind me and ran a hand over my aching ass and down between my drenched thighs. His fingers slid easily into me, pumping in and out.

I moaned and shifted trying to maneuver his rhythm. My core throbbed, hanging on the edge of release.

"Please, let me come," I begged. "I need your cock, not your fingers."

He stopped. "Tell me how many strikes do you desire."

"Ten," I whimpered.

Max picked up the paddle and I closed my eyes in anticipation.

He caressed my tender cheeks and folds, and then commanded, "Count."

Smack.

"One."

Smack.

"Two."

Smack.

I counted each strike, crying out as the sensation in my

pussy increased tenfold. A haze surrounded me as my mind separated from my body, and euphoria filled me. My orgasm was close, but every time I was on the verge of going over, Max paused and hurled me down from my high. The lashes of the paddle stroked every surface of my ass but never close enough to my swollen, throbbing core.

"How many more, Ari?"

God, I'd lost count.

"I can't remember."

Smack. My pussy spasmed.

"Please."

"No, tell me how many you have left."

I thought back over each strike. "Two more, Sir."

"Good." Max massaged my thighs with his free hand. "Where do you want them, Arya? On your beautiful ass or somewhere else?"

"My...my—"

Smack.

He hit my cheek, near my labia but too far away from...

"Please," I moaned.

"Say it. You have one more left."

"On my pussy." Everything inside me quivered and waited for the strike.

"Come for me, baby."

SMACK.

My orgasm erupted as my mind whirled. "*Max!*" I called, arching back and then falling forward against the leather of the bench.

My breath slowed, and I studied the couple on the other

side of the glass. Their intense lovemaking session against the Saint Andrew's cross ignited another quiver in my core. At the same moment, Max positioned the head of his cock at my entrance.

"Before I give both of us what we crave, tell me the truth. Why were you angry with me?"

How do I explain something I don't understand myself?

"I'm waiting."

Tears flowed once again. "Because…Because…"

Max nudged my pussy and stopped. "Say it, Arya."

"Because I need you and I know I wouldn't survive if you left me again."

"Finally, the truth." Max plunged balls deep and began pounding me.

I closed my eyes, reveling in his uncontrolled and demanding movements.

"Watch them," Max said, and I lifted my head.

The Dom fucked his sub as Max fucked me. Our rhythms were in harmony. Suddenly we all cried and came. I clutched around Max's cock, letting the intensity of my orgasm wash over me until my vision blurred.

I woke to find a cool, soft pillow under my head and the heat of a warm body behind me.

Where am I?

I must have fallen into deep subspace. Milla had talked about it, but to actually experience it was something else altogether. I remembered the out-of-body sensation during my punishment, but the last orgasm had to have sent me over the edge. I smiled inside. That was definitely a whopper of an orgasm.

I shifted to my back and caught Max's eyes watching me. His smile was content. "Welcome back."

"That was the first time I've…umm, ever…"

"Gone into deep subspace," Max finished my thought. He leaned over me and kissed my forehead. "Don't worry. I took care of you."

I arched and kissed him again, when all of the sudden I remembered what I'd told him right before I blanked out. "Max, about what I said before—"

He placed a finger over my lips. "Arya, the only way you'd lose me is if you did the leaving. I told you from the start, I'm here for good."

I swallowed. "Where do we go from here?"

"We'll take one day at a time. I won't rush you, but there's one thing you need to know. I won't allow our relationship to remain a secret much longer."

I stiffened as he gazed down at me. My hand went to the collar around my neck and his eyes followed the movement.

"You accepted the collar and everything it represents. Many would say it's the equivalent of what you refuse to be for me in the vanilla world."

I bit my lip. He was right. I'd committed myself to him last night. I now belonged to him, body, mind, and soul, and he was mine in return.

He kissed me and moved over me. My fingers threaded with his, as his lips and tongue worked their way down my neck and between my breasts. He took each peak into his mouth and suckled.

I arched into him. "I could get used to waking like this."

"Good, since that's the plan." He released my hands and moved lower, running his palms down my stomach. "I love the feel of you, skin to skin. Soft and silky."

He was right; the crisp tingle of his chest hair against my nipples went straight to my pussy.

Wait a second. Did he say skin to skin? Oh God, his hand was on my stomach.

"No! Stop." I shoved Max off me and jerked the covers up, hugging my knees to my chest."

"What's wrong?" Max's confusion was apparent.

"I'm naked." I surveyed the room. We weren't at the club. "How did I get here?"

"I told you I took care of you. After you'd gone into sub-space, I brought you home. To my bedroom, not the one in the playroom. Then I undressed you and we went to bed."

Undressed me? Oh no, he had to have seen the scars.

He tugged me toward him, but I resisted. "I don't understand why you're upset about me seeing you naked," he said.

"You saw…the scars." Tears burned my eyes.

"Yes, I saw them last night, and I've seen them many times since we reunited. Do you think I didn't notice your reaction every time my hand strayed over you abdomen? Did you think I'd reject you for them?"

"I…yes."

"Dammit, Arya, I love you. When are you going to get it through your thick skull?" I flinched at his outburst, and he released a groan of frustration. "Why won't you tell me what happened?"

I jumped off the bed. " This isn't how I wanted to tell you. You don't understand."

"Then make me understand."

"I can't. I can't. I nearly died. Don't make me go there right now. I don't want to relive it." I stumbled toward the bedroom door. I had to get out of the house.

"Please, baby. Tell me. Let me in." Max moved forward, but I stepped back.

"I'm sorry." I ran from the room, grabbed my coat and shoes, and went for the front of the house.

I stopped abruptly. How would I get home? If I called James, it would take him at least an hour to get here.

When I reached the front door, I found Aaron waiting for me.

"Ms. Rey, Mr. Dane has informed me to take you anywhere you desire."

Oh, Max.

"Could you please take me to my penthouse?"

He nodded and I followed him out the car. Before I got in, I turned back to look at the house. Max watched me from his bedroom window, and I fought the urge to go back inside and confess everything I'd been through. But would he still love me once he knew what I'd kept from him?

My phone rang, breaking into my thoughts as I climbed into the car.

"Hey, Arya. Where are you?" Milla's chipper voice rang out.

"I'm on my way home from Max's house."

"What's wrong? I know you were with him at his club last night. Did something happen?"

"No, nothing happened. Wait. How do you know I was there? I never mentioned where I was going."

Milla sighed. "It doesn't matter right now. Arya, you're upset. I can hear it in your voice."

I leaned my head back against the car seat and closed my eyes. "I let my frustrations about my feelings out on Max."

"I heard about that."

"From who? Never mind, there's more. Then I accepted his collar without a fight—"

"What?" Milla interrupted again. "Sorry, go on."

"Then I had my first experience with deep subspace and when I woke up, I was naked in bed with Max."

"So where is the bad part in all of this, besides trying to top Max?"

"Mil, he saw me naked."

She's my best friend, she should understand.

"So what? Oh, he saw the scars. Did you tell him?"

"I couldn't. I panicked and ran out of his place." I combed my hand over my face. "What am I going to do?"

"First, take a deep breath. Then think about what scares you. From the way he cared for you last night, I don't think you have anything to worry about."

"You saw us?" *Oh, man. How many people recognized me?*

"Of course. Don't worry, though. No one would think it was you, especially in the black corset, thigh-highs, and mask. You have a very conservative rep in the outside world."

"Thanks a lot."

"The reason I knew it was you was because you were with Max. People started talking the moment you two walked in. No one's ever seen him with a submissive, let alone one he'd collared. *Bella*, you're the talk of the town. The girl who captured the much-coveted Maxwell Dane."

I fingered the collar around my neck. "You're not helping."

"Ari, he's a good guy. Give him a chance. He deserves to know."

Mumbling echoed in the background. It sounded like Lex's Irish brogue but deeper.

"Who're you with? Why does that voice sound familiar?" I asked.

"You know who I'm with."

"I know you're with your Dom. You wouldn't visit the club without him. What I'm asking is who is your Dom?" Poor Lex.

"You'll find out sooner or later."

"If Lex didn't have his own little subby, I'd have to kick your ass. For two people who love each other, you're both such idiots."

"So speaks the girl who ran away from the love of her life."

"Whatever."

"Seriously, *bella*. Talk to him."

"I know you're right. Before I do, I want to go see my girls. It'll be five years in a couple days."

"Promise you'll talk to him when you get back."

"I will, but don't let anyone besides Lex know where I am. Give me a few days."

Milla sighed. "Okay. I'll hold down the fort and Jane will handle development. See you soon."

"Love you, Mil."

"Love you, too."

I ended the call and then dialed James.

"Yes, Ms. Rey."

"James, could you please get the plane ready? You should know the destination."

"Already done. I had anticipated this trip. We will be ready when you are."

I closed my phone, gazed out the window, and whispered, "Okay, my babies. Mommy's on her way to see you."

CHAPTER TWENTY-FOUR

Three days after leaving Max's house and forty-eight hours after arriving in South Africa, I forged the courage to visit my girls. As I crossed the threshold to their graves, I tightened my coat and let the beauty and sadness of the cemetery filled me. Even after five years, the moment my foot touched the soil in Cape Town, the pain of the past resurfaced, fresh and raw. My babies would have celebrated their fifth birthday today if life had taken a different journey.

Flowers filled the base of the headstone, and my heart swelled. I glanced behind me and caught James dabbing at his eyes. He'd made sure my babies were well tended.

Tears streamed down my face and I traced my girls' names.

Alyssa and Sasha.

"My babies, I wish you lived, but it wasn't your time," I whispered and leaned my head against the marker. "Your daddy and I are back together. Well, at this moment it's debatable. He doesn't know about you two.

"I know it isn't fair, but I was afraid of letting him in and then having him leave me again. Now, I've pushed him to the point where he doesn't see any hope for us."

I placed a teddy bear at the top of the tombstone and closed my eyes. "I tried to call him, to let him know I wasn't leaving him, that I needed to think. He hasn't responded to any of my messages. I don't know what to do." I shuddered, and my pain cascaded in fat drops to the ground. "I did exactly what Ian warned me against. Every time your daddy wanted more or tried to give me more, I resisted or refused. Now he's given up on me.

"Your aunt Milla was right as usual. I'm not a no-strings kind of girl. And you girls are the biggest tie that holds me to your father."

I'd hurt Max the same way he'd hurt me many years ago. I'd rejected his love to protect my own heart.

The wind intensified and blew dust into my face, causing me to cough. As I cleared my throat, I understood what I had to do. I had to give him all of me, no more holding anything back. "Ms. Rey."

I jumped and whirled toward James. "Y-yes, James." My voice came out raspy from all the tears.

"An unexpected cold front is moving over New England, and we need to leave in the next few hours if we want to arrive in Boston before the snowstorm hits."

"Give me five more minutes and I'll meet you at the car."

James inclined his head and left.

"Well, my babies, it's time for me to go home, but when I get back, I promise to make it better. And next time I'll bring your daddy to meet you."

I rose and felt someone watching me. As I glanced to my left, I saw a reflection of light. I squinted my eyes and sighed. Just a tree's shadow. All this crying must have been affecting my senses.

Shrugging my shoulders, I moved toward James, who waited for me outside the car. He took my hand as I approached him and held it tight. "Things will work out. Be honest with him and yourself."

He released me and I wrapped my arms around James's neck. "I love you, my grumpy Russian."

He squeezed me back, kissed my head, and motioned for me to enter the car. "The plane is fueled and ready, Ms. Rey."

I shook my head. "Enough with the Ms. Rey already."

Both of us chuckled as he shut the door in my face.

Eighteen hours later, I peered over my terrace toward the snow-covered city. Exhaustion from the trip to Cape Town sat on my shoulders. My chest ached, and my head pounded. Lack of sleep and crying for hours had taken their toll. I thought standing outside would help, but the chill of Boston's bitter late-winter storm had done nothing to numb the pain.

The doorbell rang, but I ignored it. My housekeeper would answer and let me know if I were needed.

I rubbed my temples, knowing what I had to do. It was time to tell Max about the past and see if we had a future together. I tilted my face to the sky, letting the snow and wind cool my cheeks.

Girls, please help your father understand. I sent my silent prayer to heaven and gazed back out into the night.

"You could catch a chill standing out here, even with your coat and scarf."

Startled, I whirled around to find Max leaning against the terrace wall. Dressed in a winter trench coat, he looked every bit the corporate executive. His dark hair blew from the wind and his sea-green eyes, shadowed from lack of sleep, were unreadable as he stared at me.

A chill ran down my spine. Until that moment, I hadn't sensed the cold, but now every muscle and bone was frozen. Max strode to me and cupped my face with his palm as he wiped away my tears.

"Who are Alyssa and Sasha?" he whispered. He stepped back, took out something from inside his coat pocket, and handed it to me.

They were pictures of me touching and resting my head against the girls' headstone. I was right. Someone had been watching me.

I clutched the photos, not saying anything as fresh tears blurred my vision. "Who gave you these?"

"Does it matter? Was this what gave you all the nightmares?"

My lips trembled. "Not them, but what happened to them...to me."

How do I explain keeping our girls from him?

Realization dawned on his face. "It was you. The one who was kidnapped," he said softly. He traced the image of the headstone. "They were mine."

I nodded. My empty hand moved over my stomach.

"Why didn't you tell me?"

"I was going to tell you, but you threw me away. You didn't want me anymore. How could I know you would want them?" A cry broke free and I slid to the ground and sobbed.

Max crouched down next to me and gathered me in his arms. "I'm so sorry, Ari. God, my stupidity cost us our babies."

I tried pushing him away, but he wouldn't let me go.

"I can't do this." I gulped for air, willing my crying to stop. I looked up, keeping my hand against his chest. "I don't want to need you or lean on you."

Sadness flashed over his face. "I need you, too. Why do you think I never gave up hope for us all these years? Or why I orchestrated the deal?"

He remained silent as I continued weeping. What I wouldn't have given to receive this support years ago. Finally, when my crying slowed, Max carried me inside.

"Let me draw you a bath, and you can relax while we talk."

I nodded, laying my head against his shoulder and directing him to my bathroom. I had resisted Max coming to my penthouse, but now he was here, and I was home.

He sat me down on the granite edge of the oversized tub and rotated the knob to start the water. "Want me to light a fire?" he asked, but didn't wait for my response and walked over to the fireplace. I'd never used it before. The luxury of having such an over-the-top en suite had been lost on me until today.

Max motioned me forward. "Come, sit by the fire. It'll be a few minutes before the bath is ready."

I rose on unsteady legs and gingerly walked over, but remained standing. I blew out a deep breath and slowly unbuttoned my coat. My fingers were cold and numb, defying me as I worked the buttons.

Max's hands stopped me, as he knelt down in front of me. "Let me do this."

I said nothing and allowed him to open my coat. A sense of hopelessness washed over me. I would have to watch him see the scars in their entirety. What would he do when he understood how much damage lay under the visible wounds? My palms stilled his, and he waited for me to say something. I took another deep breath to calm my nerves.

"Please Arya, let me see."

I shifted my arms to the side and he continued. Max removed my coat and folded it, then took off my shoes, one at a time, placing them over the coat. He stepped behind me and gently lowered the zipper on my dress. He nudged the fabric off my shoulders, but I held it up in front of me. I hiccuped from all the spent tears. He moved to face me and we stared at each other. I shook slightly as he placed his hands over mine.

"I've seen and touched every part of you. Show me what they did to you."

"The scars are deeper than you know. They damaged me." I prayed he understood what I meant.

"Let me help you heal."

Gently, he moved my hands away from my dress and let it fall at my feet. I gazed into his eyes and searched for a clue as to what he thought. He stepped back and scanned me but did not say a word. I closed my eyes, willing myself to remain still as he inspected what I'd kept hidden for years. A tremor shook my body. No more hiding, no more secrets. I was completely exposed.

When I wiped away another tear, a feathered kiss grazed the raised scars near my belly button. Stunned, I opened my eyes and peered down.

Max traced and kissed every stab wound, avoiding the one down the center of my stomach. Finally, when he finished tracing every other mark, he delicately ran his finger down the jagged line where our babies had been cut from me.

Max glanced up slightly and then lowered his head in shame. "I'm so sorry I wasn't there for you." He pressed his face into my stomach, and I felt the warm wetness of his tears.

I touched his shoulders and rubbed, trying to convey what I couldn't actually say. He held me tight as I gripped his back. All his grief washed over me. He loved our girls without knowing them.

I knelt down in front of him, cradling his face in my hands. I gazed into his red-rimmed eyes, seeing all the emotions I kept denying existed. I'd wasted so much time trying to keep Max at a distance.

But where would we go from here?

He rose without saying anything and helped me stand. Carefully, he unfastened my bra, removed my underwear, and then carried me to the tub. Pushing off his shoes, he stepped into the tub fully clothed.

"Max, your—"

He put a finger to my lips, silencing me. He gathered my hair on top of my head and clasped it with a clip he'd grabbed from the tub ledge, then sat me in the middle of the giant tub.

I sank into the water, hugging my knees as I allowed the heat and the scent of the bath to seep into my pores.

Max stepped out of the tub, and I couldn't help but reach out. "Where are you going?"

"It's okay, baby. I'm just getting a little more comfortable."

His words calmed me and I relaxed back into the bubbles. Max discarded his wet clothes, leaving them in a soaked pile, and climbed back into the water behind me. His palms slid over my stomach and drew me against his chest.

We both remained quiet, letting the steaming water soothe us. Our bodies slowly settled into each other's embrace.

I placed my hand over his as it lay across my damaged abdomen. "Who gave you the pictures?"

CHAPTER TWENTY-FIVE

Max remained quiet and then clutched me closer to his chest. "Does it matter? Let's say that the pictures opened my eyes to the true intentions of my friends."

Huh?

"Relax." He smoothed my hair from my forehead and kissed the back of my head.

"It was Jacob, wasn't it?" I had no doubt. The man hated me, especially after seeing Max and me together at the Carson Ball. Would he forever remain a thorn in my side?

"Yes. I think he believed by revealing your secret, I'd go into a rage and end our relationship."

"For being one of your closest friends, he doesn't know you very well."

Max's chest vibrated with a small chuckle. "Since you left my estate last week, I haven't been the most approachable of men." Gliding his fingers up and down my arm, he continued. "I was hurt you wouldn't trust me, even after everything we'd shared. I didn't know what to do, and feeling helpless left me in a piss-poor mood."

"But it doesn't make sense why Jacob had me followed to Cape Town and gave you the pictures. What does he gain from hurting you?"

"A lot has happened since last week. I confronted Jacob about his association with Christof and told him that any involvement with a suspected terrorist would be detrimental to himself and to the lives of his family. He insisted it was all for the kink factor and then accused me of letting you influence my decisions."

"Well, you did buy my company in order to win me back," I quipped.

"True, but you never had a say in that decision. Long story short, I told him if he wanted to continue working for MDC he'd have to sever all ties to Vladimir."

"I bet that went over well."

"To say the least. He quit and told me that he's glad you left me, and he hoped I would get my head on straight."

"Did we break up?"

"No." He released an exasperated breath. "I never corrected his misconception."

I stiffened and pulled away, but Max held me tight. "Lie back down. Let me finish." Conceding, I softened into his embrace. "I could tell Jacob wanted to tell me something, so I played along. Right before he left my office, he handed me an envelope and waited for my reaction. I couldn't believe what I saw. You looked so sad and lonely in the pictures. There was one that I will never forget; you're staring directly at the camera with such pain, that I felt my heart breaking."

Not responding to his statement, I asked, "What did you say to him?"

"I told him to get out. Until that moment, I hadn't realized what lengths he'd go to separate us. Having you followed and invading your privacy was the last straw." He paused for a moment. "Were you ever going to tell me about the girls?"

"I was coming to your house right before you found me on the balcony." My eyes filled. "I was going to see if you still wanted me after you knew the truth."

His arms tightened around me. "I'm never letting you go. Why is that difficult to understand?"

"I thought I'd pushed you away with my need to protect myself."

"Arya, I've said this before and I know it won't be the last time, but you are frustrating. Do you realize how hard it was for me to stay in that room and not come after you? I realized if I kept chasing you, you'd keep running. I decided to let you go. I was giving you space, hoping you'd come back to me. It was a gamble I prayed I wouldn't regret."

The room grew quiet except for the sound of our breaths.

After a few moments, he broke the silence. "No more secrets," he said against my hair.

"Okay," I whispered.

"No more hiding."

"Okay."

"From this moment on, you and I are together. No arrangements or separation of anything."

I turned around and put my palms against his wet chest. It

was time to accept what we meant to each other. I bit my lip trying to keep it from trembling.

Max cupped my face and searched my eyes. "I've loved you from the moment we met. I let my stupidity and fear push you away. But this is our second chance. Trust in me. Trust in us."

"Max, you don't understand. I'm broken." A tear slipped down my cheek.

He thumbed it away. "We'll figure out the rest in time. All I need is a future with you."

I shifted away from him, splashing water out of the tub. "You're not listening. I can't give you children. The doctors told me it would be virtually impossible to carry again."

Max moved forward, crowding me back. "It doesn't matter to me if you can or can't carry our children. You said virtually impossible. That means there is a chance. And if we find out you can't, we'll explore other options."

My lips quivered as his words sunk in. I gently placed my hands on his shoulders and then around his neck. "God, I love you. We've been so stupid."

Max gathered me onto his lap and against his chest. "I've waited forever to hear you say those words."

"Stupid?" I smiled at him.

He arched an eyebrow, and his hand sifted through my hair as he dipped his head down, kissing me until all thought left my mind. "Let me hear the words again."

"I love you, Max," I murmured against his lips.

Our tongues tangled, and the familiar tingle pulsed in my core. He hardened against me, sending goose bumps up my spine. My knees slipped to his sides as my heart sped up. Without a word, he lifted me, positioning me over his length. Slowly, I engulfed him, allowing every smooth ridge of him to vibrate inside of me.

A groan rumbled from deep in his throat. "Arya, baby, this feels like home."

I gazed into his fiery-green depths. Moving my hands to his shoulders, I leaned forward, teasing the corner of his mouth. His clean essence mixing with the lavender and vanilla of the bath enveloped me.

"Ari," he whispered as he clutched my hips and slowly moved me up and down.

I shook my head, pushing his arms back against the granite-lined ledge. With a rough laugh, he rested his palms on the cold stone, letting me take over the rhythm. I savored the sensation of him throbbing inside me.

Max bent his head, seeking the curve of my neck with his mouth. My back bowed as a purr escaped my throat. His lips and teeth found my nipple, drawing it into his heat. He nipped down lightly, sending a sensation of pleasure-pain to my throbbing pussy. I gasped and contracted on him, continuing my ride on his firm shaft.

His lips curved in a smile. "I know how much you like being in charge, but I'm not one to sit back and let you do all the work." With those words, he shifted, positioning me on the edge of the tub, and took over. Water splashed and dripped onto the floor as he pounded into me.

My climax rose and then exploded the moment he grazed my neck with his teeth. "Max," I moaned or shouted, I didn't know. My hands gripped his arms, squeezing so tight he'd have marks from my nails.

"That's it, baby, ride it out," he crooned. His pace and thrust increased and his jaw clenched as he erupted with his own release. He kissed the top of my head and then rested against my shoulder.

"Mine," I said.

"I'll always be yours."

For the first time, contentment consumed me. My heart had barely slowed when Milla came storming through the bathroom door.

"Arya, what the hell is going on in there? I could hear shouts down the hall. Oh shit, my eyes, my eyes. Someone kill me now." She jumped back out of the door and shut it.

"It's your own fault, Milla. Did you ever think about knocking?" Max laughed as he withdrew from me and grabbed a couple of towels. He wrapped one around himself and the other around me.

"When you guys are finished, I need to talk to both of you. We have a breach of security and we need to figure out a game plan," Milla called through the door.

"Give us a few minutes and we'll be out."

My cheeks burned thinking about what Milla had seen. Even though we discussed sex all the time, I couldn't help the embarrassment. Why was Max taking this all in stride? "You're not even a bit fazed that Milla caught us naked and getting it on?"

He leaned over and kissed me. "It's called fucking, and why are you flustered? It isn't anything more than she sees when she goes to the club with Lex. Hell, those two have put on shows of their own."

"What are you talking about? When did this happen?"

Max started laughing, stepped out of the tub, and tugged me along with him. "Baby, even Aunt Elana knew about them."

I narrowed my eyes. This wasn't funny. I wasn't that naïve, was I?

"Didn't you ever wonder where all the sexual tension around them comes from?"

"Yeah, I guess," I mumbled, lifting my robe off the hook and shrugging it on. I had a feeling I was the last one in on some big secret.

"The cat-and-mouse game they enjoy is all foreplay." Max pointed to a large robe.

"What? It came as a set. How was I to know someone would actually use it one day? Whatever. Don't change the subject. What's going on with Milla and Lex?" I folded my arms across my body, glaring at Max as he approached.

He gripped the collar of my robe, drawing me near. "My sweet, genius IQ, Arya. Lex and Milla have been in a relationship like ours since before we met. I'd say on and off for ten years. I'm not sure what surprises me more—that they kept it a secret or that you never figured it out. Aren't you supposed to be the smart one?"

I scowled but let him kiss me.

"Arya, you saw them with your own eyes at my club. Remember the couple you watched playing with the whips?"

"Oh my God, Max. We…uh…watched them…while you…um."

"Paddled your ass and fucked you senseless."

I hid my face against Max's chest. "I'm such an idiot. I even remember thinking how much they resembled Milla and Lex. I'm going to kill her. How could she keep something like this from me? She's supposed to be my best friend."

"Talk to her before you get upset. People in our kind of relationships have reasons for what they do."

I sighed. "I suppose you're right."

"Are you guys coming?" Milla yelled from the bedroom door. "I'm not sure you understand the seriousness of our situation."

"Let's go. This must be major if she is this panicked," Max stated as he opened the door.

CHAPTER TWENTY-SIX

We entered the living room to find Milla muttering to herself as she prepared drinks. She poured a shot of whiskey, downed it, and continued making drinks. Not good. She rarely drank hard liquor. This must be major.

"Milla, what's going on?" I pointed to the empty shot glass.

She ignored me and busied herself making a B&B neat, my favorite drink to calm my nerves.

I walked over, plucked my cocktail from the counter, and waited. She still said nothing. Well, if she wanted to keep us in suspense, I was going to burst her bubble with my own cryptic message.

"By the way, we have something to discuss in private. Something to do with major secrets and friends and fucking," I whispered so Max wouldn't hear.

She glanced up from her bartending with a shocked expression on her face, and her gaze shot to Max, who shrugged his shoulders.

"What's the security breach?" he asked, cutting the tension.

Milla's shoulders relaxed. "I've noticed someone using an access code to Arya's lab that we only use during mock drills. Whoever infiltrated the lab was trying to get to the core of Arcane, but they didn't realize the codes give bare minimum entry to the software."

"How did you guys find out about the unauthorized access? I never received a ping warning me." I grabbed my phone from my bag and checked my messages. "Fuck, fuck, fuck! I haven't monitored my business line since I left last week." I paced back and forth.

"Language." Max laughed as he moved to the bar and collected his drink.

Milla continued, "Lex and I've received a notice from the security protocol the moment you left for South Africa."

"Whoever it was wouldn't know every step they made was logged on the server. Who accessed the system?" I asked. The one place I felt confident was with my work. As the top security software developer in the country it wouldn't make sense to slack on my own security.

"You're not going to like this," Milla paused. "It's someone on our team."

"What? No way, our team has been with us for years. They're as loyal as they come."

"No, not our team, I mean our team in general. I'm referring to someone Max brought on."

Immediately Max's demeanor changed. "Who?" He moved over to the fireplace, resting his drink on the mantle.

"That's the problem. Each time a different initial access

code was used. Every one of us has a secure log-on to the system. Even your password was used."

Max glared at Milla, who stared back at him. "How do you know it isn't someone from your side?" Max accused.

I jumped in. "Because I know my people. They're loyal to us."

"Why? Because you have secrets on each of them? If it has to do with money, everyone is a suspect. I don't think you should rule them out."

"Max, they all could have stolen sensitive information ten times over the past five years and never did. They would lose too much to betray us. When we went public, we made them all millionaires, and they signed contracts that forfeited all their shares if they ever compromised our intellectual property."

And thank God Lex had insisted everyone sign nondisclosure agreements years ago, too.

"It could still be someone trying to frame my people," Max retorted.

"This isn't about sides. I told you from the beginning only a handful of people know the real development we do. Even then, they simply work on and have access to their part of the project. I'm the sole person with complete, unilateral access to all sections of the system."

"Are you telling me that all the time and energy our people have put into this project was for show?" He stalked over to where I stood at the bar. The relaxed glow from our lovemaking had all but evaporated.

"No, each person worked on their integral part. Without

their work, the software doesn't function correctly. It's like putting connecting pieces of a puzzle together."

"Let me get this straight. Arcane's puzzle master is you, and the one person who can work the system is also you?"

The way he towered over me made me think that maybe I should lie. "Well…technically, uumm…you see." I moved back as Max crowded me.

"Spit it out, Arya, before Max busts a vein," Milla said from the safety of the kitchen.

Max trapped me against the bar with his arms.

"Don't be mad, but the only way I could assure the confidentiality and security of Arcane was to keep all the program launch codes in here." I tapped my head.

At this moment, I sensed my brilliant plan wasn't very bright. Lex and Milla constantly badgered me about the risk of keeping everything to myself, but until now, I hadn't seen that maybe keeping a backup set of codes and instructions would have been a better idea.

"Did you even comprehend what kind of risk you're taking?" Max leaned into me, clenching his jaw.

Oh hell, I'm in big trouble.

"Ari, I'm out of here. Call me when he calms down. This isn't the right time to be strategizing." Milla moved to leave the penthouse.

Max turned his face to Milla, while keeping me caged between his arms. "You stay right there, and get your lover boy here immediately. I can't believe you two let her put her safety at risk. Please tell me my sister wasn't in on this decision too."

I shrugged my shoulders. I couldn't throw Carmen under the bus, could I?

"Arya, you're the smartest person I know. How could it escape your mind that you were setting yourself up to become the perfect hostage for someone hoping to profit from stealing the software? If the government's willing to pay such a high price for it, don't you think other countries would do anything to get their hands on it, too?"

I hated it when he was right. "I'm sorry. I didn't think about it like that."

"After what happened to you, why would you put yourself at risk?" He cupped my face and touched his head to mine.

"My thoughts were about succeeding. All I had was my work." My hands clutched his shoulder.

"You have me now. I won't let you put yourself in any more danger. At least you have James with you most of the time."

I closed my eyes, enjoying the feel of having someone who was completely mine.

"I hate to disturb this Hallmark moment, but we need to get back to the issue of the breach," Milla announced.

"I still don't believe it's someone from MDC," Max said while holding me.

"Sorry to burst your bubble, but our paranoid Arya created a tracking program that activates when any R & D product is accessed outside of ArMil. The program was traced back to your building, specifically the eighty-first floor."

"But that's my floor. The only two people on the team from my department are Jane and myself."

"You forgot Jacob," I interjected. "He's been nosing around

the team for months, asking for detailed information that only computer techies are interested in, not mergers and acquisition suits. Besides, he hates my guts and reminds me constantly that I'm not worthy of his presence."

"He may not prefer you for me, but I doubt he hates you," Max insisted.

"Keep believing that. He thinks I've gotten you in my clutches again, and he doesn't like it one bit." I kissed the scowl from his face.

"God, you two make me sick. I wish Lex would get here already," Milla grumbled.

The doorbell rang and she rushed to answer it. In the few seconds it took Milla to return, I heard the commotion of a loud, whispered argument. If Max was right, they held the top prize for keeping their bedroom antics separated from real life. What a whopper of a secret. For over ten years; hell, that would make her barely out of high school.

"Let it go. We'll deal with it later," Lex muttered as he crossed into the living room. Milla followed, frowning at his back.

"Do we need to leave you two alone to sort out your lover's quarrel?" Max jested.

"Fuck off, Dane." Lex slumped down on the couch, running a hand through his blond hair.

Max held up his hands in surrender and moved around to the back of the bar to fix another drink. He made two and handed one to Lex, then sat on the recliner next to him.

"I take it you and Arya have sorted out your differences," Lex said. He took a sip of his drink and winced. "This will definitely take the edge off." He gestured to the glass.

"It's the least I can do for letting me know where to find her."

Now it made sense. No one but Lex and Milla knew I'd gotten back from South Africa. From the interaction of the two men, they'd finally come to terms with the past and rekindled their friendship. "I see you both have made nice and decided to play together in the sandbox." I smiled as both men scowled at me.

"Forget about all our personal issues for a moment and figure out how we're going to protect the most critical piece of software we've created to date."

"So eloquent with the dramatics, Lex."

"Shut up, Mil."

Both Milla and I moved into the living room. I sat on the armrest of Max's chair and she sat across from us in her own recliner, away from Lex.

Max put his hand on my terrycloth-covered knee and squeezed. "Okay, this is what I propose," I said. "We're going to proceed as planned, but with a few changes. I'm going to duplicate Arcane with an altered code, essentially creating a worm inside the program. This way the government software is safe and completely separate, and the only people who'll know where it is, is us."

"In English, please," Milla interjected. "I may have co-founded the company, but you're the brains and I'm the brawn."

"So what does that make me?" Lex asked

"Our bitch," Milla retorted.

"You're going to pay for that," Lex muttered.

"Give it your best shot."

Lex moved off the couch.

"Children, please. Let's be nice to each other," Max jokingly reprimanded.

"Shut up, Max," Milla and Lex grumbled in unison.

"Are they like this all the time?" Max asked, gathering me into his lap.

"Yep, ever since I've known them."

"See what I mean? Sexual tension," he whispered in my ear.

I observed the annoyed couple. Watching them now and thinking back to their interactions over the years, I had been oblivious to the fact their issues were a precursor to sex.

I whispered back, "It was foreplay?"

Max nodded.

Lex heard my not-so-quiet statement and growled. "Can we get back on subject? Explain to Milla and the rest of us what you mean by *worm*, and use small words so we idiots of the world understand."

I laughed. "Okay, Mr. *I graduated from college at seventeen*. By *worm*, I mean putting a hidden tracking virus in the software. You can't detect it unless you search for it, and once it's activated, every transmission in and out will have a happy little bug attached. We'll know who's trying to access Arcane, and who will use it once it's stolen."

"So this is like malware, but for our benefit? Oh no, that means—" Milla leaned forward on her recliner and moaned "—that you'll need help attaching this worm to Arcane."

"That's right. Let's give the prize to the grumpy nonprogrammer." I smiled.

"Can it, Rey."

"Suck it up, Castra."

"Tell us exactly what you need us to do." Max interrupted our banter. "I'm sure all of us will help if we can."

"I know the three of you are the furthest thing from techies, but I'll need you to put your big-girl panties on and help me reformat code."

Max turned me toward him. "I assumed all the time in the lab learning coding was your sick way of torturing me for taking over Carmen's spot."

I coyly peered at Max and smiled. So what if I received pleasure out of making him suffer learning script? He was the one who had invaded my personal space. "You did learn a valuable skill to add to your résumé."

Max shifted me to the side and lightly smacked my butt. I gave him an exaggerated scowl and continued, turned back to face Lex and Milla. "I know I promised to never make you code again after our first project, but this is important. I don't trust anyone besides you three. That means you two are back on duty."

They both groaned simultaneously and nodded.

"For the next week, you won't see much of me. I'll have Kerry cancel any noncritical appointments, if not all of them." I jumped up, surprising Max. I clutched my robe and headed for my bedroom.

Max chased after me. "Where are you going?"

I searched for my favorite T-shirt and yoga pants from my closet. Finding them, I tossed them on my bed. "I need to get to the lab ASAP."

Max caught me around the waist before I ran back to the closet in search of shoes. He drew me against his chest. "Arya, calm down. Less than two hours ago, you were falling apart in my arms. You need to recharge before you lock yourself up in your lab and play Vanessa-Mae nonstop."

He meant well, but I couldn't possibly relax with the possibility of someone stealing my software. "Max, do you know what's at stake here? If Arcane is stolen, not only would I lose everything, you would, too."

Max turned me around but didn't release me. "What do you mean, lose everything?"

"The contract is for exclusive security development for the Defense Department, at a cost of two billion a year for fifteen years."

"What's the catch?"

"If we don't fulfill the terms of the agreement, we would forfeit any money earned to date on the project and lose this, as well as all of the other twenty-five government contracts we have outstanding."

"What?" The shock on Max's face told me Lex left out significant specifics on the deal as a whole. "Who made that asinine decision? Lex or Carmen? No, don't tell me."

Max sat on my bed, hunched over with his elbow resting on his legs and his head cradled in his palms.

"It was a mutual agreement. Most people don't reject an opportunity from the United States Department of Defense. Let's say they can be very persuasive."

"They strong-armed you, in other words. It's too late to second-guess all the arrangements made to date, but from now on, think about what you're risking before you jump in head-first. Out of curiosity, what did they use to persuade you to accept the offer?"

"They promised Milla a shipping contract for freight delivery to bases around the world and Lex a position on one of the subcommittees for the International Trade Commission. I was given an exclusive right to provide security and encryption software through my various companies."

"And?"

I bit my lip and hoped he wouldn't be upset. "And they agreed to let me buy land and build a house in a particular cove on Kauai."

Max smiled at me with a calculated gleam. "So you're the one I've been fighting to get that land? For three years, this anonymous bidder blocked every attempt at government approval. First, it was preservation land, then it was public-use land, and then all of a sudden an unknown company called ANR owned it. I guess I know what that stands for now. Do you know how many people I called to find out who was behind that organization?"

"They'll use any means necessary to get what they want. Not unlike someone else I know." I moved toward Max and glided my hands through his hair.

His head came up and he smiled. Some of the worries eased from his eyes. "You're easily convinced with the right tactics. For me it's all about pushing your limits."

I hummed as my core awakened with the memory of being at the club.

Max got to his feet, handed me my clothes, and leaned

down to kiss me. "I know exactly where your mind went. I should paddle your ass for keeping the contingencies of the deal from me."

I quirked an eyebrow and untied my robe, letting in fall to the ground. Stepping back, I dressed with slow, exaggerated movements.

"You're playing with fire."

"So what are you going to do about it?"

Max walked out my door, pausing to look back. "Nothing. You have a company to save, and I need to find some clothes. I bet Milla has something of Lex's over at her place. Get to work, Rey."

CHAPTER TWENTY-SEVEN

Finally a few moment alone," I said to myself as I sat in the gardens of the Blantyre Hotel.

Max had insisted I needed a night out away from my computer, so I'd spent the better part of the evening hobnobbing and making business connections at a banquet for one of my favorite charities. It was also the first event Max and I had attended as a couple.

After all the press I received following the balcony video of me from Miami, I was surprised that most of the people at the party weren't as fazed about our relationship status as I'd expected. Well, it made sense, since I remembered seeing some of them at the club.

"What are you doing out here?" Max walked up behind me and placed his hand on my shoulder.

I beamed at my sexy man. He worked a suit like no one else. Who was I kidding? He was hot all around, with or without clothes. He shot me a knowing smile that sent wetness straight to my pussy.

"Thinking. And I needed a few minutes to breathe."

He toyed with the clasp on the back of my collar and then caressed my cheek. "Thinking about what?"

"Us and the number of people here tonight that I saw at the club."

"You won't be wearing a mask the next time we go."

"Is that right?"

"Any objections? As I recalled, you enjoyed yourself." He held out his elbow. I stood and tucked my arm into his.

"Maybe I'll be the one to strap you to the bench and have my wicked way with you."

"That is never going to happen, baby. I'm not a switch and never will be. You may enjoy a little control in our lovemaking, but I don't think you'd enjoy the scenario as much as you believe. You're a true submissive and I'm your Dominant."

He was right. The whole domination thing sounded fun in theory, but bondage was my kink. I loved the playroom and all the restraints. Especially the way the binding rubbed against my skin and the sensation of being utterly helpless to every demand placed on my body. I could imagine the slide of Max's cock between my swollen, wet folds while strapped to the cross.

"Whoa there."

Lost in my fantasy, I hadn't realized I stumbled until Max caught me.

"If you don't stop that train of thought, I'm going to position you against the wall of this hotel and fuck you senseless, not caring who sees us."

I touched my damp, flushed face. "Sorry."

"Don't be, but I expect you to do something about this as soon as we're alone." He took my hand and placed it over the erection hidden under his tuxedo jacket.

My core reverberated, and I licked my lips. "With pleasure. You do know it's a two-and-a-half-hour drive back to Boston?"

"Good. Let's move faster. I've called Aaron to bring the car. He'll be waiting for us. The sooner we get out of here, the sooner you can relieve the hard-on I've had since I saw you wearing that dress, knowing you were naked underneath." His gruff voice told me he both loved and hated my outfit. I'd chosen the form-fitting gown with a plunging front especially for that reason.

I paused as we approached the steps leading into the hotel. "There's no way to leave without going through the ballroom."

"Smile, try not to engage anyone, and we should be out of here in twenty minutes."

I scanned the occupants of the ballroom and counted at least three hundred people to pass. "I think your estimate is a bit optimistic. What will you give me if it takes longer?"

"Multiple orgasms."

My steps wavered. "I can live with that."

We worked our way through a crowd that seemed determined to chat with us at every opportunity. By the time we approached the hotel exit, the twenty minutes had become forty.

Aaron opened the door of the limousine and I slid in, followed closely by Max.

I closed the partition, sealing us into the cabin and glanced at Max. "I'm ready to collect on my bet. Any objections?"

Relaxing back into the seat, he adjusted his pant legs and smiled. "None whatsoever, Ms. Rey."

My eyes roved to his straining erection, and I licked my lips.

"Are you hungry? Would you like to stop for dessert?" he quipped.

"I believe I'm craving a different type of dessert."

"What would that be?"

"You." I slid off the seat, crawled across the limo, and stopped between his knees. "Do I have permission, Sir?"

Sucking in a sharp breath, he nodded. I smiled and leaned down, inhaling the intoxicating musk through his pants.

"Pull him out, Arya. He's been waiting all night for some attention."

"Yes, Sir." I sent him a saucy smile, bit my lip, and preceded to follow his command.

With slow, precise movements, I undid his belt, drawing the leather through the metal buckle. Next, I tugged his shirt free. I continued with the button of his trousers and then used my teeth to slide the zipper down.

"Arya, don't make me punish you."

I tilted my head, feigning innocence. "You don't like what I'm doing?"

"My cock better be in that luscious mouth in thirty seconds or you forfeit any pleasure I promised you."

"I get the message, Sir."

"Good."

I reached into his slacks and pulled out his raging hard-on.

It appeared larger than usual as it bobbed against his white tuxedo shirt.

Before I could grip him properly, Max grasped the base of his cock and pointed the large plum-shaped head toward my lips. His other hand moved to the back of my neck. "Open up."

A groan erupted from his chest as I started sucking.

"Oh, yes. That's the way I like it." His threw his head back against the seat, and his eyes closed tight. His hold on my hair increased as I hollowed my cheeks, taking him deeper.

My tongue worked the throbbing vein on the underside of his engorged cock, and another moan escaped him. I savored the salty sweet cream dripping from his tip; he was already close.

"Touch yourself while you work my dick."

My hand traveled between my legs, gliding through my swollen slit. I plunged two fingers into my core and pumped as my palm rubbed my throbbing nub. I worked both my body and his, bringing our orgasms to the cusp.

At once, I exploded around my fingers, crying out, but not stopping my ministrations.

"Ari, stop right now. I'm going to blow and I promised to make you come over and over again." His words sent another flood of moisture to my aching pussy. I released him with a pop and pulled my saturated fingers free.

Without warning, Max lifted me onto his lap, raised my dress to my waist, and impaled me on his cock. I cried out from the pleasure-pain of the sudden invasion. He raised my fingers to his lips, licked them clean, and then commanded,

"Place your hands on the back of the seat and ride me while I make use of this plunging neckline."

I followed his directive and positioned my knees against his thighs. I worked his cock in and out of me while grinding my pelvis against him every time I lowered back down. My movements remained slow and sensual at first. Then as I felt the scrape of Max's teeth against my now exposed nipples, I rode him harder, loving the sound of his shallow breath against my sensitized peaks.

"That's it. Keep moving as I feast on your fabulous tits."

I lifted my thighs and slammed down. We both groaned, and I continued my onslaught until another wave of ecstasy cascaded through me. I threw back my head and scratched the leather of the seat with my nails. My inner walls convulsed around his giant girth as they milked my release.

Max clutched the back of my head, bringing me forward and taking the last of my cries into his mouth. We stared at each other and my heart fluttered, seeing the depth of his emotions.

Twice more I erupted before he held my hips, stopping my now-slow pace. "Turn around. It's time for me to work that pussy."

I pivoted on wobbly legs with his help. Breathing heavily, his hand slid down my back positioning me against the cushion of the seat closest to us. I rested my sweat-sheened face against my forearms as my heartbeat pummeled in my ears.

His cock slid down the crease of my bottom and slammed into my dripping pussy. He rubbed against my inner walls, sending shock waves to my toes. Slow and steady, he slid in and out of me.

I needed him to stop being gentle and fuck me. He knew what he was doing. He wanted me to beg. After countless orgasms, I wouldn't be able to come unless he did something to push me over the edge.

"How do you want it?" he finally asked. "Hard and fast or soft, with me taking my time?"

"Fast," I answered. "I'm going to come. Please!"

"Your wish is my command." The force of his pace increased, rough and unsteady.

My core quickened and my hips rocked back. I reached behind me, squeezing his ass, hoping to make him hammer harder, but he pushed my hand away. "This is my show. You're there, baby. I can feel it."

Every inch of my body begged for relief. His fingers glided across my clit, and I shot forward.

"Max," I wailed as it hit. Spasms ravaged me, the exquisite pleasure spreading through every part of my body.

"That's it, baby, squeeze me tight," he crooned. "Ride it out while I finish."

His thrusts became frantic, his muscles tightened while he pistoned in and out. The rough breath grazing my skin told me he was close to coming. I closed my eyes and let the continued waves of pleasure thrust me into another free fall.

We both cried out, not caring if Aaron could hear our pleasure.

Max pulsed inside me and collapsed with me against the leather seats. "I love hearing you come," he murmured against my ears.

Struggling to steady our breaths, I entwined my left hand

with his, and he gave me a slight squeeze. "Wow." My brain hadn't regained its function.

"That's an understatement." Max lifted me into his arms and sat back half naked against the seats.

I yawned and snuggled into his warm body. The cab of the limousine smelled of our lovemaking and slowly sent me into the sleep I'd suppressed for days.

"We have at least an hour and a half before we get home. I'll take care of you," he said against my forehead.

"I know you will," I sighed. "There's no other place..." I trailed off.

"What place?" He tickled me to get my attention.

My brain fired a short flare. "No other place I want to be than in your arms."

He cradled me tighter against him and chuckled. "Same here. That is until you lock yourself in the lab again."

"Only for one more week and then I'm all yours."

"Promise?"

A nudge pierced through my haze. *Oh yeah, I never answered his question.* "Yes."

"Good, because after the software transfer, I'm taking you away."

"A vacation sounds good. Where are we going?" Who cared? Right now, I needed sleep.

The last thing I heard him say before my exhaustion got the best of me was, "If everything goes according to plan, by the end of the week, the collar won't be the only commitment you've made to me."

CHAPTER TWENTY-EIGHT

She's all yours, General." I pushed back from the conference table in the lab and handed General Ansgar and his team the final security codes to Arcane. With three more labs attacked and an increase in threats against me, I refused to take any chances of compromising the project. Consequently, I decided to shift all my work from my project lab on the outskirts of Boston to ArMil's facilities inside our headquarters, where the possibility of bugging was virtually nonexistent.

"It's been a pleasure doing business with you, Ms. Rey. We'll release the overview of the project in a few days."

"No one outside of the ArMil team with the exception of Mr. Dane"—I glanced at Max, who nodded and returned his attention to his notes—"knows we've transferred ownership. In the next few hours, Arcane's protocols will implement throughout the areas we've outlined." Kerry passed out the schedule as I sat.

"Explain what you're planning for the copy software you've

developed. When I spoke with Mr. Dane a few days ago, he informed me you're working with a few of our agents to locate the broker auctioning the program. But his details were limited, at best."

"I understand your concern, but we've been told to keep any information about the ongoing investigation confidential, even with you."

He laughed. "I knew hiring your firm was a good decision. You follow procedure. I can respect that. Make sure you take into account the increased need for safeguarding yourself and your staff."

I smiled at the general. He might not have understood the technical aspects of the project, but he understood the necessity for discretion and the associated security ramifications.

"Protection has already been put into place," interjected Max without stopping his perusal of his papers.

Oh, really? His tone told me there was more in place than the logistics we'd discussed.

"Well, ladies and gentlemen, I will see myself out. It was a pleasure doing business with you. My team will stay in touch."

"Thank you, General." I rose and shook his hand. I walked over to a panel on the wall and typed in a code. At once, all unauthorized electronics activated and the steel doors opened.

Immediately, the room cleared of all military personnel, and we all relaxed with a collective sigh of relief.

"I'm never putting myself through that again," Lex announced while propping his feet on the conference table.

"We're not off the hook yet, but more or less we're there." Milla sighed and leaned her head against the back of her chair.

I strolled over to where Max sat and placed a hand on his shoulder, leaned down, and whispered in his ear, "Are you ready to go?"

He stroked the side of my face. "So eager to leave, my love."

"You did say to be ready as soon as the transition took place. My bags are packed, no reason to wait."

"Where are you two off to?"

Rising to my feet, I said, "I'm not sure. All we packed were sundresses and bathing suits, so I'm guessing somewhere tropical."

"Sounds like fun. We could all use a break after the slave driving you put us through over the past few weeks. Want us to join you?"

"Not this time," Max said and stood, placing his hand on my lower back. "This is for Arya and me only."

"Message received loud and clear," Lex said. "Besides, Milla and I have an appointment for this evening that we can't miss."

Milla straightened in her chair and smiled at me, pretending she hadn't heard Lex's words, but the flush of her cheeks gave her away.

We still hadn't discussed their relationship in depth, and her reluctance to give any details meant things were complicated. I wouldn't push.

"Go have fun. I don't think you'll have much use for clothes with the way Max is ogling you." Milla winked and blew me a kiss.

I woke to the smell of tropical flowers and the rush of ocean waves crashing against the shore. Keeping my eyes closed, I smiled, stretched, and lazed back into the soft sheets.

Two hands crept around the sides of my body, caging me. "Good morning, Mrs. Dane."

I opened my eyes and stared into a breathtaking shade of emerald. My heart clenched at the love peering down at me.

God, how could I have gotten lucky enough to get a second chance with this magnificent man? I traced the day-old stubble showing on the gorgeous face. "Morning, Mr. Dane."

Max nuzzled into my hand, kissing the palm. "Time to wake up, baby. We need to explore the property my wife stole out from under me."

"Oh, is that right?" I arched into another deep stretch and grazed my already sensitive nipples against Max's bare chest.

A scowl formed over his brows but didn't touch his eyes. "You aren't playing fair, Mrs. Dane."

Threading my fingers through his hair, I drew him to me. "You like saying that." I bit his lip and then captured his mouth.

"Do you blame me?" he murmured. "I've waited forever to have you and never expected you'd agree so readily when we got here."

I wrapped my legs around his waist and flipped him onto his back, rubbing my tender pelvis against his growing erection. "It was the way you convinced me." I stared into his sexy sleepy face. "Are you sure you want to get out of bed?"

Fire shot through me, straight into my pussy, as he slapped my ass and squeezed it. "We've spent the past two days doing nothing but eating and fucking, Ari. I know you're sore even if your appetite for my cock is insatiable."

"I suppose you're right." I leaned down, resting my head on his chest and listening to his heartbeat. *I loved this man so much.* Tears blurred my vision, and I snuggled close.

His hand worked its way into my hair as he held me tight against him. "I love you too, baby."

Inhaling deeply, I closed my eyes and smiled at the memory of his proposal. An hour after touching down in Kauai we arrived at Wailua Falls. Max covered my eyes with a soft ribbon and guided me out of the car, until the sound of rushing water echoed all around me. When he untied the silken mask, I found myself on the banks of the falls, surrounded by more than a dozen paintings positioned on easels. In each one, he'd used his skills to capture a special moment from our past. From the first time our gazes locked in the training tent in Cape Town to the night he'd collared me in front of the mirror. The pictures depicted the love he felt and my own emotions, ones I'd refused to acknowledge. I was lost in my perusal of the paintings until I noticed Max on his knees behind me.

"Arya, five years ago you filled a void in my life I hadn't realized was empty. Through my own stupidity, I lost you, and now that I've found you again, I want to bind us together forever. You're my heart, with you I feel whole." He held my hands in his, kissing the tops of each and peered at me. "Never again will you fight battles alone. I promise to stand with you through everything. I love you, baby. Marry me."

Tears blurred my vision. This was it. Everything I ever wanted. It was time to make the leap. I nodded, cupped his face, and used my thumb to wipe away his own wet cheeks.

"Say it, I need the words."

"Yes…yes…I'll marry you. Make me your wife."

A visible tremor passed through him and he relaxed. Cradling his arms around me, he buried his face in my stomach. "We'll be married as soon as possible."

A laugh burst free. "Hold on there. I just got engaged and I don't even have an engagement ring."

He grinned at me with mischief in his eyes. "Look at your left hand."

I lifted my arm and examined an emerald-cut pink diamond surrounded by white diamonds in a platinum setting. My breath hitched. "It's beautiful." Then I frowned. "When did you put this on my finger?"

"While you were looking at the paintings."

"Sure of yourself, weren't you?" I cocked a brow.

Grabbing my outstretched hand, he stood. "With you I'm never sure of anything. I only hoped." He kissed my forehead. "I'm going to make you happy. I swear it."

I stood on my tiptoes, captured his mouth, and murmured, "We're going to make each other happy. So how soon is soon?"

"What about tonight?"

My heart fluttered, and for the first time in my adult life, I didn't hesitate. "Okay."

"Really?"

I wasn't the reckless type, but this was right. "Make an honest woman of me."

Lifting me into his arms, he spun me around, and slid me down his firm body. "With pleasure."

A squeeze against the tickle spot on my hip snapped me out of my daydream. "Hey," I admonished.

"Come on. We're going snorkeling, and then after we'll eat breakfast."

"Okay, okay. Let me go freshen up, and I'll meet you downstairs in a few."

"Not going to happen. As soon as I leave this room, you're going to roll over and go back to sleep."

I crawled off him and frowned but didn't deny his accusation. So what if I wanted to peruse the pictures he'd painted in more detail in my dreams? *Speaking of…* "Where are the paintings? We've christened every room of this house, and I don't remember seeing them."

"I had James and Aaron stow them on the plane."

My cheeks burned. "I hope you covered them again. James is like my stepdad, and I don't think I could ever look him in the eye again if he's seen me in so many intimate poses."

Max slid his fingers into my hair and drew me to him. "Stop worrying about it. If he doesn't know about your extracurricular activities by now, he isn't as sharp a bodyguard as we all assumed."

"Knowing and seeing are two different things," I grumbled, as he kissed me again.

My cell phone rang and we both groaned.

"Let me get that." He stretched over to the bedside table, picked up my phone, and scowled at the display. "This better be good, Duncan. Arya's on vacation with her husband."

Husband. I liked the sound of that.

All of a sudden, Max's demeanor changed. "Wasn't anyone with her?" He ran a frustrated hand through his hair.

They were talking about Milla. What did she do now? A dread settled in my stomach.

"No, we're on our way. Fuck. No. I'm not going to be able to keep her calm when she finds out."

Whatever it was, it was bad.

"We're on our way. Increase security on everyone. I don't care if Aunt Elana resists. Tie her to a chair but keep her safe. James will kill you if she isn't protected."

I heard yelling through the phone as my heart was on the verge of leaping out of my chest. I scooted over to Max and buried my face against his side.

Max sighed. "I'm sorry, Lex. I can't imagine what you're going through. We'll be there as soon as we can."

He hung up and held me tight. Tears flooded my eyes. "Tell me. I can handle it. Did something happen to Milla because of Arcane?"

"That's a distinct possibility. I don't know how to tell you this."

I clutched his back. "Please, spit it out."

"Milla's been kidnapped."

Less than twelve hours later, we landed at Boston's Logan Airport. After Max relayed to me the conversation he'd had with Lex, we left Hawaii and spent most the trip in a state of anxiety, determination, and fear.

I'd contacted every agency that owed me a favor, as did Max. Now all we could do was wait and see if there were any ransom demands.

I leaned against the kitchen island in my penthouse, took a swig of B&B to steady my nerves, and, with shaky hands, set the glass on the counter in front of me.

"Arya," Max pushed my phone into my hand. "This British prick at MI6 won't talk with anyone but you, since you're their primary contact." The doorbell rang. "That's the extended security team. I'll let them in."

I brought the phone to my ear. "Larry, please tell me, you have some good news to share"

Larry filled me in on the logistics of the plan, which involved stepping on toes and ignoring bureaucratic procedure. I felt no sympathy for him, I'd lost count the number of times I'd bailed his ass out of a bind. This was the least he could do. I finished the call and walked into my living room. The place resembled Def-Con Central. James lurked in the corner as computers and people occupied all available space.

"Wow, taking over much?" I said to no one in particular.

Max came over, put his hand on my waist, and kissed my hair. "I know, I know. We decided setting up shop in your penthouse would be best, especially with all the security you have hidden in here."

He had a point, but I didn't have to like it. I crossed my arms and glared as an agent brought in ten boxes of pizza. "Do not put that on my mahogany table, or I will kill you with my bare hands. There's a counter behind you at the bar. Use that."

The agent paused in mid-bend and went to settle the boxes on the counter.

"Why couldn't they congregate at your estate? It's large enough to house a small army."

"My house isn't as secure as the penthouse. And it's your estate now, too."

"I know. Sorry for being grumpy." I released a deep breath. "I'm so worried, Max."

"We all are, baby."

"I think I'll go to the lab where the copycat is stored and make sure nothing is moved."

"Negative, ghost rider," Lex called as he entered from the hallway leading to my office.

When had he arrived? I ached seeing him. His eyes were bloodshot and hollow. I ran to him, hugging him close. His body radiated tension, but he sagged against me and held me tight.

"Oh Lex, what are we going to do?"

"I don't know, Ari. She's everything to me."

That one statement broke my heart. "We're going to find her." I promised, then hiccuped as fresh tears clouded my vision. "It's all my fault—they wanted me."

"That's why you aren't going anywhere." He gestured toward Max for support. "I'm sure your new husband will agree."

"Absolutely," Max voiced in his no-nonsense way.

I stepped out of Lex's embrace. "I'm not going to stay hostage here." Moving to a counter, I seized a bunch of napkins and handed them to the agents eating like slobs in my home. "I have a company to run, and I have to make sure my lab is untouched."

"I checked it. Nothing has been moved."

"Lex, you wouldn't know if someone tampered with my protocols. I'll be gone for a half hour to an hour tops. If you want, I'll take a few of these bottomless pits and James. They'll make sure I arrive home safe and sound."

"*No*," Max commanded.

"Don't use that voice on me here. I'm going."

"No," Lex echoed Max's sentiment.

"Get over it, boys."

"Don't make me call Elana." That was a low blow, even for James. Thank goodness, Aunt El was sequestered on the Dane estate and not here to add to my headache.

"You're supposed to be on my side."

"Mrs. Dane, I understand your frustration, but protecting you is our main priority, in addition to locating Ms. Castra."

I moved to the closet, and grabbed my coat and the keys to my Porsche. "I'm going with or without you." All three men stalked toward me. "Guys, I don't think you comprehend that the software can help me locate Mil. And I will do anything to get my sister back." A tear spilled down my face.

All three men released a collective sigh. Max approached me first. "Fine, go. But make sure you don't take off your tracker."

"Like I would. It's attached to the back of my collar." I inclined my head to James. "Are you coming, Pops?"

He nodded and signaled to three agents to follow him.

I gave Max a quick peck before I headed into the waiting elevator.

The moment the doors closed, James spoke. "Mrs. Dane, I want to stress again the foolishness of your plan. You are placing yourself in unnecessary danger."

"She's my sister. I will do whatever I have to to get her back."

"Even with the assistance of these agents, I cannot guarantee your safety. Please reconsider."

"No. Now let's get moving."

I slid into my car, fastened my seat belt, and waited as James took the seat next to me. One agent moved to drive, and the other two entered a vehicle that would follow behind us.

My phone beeped, and I glanced at the message.

Don't do anything stupid. Come home to me. If you aren't back in one hour, there will be hell to pay.

I laughed at Max's veiled threat.

I inhaled deep and prayed as we drove. *I will find you,* mera behna.

James took my hand in his and squeezed. "We are about to pull up to the lab. Do not leave the vehicle until I give the all-clear."

I nodded. Sweat prickled my skin.

He exited the car and returned almost immediately. "Mrs. Dane." James's voice was somber. "Ari, this place isn't secure. Please don't fight me on this. Wait for me to return. Once we've inspected the building, you can come in."

He called me Ari.

My lips trembled, and I wrapped my arms around myself. "Okay, I'll stay put. Be careful."

Ten minutes passed, and James hadn't returned. My stomach twisted in knots. I hated feeling helpless. Why hadn't I listened to Milla and learned to shoot a gun? Then I wouldn't be defenseless. God. I hoped she took her own advice and gave them hell.

A knock on the door startled me out of my thoughts.

One of the agents opened the door, and I stepped out. "How long do I have in the lab?"

"No more than twenty minutes."

"Well, let's get moving." I tried to push past the agent, but he blocked my way.

"I'm sorry, but you must come with me." He grabbed me by the waist and covered my mouth with a sickly-sweet-scented cloth.

I screamed and struggled against the hold. Another man came into view with his hand raised, and everything went black.

CHAPTER TWENTY-NINE

I awakened with a deep pain searing through my head. Blood dripped down my forehead and into my eyes, blurring any possibility of seeing my surroundings. I winced as I struggled against the ropes binding my wrists. My heart pummeled out of control as fear consumed me. Where was James?

Oh God, not again.

Calm down, Arya. Think.

The faint sound of another person breathing echoed in the small, closeted room. I rocked my body trying to rotate away from the wall I faced.

"Hello? Is anyone there?"

A moan sounded in response.

"Please tell me who you are. Are you hurt?" I finally flipped my body to the other side. A beaten Milla, barely covered in shorts and a tank, lay on the floor. My heart sunk and cried out. One eye was swollen shut, and cuts, welts, and bruises covered most of her exposed skin.

"Oh Mil. What have they done to you?"

I scooted my bottom until I neared Milla. I leaned into her face. "Please, *mera behna*, I need you to be okay. Please wake up."

Milla moaned louder and blinked one eye open. "Arya?" she breathed.

"It's me."

"You look like hammered shit."

A tear rolled down my face. Trust Mil to use humor at a time like this. "You're no pageant queen, either."

"How long—" she winced "—have they had you?"

"I don't know. I was at the lab, waiting for James to search the facility and give me the all-clear to go inside. When an agent came to get me, I didn't think anything of it. The next thing I know, someone knocked me out and I woke here." I struggled with the rope binding me. Then I remembered the restrain-manipulation techniques James taught me, if I ever was in this situation. I twisted my wrists in a figure-eight pattern and hoped the shifting of my hands would loosen the rope. "I know you're scared, but we'll get out of here. Lex and Max will find us."

"Promise me, no matter what, don't let them access the system."

"Who are they? Who's got us?" One of the knots released, allowing me a little more movement.

"Jacob. And I think he's working with a broker for the deal."

"What?" Dread crept in. "It has to be Vladimir Christof. They were at the club together."

"Oh, shit, Arya. Did he recognize you? Fuck!" she cried. "I hurt so much."

"Stay still, Mil. I'm almost loose. Then I'm going to help you. And no, he thought I was Max's new flavor. He made some comment about knowing Max was my former lover."

"Now it makes sense why they took me. Jacob had to have found out that you kept all the codes to yourself and he knows if he had me, you'd do anything to find me. Oh God, what about Lex?"

My hands came free, and I immediately gathered Milla in my arms. "I don't know. We have to figure out how to get out of here." Milla whimpered, and I held her closer, rocking her back and forth. My dear friend captured because of me.

"Ar—"

"Shhh," I continued to rock her. "Don't use your energy."

"No listen, there's something else you need to know. It has to do with Africa. Jacob—"

At that moment, the door opened.

"Stay quiet, Mil. Let them think you're still out."

She nodded her response as Jacob entered the room.

"I see you're awake and figured out how to untie yourself." He frowned and continued walking toward me. "Too bad your friend over there isn't as tough as she acts. Lex's whore couldn't give me the details I needed. Maybe you'll be more accommodating."

Rage filled me. The lying two-faced bastard was supposed to be Max's friend.

Jacob strolled around us, shaking his head with his hands in his pockets. "I'm never going to understand how two foreign tramps made it so big."

"It's called using our brains, fucker."

"Tsk-tsk. That isn't very polite. I would have expected Max to have trained you better."

I ignored his comment. "Why? I don't understand why you're doing this."

"I'm tired of living in the shadows."

"Whose shadows? That doesn't make sense. You came from money. You can do anything you desire."

"Max's, for one. Even with his father's scandal he came out on top."

Then it hit me. "You wanted it handed to you, right? Poor little rich boy, sixth in line to the family fortune. God, you're pathetic."

"Keep telling yourself that. Unlike your name, mine opens doors."

"How did that work out for you?"

"Better than you think. Right now, we're negotiating with your ever-loving adoptive brother. What do you think the two of you will go for?"

"Lex will find you before you know it."

I prayed the tracker on my collar worked.

"Don't hold your breath. My investor's underground connections far surpass Lex's. Maybe I can get a little more out of your new fiancé."

Max. He'll find me. I know he will.

"You aren't making any sense," I hissed. "By taking us, your reputation will go down in the gutter. Don't you think people are going to notice that at the same time both Milla and I go missing, you're nowhere to be found?"

"Don't worry about those details. I have a plan." He

crouched down and attempted to touch Milla's face, but I shielded her with my arm. "Too bad she's out of commission. I've wanted a taste of her gorgeous, submissive body for years. Maybe after our negotiations with her master, I'll take a little taste of her."

"You touch her and I will kill you."

My head jolted back as he fisted my hair in an excruciating grip. "At this moment, you're closer to death than I am."

With a sudden jerk, he released my scalp, and shook his head in dismay. "I will never understand how a man like Max, with his impeccable background and breeding, ever fell for you. Some submissive you make. You talk too much, you're a cold bitch, and you possess no pedigree whatsoever. If it weren't for your interference, Caitlin and Max would be happily married and she wouldn't be pining over that stupid Brit."

"Don't even pretend to care about Caitlin. All you really wanted was access to Max's money. Is that what you think will happen with Vladimir Christof? That he'll give you free reign to his empire if you play wingman for him?"

Jacob hauled me up with his biting grip. "Be careful or Milla will be the only hostage returned."

My wrist snapped as he twisted my arms behind my back. I screamed as pain shot through my hand.

"I want to introduce you to someone. He's waited many years to meet you again."

My mind whirled as my scalp prickled and all the hairs on my body crept straight up. "Hello, Ms. Rey. Remember me?"

I glanced at the man who had entered, a man I knew only as Greg. My body heated and the rage I'd held tight for five years burst free. "You monster!" I kicked out with my feet and thrashed against Jacob. Tears poured down my face, the pain I'd put to rest consuming me. "How could you? How could you do that to those babies? You're a monster," I panted.

"Oh, now that's not very becoming behavior from a world-renowned philanthropist. Wouldn't you agree, Mr. Brady?" he asked Jacob, as he strolled to stand in front of me and ran a finger down my cheek.

I flinched at his touch and spit in his face.

The next second a slap jarred my head and fire exploded throughout my cheek. "You better get yourself under control before the boss gets here. He won't be as lenient as I am." He gestured to Milla. "Ask your friend over there. Between Mr. Brady and myself, we taught her the rules of true sadism."

Oh God, what did they do to her? Milla still laid motionless on the ground.

"You bastard."

"Yes, but then I'm a baby killer, if you remember. Now let's get her to the boss."

Jacob shoved me forward, through the doorway and up two flights of stairs. I stumbled twice trying to glance behind me. They'd left the door open. Milla could escape.

Please, mera behna, *be strong enough to find help.*

We entered what appeared to be the rooftop deck of one of the warehouses, near Boston Harbor. I scanned the area, trying to figure out where we were. I recognized the nearby buildings; this was Excalibur, a nightclub known for its shady clients.

"Boss, we've got her. She woke a few minutes ago."

A person lounged behind the curtains of a cabana. "Bring her here."

Fuck. Christof!

"Welcome Arya, or should I refer to you as 'mine'?" Christof chuckled and motioned me toward him. "I knew you were a most worthy adversary."

I glared, taking in the pristine appearance of the one man I feared more than the murderer of my girls. His ice-blond hair and crystal-gray eyes created the aura of a calm fallen angel every woman would desire. He seemed friendly and casual, dressed in white linen slacks and a navy polo shirt, but his calculating gaze gave away his true self.

Evil.

Jacob released my arms and I fell forward. I caught myself before I hit the ground, grinding my teeth against the pain in my wrist. I stumbled onto a nearby lounge chair. Christof traced my collar and fingered the triskele at the clasp. I stiffened, praying he wouldn't notice the tracker.

"I should have known Max could not resist making you his again. I would have assumed that he would have lost interest when he realized you no longer possessed the traits necessary for a true submissive. But then again, you were very convincing. You fooled me. Your pose and admiration for your master were quite desirable."

I tried to remain calm. Keeping a level head was the only way I was going to survive this. "Why am I here?"

"To activate your program, of course. I found your hiding place, and while you were on vacation I brought the server here and procured Ms. Castra."

Shit, shit, shit. He had the duplicate software. He must not have activated it, or the worm would have infiltrated his whole system.

"How did you get it? It isn't ready. We're still in the prototype stage. I—"

"Don't underestimate me, Ms. Rey, or should I say Mrs. Dane?"

"What?" Jacob shouted. "You conned him into marrying you?"

"Quiet, Mr. Brady," Christof glared in Jacob's direction and then turned back to me. "As I was saying, I know you've run a successful test and are ready to launch as soon as the funds have cleared."

How would he know all this? Even if Jacob were behind the break-ins, he couldn't have learned that kind of information.

"Why are you surprised? There is a lot of information you can acquire when you know the right people. Discovering your secret marriage was much easier than learning your software was complete and its hiding place, but then I have plenty of resources to assist my cause."

He gestured with his hand and two men in leather jackets and black slacks brought a blood-covered woman out from another cabana and threw her on the ground at my feet.

My stomach rolled, as I scanned and then recognized the slumped form. Jane Erickson. No, she wouldn't betray Max.

"Like you, she fell in love with the wrong man. Lonely women are such easy prey."

Huh? Jane was breathtaking; she could have any man she wanted.

"When Ms. Erickson figured out that her secret crush had eyes only for his former lady love, she sought out his dear friend for comfort."

"Why?" I asked Jacob. "What did you get by seducing her? She's a good, kind person."

Jacob walked with his hand tucked into his pocket and paused in front of me. "Sex, of course. She is a hot piece of ass, and she had access to Arcane. Too bad no one knew you didn't trust your own people."

Thank God for my paranoia.

"You owe me, Mrs. Dane," Christof interrupted. He glared at Jacob, commanding his silence. "And launching this software will be the perfect payment for my many losses."

"I owe you nothing. You—"

"Oh, but you do. Don't fool yourself. Your involvement many years ago cost me men, time, and money. Retribution for crossing me is typically very stiff, but I decided you'd have other uses."

A chill went down my spine. I didn't have a choice but to help him. Well, until I knew Milla escaped or Max had traced us to the warehouse.

"If you know the software is active, then why haven't you implemented the program? Any trained analyst can operate the components."

"I may not have your level of intelligence, but I am hardly stupid. I know all about how the wrong order of activation can corrupt the system. You are here to make sure everything runs smoothly."

"If you'd done your research, you'd know I don't work well

under pressure. What if I accidentally damage something?" It was a long shot, but maybe he'd believe that.

"You may hate public speaking and socializing, but you are renowned for working best in situations of high stress. If it wasn't for your performance at Def Con, we would have never crossed paths."

Until this day, I'd never regretted attending that stupid conference. No. I shook the thought from my mind. Without the Def Con challenge I wouldn't have my company or have met Max.

"What if I refuse?"

"We have ways of making people cooperate. Plus we know your weakness."

"And that is?" I retorted.

"Your family, including your very hurt friend downstairs."

"You're a bastard, Christof. Does abusing a helpless woman get you off?"

His eyes crinkled at the sides. "You have a lot of spirit, Mrs. Dane. I hate to disappoint you, but I wasn't the one who abused your friend or Ms. Erickson. That honor belongs to my associate, Mr. Brady, and his companion. I may not enjoy his type of kink, but who am I to deny him his vice?"

Fury filled me. These men represented the scum of the earth, and Christof was no different. "If you think I'm going to help, you're out of your mind. You might as well kill me, because I won't do it."

"Shut that bitch up." Jacob stalked over and slapped me across the face, propelling me to the ground.

My vision blurred and my eye started to swell. The continuous throbbing in my head dulled the pain in my face and wrist.

"Get control of yourself, Brady, before I lose my temper and teach you a lesson." Christof commanded in a cold, emotionless tone. He crouched down in front of me, extended his hand, and helped me to stand.

"She's of no value, Vladimir. Let's be rid of the two whores. I'm sure Jane can figure it out." This man had the nerve to believe Jane would help him after what he'd done. The stupid prick.

"Stay out of this, Brady. I have not asked for, nor do I require, your counsel."

"He's right, I'm of no value. Please listen to him. Let Milla and me go."

"I cannot do that. You're priceless to me, Mrs. Dane. I've had plans for you for many years. I initially thought to lure you in as part of my team. You see, I'd rather have you work for me than against me."

He ran a finger down the side of my face and throat, and I cringed. "Sorry, but you're not my type."

"I take no offense, *myshka*. I'm a very confident man with no shortage of women to warm my bed. Having you as my mistress would have made things easier, but we can't get everything we want—although soon that will be remedied."

I glared, not voicing a response.

"I must say"—he peered at Jacob—"I was very upset when Mr. Brady almost killed you in his overzealous need to remove you from his dear friend's life. Lucky for him, he only intended for you to miscarry; otherwise, he wouldn't be standing before us today."

"What?" I gasped as my mind spun, and I clenched my fists under the table. Nausea engulfed my stomach and I inhaled deeply, trying to keep my mind focused.

He was behind my babies' murder. It wasn't a random act of violence. My heart screamed, remembering the attack. There was a special place in hell for men like him.

"As a present to you, I took care of the man responsible for your pain. I don't tolerate interference with my plans. You should be happy Dave died a painful death."

Bile rose in my throat. "But he didn't. That fucker over there," I gestured with my head to the left. "Greg is the one who attacked me, Dave was the driver. He wanted to sell my babies."

Christof's mouth tightened and his eyes pierced Greg's, who shifted back and forth where he stood, uncomfortable with the scrutiny he was getting.

"I see. Well, I'll deal with that now."

He motioned to his guards, and they shot Greg through the head.

"The only things I hate more than disobedience are disloyalty and lies."

I stood frozen. My tormentor was dead. But I felt nothing, no relief, no closure, nothing.

"Now that the unpleasantness of your past is resolved, let's get down to business." Christof motioned for me to join him under the canopy where a table was set.

I followed in a numb haze. The realization hit me; I was never leaving this place alive. The stairwell door came into view as I approached the table, and I prayed Milla found an escape.

I sat across from Christof and stared at my plate. I hadn't eaten since my flight home, but the mere notion of food soured my stomach.

"Please eat," Christof said politely, but the edge of command lay underneath. "Once we're finished with lunch and you have a chance to freshen up, we'll get to work." He regarded Jacob as he approached. "Why are you still here? You should be in the lab preparing for our guest."

"She's not a guest," Jacob countered.

Christof dropped his fork and jumped up. Jacob instinctively stepped back, but Christof caught him by the collar. "You are alive today only because of our mutually beneficial agreement. Don't make me regret our association."

I turned my head away when Jacob's gaze caught mine. The hatred emanating from him frightened me. If Christof didn't kill me, Jacob would.

At that moment, one of the guards ran up the stairs in a panic. "Sir, we have a situation."

"What is it?" he hissed without releasing his grip on Jacob.

"Ms. Castra has escaped."

CHAPTER THIRTY

W ho was watching her?" Christof shoved Jacob away and glared at the guard.

Relief washed over me. *Get help*, mera behna.

"She was unconscious, sir, and we didn't expect her to wake."

Christof picked up his drink, swallowed deep, and then pinned Jacob with an angry stare. "Brady, your skills are becoming rusty. When I say make sure she can't inconvenience us without killing her, that means make it so she isn't strong enough to walk."

Jacob pulled out his phone and scanned the screen. "Let me find her. I put a tracker on her in case this scenario arose."

Shit, where would he have put it? No, Milla was too smart to let herself be tracked. I'd taught her how to debug herself. I prayed she was strong enough to find it and get it off her.

"Oh, Arya, don't look surprised. I do know my way around technology, no matter what you may believe. How do you think I acquired all the passwords of the MDC team?"

"By seducing an innocent woman," I retorted.

Jacob yanked my head back with my ponytail, practically tipping my chair over and spoke through gritted teeth. "You're nothing but a whore. What would you know about real intelligence? I think I'll take a few hours in private and teach you true discipline and then find out if the pussy Max has permanently attached himself to is worth the price."

Bile rose in my throat.

"Release her, Brady, or I'll lodge a bullet in your head."

Jacob visibly shuddered and released his hold on me, forcing my chair forward again. Lucky for me, I caught myself with my good hand, before my head hit my plate and the food on it.

"Arya, please finish your meal before it becomes cold. I think I will have a word in private with my associate."

Jacob and Christof moved to another cabana area on the edge of the roof. Picking up my fork, I went through the motions of eating without tasting any of my food.

I had to think of a plan to get out of the building.

Fifteen minutes passed and Christof hadn't returned. Curiosity got the best of me and I peered toward the tent. The shadows of the men in discussion glowed through the thin material of the coverings. Then a shot rang out, and one figure fell to the ground. Christof strolled in my direction as if he hadn't a care in the world.

"Please excuse me for keeping you waiting." He smiled and ran a finger down my swollen eye, *tsk*ed, and sat next to me. "I am happy to inform you that my business relationship with Mr. Brady has been severed."

I remained still and peered out over the harbor. In a less than an hour, two people had lost their lives, and no one was fazed but me. Max was right; I hadn't considered the ramifications of being the puzzle master of the software.

"I see you have lost your appetite. Understandable, considering the events of the past few moments. Boris will take you to your chamber to rest. Then we will reconvene in the basement lab." He checked his watch. "Let's meet at three thirty. That will give you a little over one hour to freshen up."

I nodded and moved without thought toward the guard.

"Arya," Christof called, and I paused at the door to the stairwell. "No harm will come to you. You are more valuable to me alive than dead."

Two hours later, I sat in front of the terminals confiscated from my lab, hoping and praying my plan would execute without incident.

"Are you ready to begin, Arya?"

"Yes, but having a gun trained on me makes me nervous. If you wouldn't mind having your guard point that thing somewhere else, I'd feel a little more confident about my task."

With a nod from Christof, the thug lowered his weapon and observed us.

His hand trailed down my back. "He doesn't approve of my fascination with you." It took all my willpower not to cringe. "Now that we are here without the presence of Mr. Brady, I will admit you were too good for the likes of him. I think what he disliked the most about you was that you weren't impressed by your friends' wealth. Too bad he didn't know you were an heiress in your own right."

I slanted my head and narrowed my eyes.

"Come now, we all know of your inheritance from your maternal grandmother, but maybe you didn't know about your father's family."

I pushed back from the computer, folded my arms across my body, and glared at Christof. "What the hell are you talking about?"

A chilling chuckle left his mouth. "Don't tell me you didn't know that your father was one of the estranged sons of Minesh Rey?"

"Of course I knew that. He disinherited my father and uncle when they left their family's business. All the wealth went to the younger brother, who followed in my grandfather's footsteps."

Why did he care about my family tree? Yes, I had money in my background, but none of that had made any difference while growing up. Aunt Elana did well by me, and that was all that mattered.

"Your disgust with your family's money is the reason you are unique. We come from similar backgrounds. I think if you open yourself to the possibilities, you and I could have a very lucrative and prosperous future."

He sank to the ground in front of my chair and threaded his hand into my hair. "I'll have to train you to favor me with the same gaze you gave Max. I am sure in time you'll learn to care about me as well."

Milla, please have found help.

"Sir," the guard interrupted, "I think we need to continue on our task. Our window of launch is limited."

Releasing his grip on my head, Christof stepped back. "Right as usual, Olaf. Arya, we will continue this discussion later. Now it's time to get to work."

I bit my lip and stared at the monitor. Inhaling a few deep breaths, I steadied my mind and typed in code. From the corner of my vision, I spotted the cameras trained on me. Shit, he was recording every move I made.

Line by line I entered commands that corresponded with the ones for the actual program. No one would detect anything was amiss, but once launched, the program would operate a different system altogether. Sweat trickled down my spine as I prayed this farce would work.

My heart jumped as a blip of code appeared on my screen, using the language I'd taught Milla to relay secret messages when we were in school. My eyes teared, but I held them back.

Mil, are you okay?

This is Lex. Mil's on her way to the hospital. We know where you are. Stay on the system as long as possible.

Is Max safe?

He's fine. We're going to get you out.

Lex, he's not going to release me.

Yes, he is. Type the code. We're monitoring the system. Act natural. I'll let you know when to go live.

My hands shook.

"How is the process going?"

"Fine," I snapped. "Considering I'm coding something that requires four analysts with only one useable hand."

"I have complete confidence in your abilities. I also have my own programmer watching you, so we'll know if you are accessing areas you shouldn't be."

Obviously, he wasn't as smart as Christof expected, or he'd have already notified everyone that I'd hacked the grid.

"Then why isn't he activating the system?"

He ignored my snarky comment. "Perhaps it's time for refreshment. Here." He thrust a glass of water in my hand. "Drink, you're flushed. I don't want you to become ill, and I can see your temper is piqued."

Stay calm, Arya.

Taking the glass, I sipped the cool liquid that resembled water, but tasted nothing like it. "What did you give me?"

"A small stimulant to give you some energy as well as a tonic to ease some of the discomfort from the beating you took earlier."

Oh well, what the hell. I drank the liquid down. My body hurt too much to refuse any pain relief.

After handing him the empty cup, I asked, "Aren't you a sadist? Wouldn't my discomfort please you?"

"No, my dear. I abhor abuse for the sole purpose of abuse. What happened to Ms. Castra was a shame, but necessary. When we play, you'll learn the difference."

"You contradicted yourself."

"I guess I did. You are quite intelligent. I can't help but anticipate our future together," he hummed. "Now back to work, *dorogoy moya*. Then later we will have our first visit to the dungeon." He kissed the top of my head and sat on the sofa behind me.

"I am not your dear. I belong to someone else."

"Tsk-tsk. Such spirit."

I fixed my gaze to the screen and resumed typing. For the next three hours, I coordinated the codes for each part of the software so they would run without overlapping the programing and causing it to crash. A few more strokes and the program would activate.

The screen blipped again. *Launch*.

"I'm ready, Christof. Once I hit the final key the program will be equipped."

"Magnificent." He moved behind me, leaning close my ear. "Call me Vladimir. Especially since soon we'll become more intimately acquainted."

The hell we would.

"Please do the honors."

"Why not." He reached over and pressed the Enter key.

The system activated, and the program showed the locations of all bases in the world, including unlisted centers. Too bad he didn't know most of the information was false.

"Wonderful. Now we'll celebrate." He turned to Olaf. "Prepare the jet. My guest and I will be leaving soon."

Olaf nodded his head and opened the door, but the second he entered the hallway gunshots sounded.

Christof grabbed me out of my chair and hissed into my ear, "What the fuck have you done, *myshka*?"

I panted, "I'm not your little mouse."

"You are coming with me." He forced me through the door and into the hallway, drew a gun from the back of his waist, and hoisted me up the stairs.

I stumbled, gripping the railing for balance. My head spun from the drink Christof had given me. "Let me go. I'm of no use to you now. You have the recording and your software is active. Please." I lost my balance again and fell.

"*Der'mo*, you are drunk." He threw me over his shoulder and ascended the stairs.

My head roiled from all the movement, and my stomach lurched. Shouts sounded all around me, and I bobbed up and down on Christof's back.

Suddenly, the stairs collapsed and the world went black.

CHAPTER THIRTY-ONE

Arya, baby, please come back to me. I need you."

Max!

His voice echoed in my mind, but my body refused to respond. Every inch of me seemed permeated with pain and screamed for relief.

Milla. I had to find her.

Please, someone make the beeping stop. My head can't take anymore.

"Nurse, she's crying. Help her!"

"Sir, you have to stay calm. This is a good sign. It means she's waking."

"What about the swelling?"

"I wish I could tell you, but it's too soon to know. She's only been out of surgery for a few hours."

The beeping grew louder. If it didn't stop, I was going to lose my mind.

"Sir, I need you to hold her down. Her blood pressure is too high. She's having a seizure."

"Save her, before you do anything else!"

"I'm paging the doctor."

No, I'm awake. Please, someone make that noise stop.

"Max you have to get out of here. If not to run your business, at least for a shower. Arya would want you to take care of yourself."

"What am I going to do, Lex? It's been three days since the surgery."

Three days? Surgery? Oh God, the explosion. The last thing I remembered before the world went dark was Christof running up the stairs.

"I don't know." Lex exhaled. "All we can do is wait and pray."

"I can't lose her," Max sobbed with his head resting on my stomach. "I've barely gotten her back."

Don't cry, I'm here.

"You're not. None of us are losing her. She's strong, plus she's got something else to live for."

Max's hand caressed my stomach. Why was he doing that? *Oh God, I couldn't be. No, it's probably something else.*

"Arya is a champion fighter, both our girls are. It's taken all my effort to keep Mil home."

Max's head lifted off me. "I'm sorry, man. I haven't asked about Milla. I've been so wrapped up with Arya."

"She's doing better, but she's pissed as hell. She hates feeling helpless. That fucker did a number on her. If Jacob weren't dead, I'd be the first in line to kill him."

What did he do? I wish this fucking body would move.

"How could I have been so wrong about him? Why didn't I listen to Arya?"

"Hell, we've known him since we were kids. His warped sense of entitlement got the best of him. I can't believe he'd gotten himself involved with Christof."

"Well, he made his grave and now he has to lie in it." Max released a deep breath. "How are you handling the invasion of the Castras?"

"As well as can be expected when you're the nonpracticing Catholic lover of their wild child daughter and a member of a family they can't stand."

A knock sounded on the door. "May I come in, gentlemen?"

"General Ansgar, what can I do for you? As you see, we aren't prepared for company." Max's fingers feathered across my immobile forehead.

"I understand, but this is a matter of national security. We need to speak with you." He paused. "Actually this concerns all of you, specifically your women."

"Right now our priority is to protect them. Making life easier for you is the least of our worries," Lex interjected.

"Under the circumstances, I expected your hostility, but without your assistance we cannot safeguard any of you from future aggression."

A resigned sigh filled the room.

"Take a seat, General. Lex and I will answer what we can, but our women, as you put it, tend to march to the beat of their own drums. If I had any say, they wouldn't have become involved with your project in the first place."

"Duly noted. I ran into Elana Rey a few moments ago. She's already warned me not to upset you." He chuckled. "For such a wisp of a woman she isn't easily intimidated."

"That's an understatement."

I warmed, thinking of Aunt El and the Mama Bear side of her personality that would destroy anyone who thought of harming her family.

"Let me get to the point. We need to know if she activated the software and where the data is stored. Every attempt to contact Ms. Castra has been hindered."

Lex grunted but didn't comment.

Relief flooded me. Lex would protect Mil the same way he'd done for me in the past.

"Our teams have scoured all of your labs, but then again Ms. Rey is a security expert."

"Mrs. Dane," Max corrected.

"Yes, Mrs. Dane. Would either of you gentlemen have any idea where your wife or Ms. Castra would have sent data collected from the virus they planted in the copycat software?"

"No sir, I'm sorry. I understand your sense of urgency, but until Arya wakes up none of us will know."

Shit, this meant Christof was alive. Damn, this wasn't over. I willed my body to cooperate. I could give the general his information, and then he'd leave me to recover with my husband.

"What about you, Mr. Duncan? Do you have any information that could help us?"

Please keep your mouth shut, Lex.

"No, and before you ask, there will be no access to Milla.

She's very fragile right now and has been through too much. I won't have you upsetting her."

He was dead if Mil ever found out he said those words about her. Though I understood his need to keep her safe.

Wait, if he described her as fragile, that meant she wasn't well.

"Gentleman, I recognize your desire to shield your women, but with Vladimir Christof free, they are both in grave danger. This is the second time Mrs. Dane and Ms. Castra have hindered his plans. He won't take it lightly."

"Security measures are in place, General," Max stated coolly as he continued to hold my hand.

"I see there is no point in pushing either of you any further." His footsteps echoed to the door. "But if you think of anything, please let us know."

The door shut, but both Max and Lex remained quiet.

After a few minutes Max broke the silence. "I don't think he believed a word we said. You know he isn't going to let this go. Ari told me how he got each of you to agree in the first place."

"I'm already on it. Our contacts at the agency have been scanning the data since our girl genius activated the program."

"So why the secrecy with the general?" Max's grip tightened on my hand.

"Because there's suspicion that someone from the general's group tipped off Christof."

"Fucking hell, Lex. Were you going to let me know any of this?"

"Arya thought the less you knew, the safer you'd be. This way you wouldn't be lying when questioned. I'm a former gangster's grandson. I've trained from birth to skate the truth.

You, on the other hand, need lessons. Especially when playing with the big dogs."

"Can the jokes right now, Duncan."

Lex ignored the reprimand. "You've been under surveillance since the kidnapping. All of us have, but some of us know how to maneuver around tails. Plus, letting them keep tabs on you allowed me to transfer the data to the right hands."

Lex and his connections. A small twinge of a smile tugged at my lips, but the rest of me remained immobile. This sucked.

"I swear to God, as soon as she awakes I am going to wring her neck. If I didn't know how much she loved me, I'd think she didn't trust me."

Lips brushed my forehead, helping me conjure the strength to speak. "Are you—" my throat burned from dryness "—are you going to kiss me every time you want to choke me?"

"Arya, baby. You're awake." Max sobbed, gathering me in his arms. He ran more kisses over my face and held me to his chest. His body trembled against mine, and his love for me radiated into my being.

Why did I ever think to keep us apart?

My eyes still weighted heavily, but I managed to open them a little. The light pierced my vision and I winced, closing them again.

"Rest and take it slow," he whispered against my hair, rocking me back and forth. "God, Ari, I thought I'd lost you. We all did."

"Not me," interjected Lex. "You're resilient. I've always known that."

"Shut up, Lex. You're such a kiss-ass."

I tried laughing at their relieved banter but grimaced at the contraction of my abs. "Holy shit. Everything hurts like a bitch."

"And she's back." Max chuckled and his grip loosened. "What are we going to tell our kiddos about your potty mouth?"

I opened my eyes, ignoring the discomfort and stared in confusion. "What?"

Max gave me a sheepish grin. "We'll discuss that in a minute. Right now we need to talk about keeping secrets from your husband."

EPILOGUE

This celibate thing is pissing me off, Carm. I'm not going to break. It has been three months since the explosion."

"Stop right there. I do not—let me repeat—I do not want to hear about my brother's sex life."

"Well, deal. Milla's off in Italy with her family, and I won't risk having her superconservative mother listening to our conversations."

"What about Lex?"

"He's nursing a broken heart. I'm not adding to his pain." Sometimes I wanted to strangle my stupid best friend.

"Hey, I have a broken heart, too."

"That doesn't count. You did the breaking up for stupid-ass reasons, something you and Mil have in common."

"Fine," Carmen groaned through the phone. "Here's my advice."

"Okay, I'm listening."

"Seduce him."

"What?"

"You heard me. Max is freaked out about harming you or the babies."

My heart warmed at the mention of my miracles. Max was right. *Virtually impossible* meant "slightly possible." "He'd keep me wrapped in a bubble if I'd let him. You wouldn't believe the argument we had when I told him I was going back to the office."

"I can imagine. You told me the doctors cleared you for all activity. I'm assuming sex is included?"

"Yes. She doesn't see any restrictions until close to the end of the second trimester. With the scars on my uterus, she thinks I shouldn't risk too much activity after twenty-three weeks, but until then, I'm home free."

"Good. Then go put on one of those outfits and knock his socks off. I'm not going to tell you what to do or say, because that's gross."

I leaned against the windowsill and gazed out at the grounds of Max's estate. I guessed it was my estate as well. "What if I fuck it up?"

"In the words of our MIA Milla, you're supposed to fuck it up, with an emphasis on *fuck*."

I groaned. "Not helping."

Carmen laughed. "Relax. Enjoy yourself. Make sure to get as much as you can, because you're in for a lengthy drought in a few months."

"Yes, yes, I know. Love you."

"Love you, too."

I set the phone down and checked my watch. I had exactly

one hour before Max would be home. Thank goodness, I'd given the staff the weekend off. I wouldn't want any of them seeing me running around the house like a crazy person.

I pressed my palm against the identification plate, and the playroom's wooden door unlocked. My heartbeat accelerated, but I couldn't understand why. This space wasn't taboo or forbidden, but I still felt I was breaking some kind of rule.

I strolled into the dressing area of the playroom and went straight for the corset ensemble Max had selected for our night at the club. I slid over the soft, silky material and closed my eyes as the image of lying across the bench popped into my head. My mouth watered at the memory of Max, bare-chested, administering my punishment. I gasped as my core contracted, shaking me from my daydream.

I glanced at the clock; I'd lingered in the same spot for twenty minutes, leaving me only forty to get ready.

I dressed as quickly as possible, but I kept the ties around my stomach loose. My swollen breasts spilled over the tops of the bra cups as I clipped my stockings, making me laugh. I very nearly felt like a buxom burlesque dancer with these melons.

I moved over to the vanity, removed my makeup, since Max preferred me with a natural face, and released my hair from its bun. Giving myself one last survey, I slipped on my shoes and walked back into the playroom. As gracefully as possible with my growing belly keeping me off balance, I lowered myself onto the sapphire-blue kneeling pillow.

I flinched as the beep of the lock alerted me to Max's arrival. He was early.

Please let this work.

I lowered my head and waited for Max to approach with my heart close to beating out of my chest. His breath hitched when he entered the room and my confidence increased.

"What're you doing?" he questioned with a gruff voice.

"Waiting, Sir." I kept my head down.

He approached and traced his fingers down the back of my neck. Goose bumps prickled my skin. "Why?"

"Because you need this." My lips trembled. "I need this."

He released a sharp groan. "Do you realize you're trying to top me? You forget. *I* decide when we use this room, not you."

His harsh tone cut deep, and my shoulders slumped in response as tears burned the back of my eyes and throat.

Rejected.

Not looking toward him, I rose, filled with resignation. "I'll go change."

I was already moving toward the dressing room when he grasped my arm. "Baby, don't cry."

I struggled. "Please Max, let me go. I feel humiliated enough."

He gathered me against his chest. "I'm never letting you go," he whispered. "This isn't how I planned for this weekend to start." He leaned over to the counter, while keeping me in his hold. "Now open this box before you jump to any more conclusions."

"What is it?"

"Something I bought after a conversation I had with Dr. Morris."

"Why would you need to talk to my obstetrician?"

"Arya, open the box," he commanded, not hiding his frustration.

"Fine." I took the box from his hands, set it on the table, and peeked inside. "Oh."

"That's right, oh."

A delicate pink lace-and-satin bustled-back slip with garter sat nested in tissue. He hadn't rejected me.

I'm an idiot. Stupid pregnancy hormones. I moved toward him. "I'm—"

"Shhh." Max placed a gentle kiss on my lips, silencing me. "I don't want anything too constrictive against your body." He stepped back, shaking his head. "This won't do."

"Max!" I gasped as he ripped my bustier from top to bottom.

He caressed my back, trailing his fingers over my spine and around to the slight swell of my belly. I leaned into his touch, no longer ashamed of my scars.

"I love your naked body, especially these." He cupped my heavy breasts. "I've been dying to taste them." He licked the tips and drew back.

A moaned protest escaped my mouth.

"Go put on your present while I prepare your punishment."

I stared into his desire-glazed emerald eyes. "What did I do?"

He arched a brow, gave me a slight smile, and pointed to the pillow. "For thinking you could top me into playing."

It worked, didn't it?

He walked over to the cabinet, slid a drawer open, and extracted his instrument for discipline.

My breath hitched as excitement ran through my body and wetness pooled between my legs.

The slap of the paddle against his palm echoed throughout the room. "You wanted to play, Mrs. Dane. Let's play."

Want to know what happens next for Milla and Lex?
Please see the next page for a preview of
Book Two!

Thirty minutes later, I came out of the shower and examined my reflection in the vanity mirror. Hazel eyes speckled with green stared back at me. Good genes gave me a more youthful appearance than most twenty-nine-year-olds, but the last few months had taken their toll on my body.

I shifted my hips from side to side and grimaced. The sexy curves I'd become notorious for were a thing of the past. I'd lost so much weight that I no longer resembled the wild-child heiress of one of the world's greatest shipping fortunes. The outspoken and independent woman, on whom the tabloids loved to report, had disappeared.

The fire is still in there Milla. You just need to find it.

Who was I kidding? I had never been the girl everyone believed. My forthright manner was the only true aspect of all the reports. What would the world think if they knew I'd had only one lover my entire life and not the numerous suitors everyone assumed I'd had, or that I hadn't engaged in any of the scandalous things I'd given the press to print?

The only people who knew the real me were my best friends, Arya and Carmen, and even they didn't know me as well as…I closed my eyes and inhaled.

Lex.

He understood who I was and accepted me, flaws and all.

My phone beeped, reminding me I was already late and had spent too much time reflecting. I hurried to the closet, pulled out the couture gown the tailor had refitted earlier in the morning, and dressed. I moved to the oversized vanity in the bathroom and sat down to apply my makeup.

"A little concealer will hide those depressing circles, Mil.

Let's sex it up for our last gala in Italy," I mumbled to myself.

I loved my cosmetics, clothes, and glamour. It wasn't as if I couldn't live without it, but it was so much fun putting on a new shade of eye shadow to enhance an outfit. Tonight I'd use my products to help cover the sadness and to pretend the past six months had never happened.

Emotionally broken or not, I had to put on my big-girl panties and represent the firm Arya and I had worked our asses off to build from scratch.

I smiled to myself. Two girls from completely different backgrounds became best friends and created the world's first female-founded billion-dollar technology-development firm. Ditching high school was the only thing on our agendas the day we met, and now we couldn't imagine a life without each other.

As I finished the final touches on my face, I realized I hadn't slipped on the one piece of jewelry I always wore somewhere on my body.

I walked into my room and toward the childhood picture of me with my siblings, which was positioned on the far wall of my bedroom. The mischievous smirks we displayed paid tribute to the love we shared. I tapped the side of the portrait and it shifted to the side, revealing a safe tucked into the wall. I disengaged the lock with my fingerprint and opened the door. Slowly I pulled out a purple velvet pouch. I loosened the string and tipped the contents into my palm. A banded ring in platinum with marquise and round, brilliant-cut diamonds fell out.

I sighed, clutching the ring in my fist, and held it to my heart.

What we have is special, Milla. I won't touch you until you wear my ring and belong to me completely.

At nineteen, I held no comprehension of the great significance of those words, but I had taken the ring and made the vows. Now at twenty-nine, and with six months of reflection and healing, I understood the depth of what those words meant to him and how much hurt I caused him over the years by withholding what we'd shared from everyone.

He'd made no secret that he wanted a very public relationship, not just a private one, but I was too selfish and enjoyed playing the rebel too much to care.

A shiver crept up my body and I shuddered as a hiccup escaped my lips.

I had finally agreed to wear the ring at all times when my world fell apart. He deserved better than me.

What is wrong with you, Milla? Where has the confident, no-holds-barred girl gone?

I shook my head, trying to clear another rebuke from my mind. I couldn't lie to myself. I had to find that girl again. I knew she was hiding somewhere deep inside. Besides, if she didn't make an appearance soon, Arya was going to kick my ass trying to get her back.

My phone ran with the "Jingle Bells" tune and I squealed. Speak of the devil. Well not really speak, but think. I rushed to answer it.

"Hello."

"Hey there, *mera behna*. I miss you."

My heart lit up at the sound of my best friend's voice and the standard Hindi greeting she gave me.

Arya Rey Dane was my sister in everything but blood. I quickly strung the ring on a thin platinum chain and slid it around my neck, making sure to hide it under the high collar of the gown.

"What's wrong?"

How would she know that I was feeling sad?

"Huh? What makes you think something is up?"

"Well, for one you responded to my question with a question. Second, your voice gave it away. Third, you didn't answer me with your haughty Italian heiress greeting of '*Pronto*.' You said 'hello.'"

I never used that phrase and she knew it. It was a running joke between us. It was our way of telling all the pretentious Italians from us ruffians.

"Yes, yes, Miss Genius I. Q. I forgot my Italian etiquette. I've been hanging out with your half-Indian ass too long."

"My ass is huge right now, and you would know that if you were home. And don't say we video-conference, because it isn't the same. I need the deliverer of my chocolate croissants here in Boston with me. Max doesn't go to the same bakery as you do."

I couldn't help but smile at the joy hidden around the whining I heard in her words. She finally was going to have the family she'd wanted all her life.

She'd spent five years building herself up following the deterioration of her relationship and devastating loss of her babies. Finally, she had her fairy tale. After reuniting with the love of her life, she was expecting twins again.

"I know, *bella*. I will be home to see the giant whale you have become with those boys."

"I miss you. *He* misses you."

My breath hitched. "Why would Max miss me? Isn't he your husband?"

"Don't be a smart-ass." Her voice grew stern. "You know who I mean."

"I know, Ari. I just don't know what to say to him or what to do to make it better. How is he?"

"How do you expect? He's been with the same woman for a decade and she left him. Something we still haven't discussed, by the way."

I winced. I'd avoided any conversation regarding my relationship with Lex Duncan. Especially the part where I'd never told her he was the Dom I'd been with for years. Or that he was even more then my Dom.

"Is he…is he…?"

Do I really want to ask this question?

"No, he isn't seeing anyone, you moron. For some reason he loves you and takes the commitment he made to you seriously."

Relief flooded me. "Pregnancy is making you bitchy."

"Ya, well let me count the ways I am pissed off at the whole lot of you. First, my two best friends lied to me for years, pretending to see different people when they were together the whole time. Surrounding me with overwhelming sexual tension and making me think it was love unfulfilled."

I cringed. "Yeah, well, there were personal reasons for all of that."

"Second, when I found out they were a couple, they left out a tiny detail that they were more than Dominant and submissive."

"Well you see—"

"Shut up. I'm not done."

"Sorry I'll zip it."

"Third, my other best friend and sister-in-law, Carmen, has become a complete workaholic and has no time for me. Fourth, I don't have you here to keep me sane while I'm on bed rest and prevent me from killing my overprotective husband. And fifth—" Arya sniffed and her voice cracked "—I'm scared out of my mind that I will lose these babies, too."

My heart ached for her. She'd been through so much, and by some miracle she was pregnant again. "Don't cry, *mia sorella*. I'll be home soon."

"I'm sorry. I'm just a big, pregnant, hormonal, fucking mess."

I shook my head. "Language! Max is going to kill you if the first words those kids utter are *fuck* or *shit*. For someone so proper you have the mouth of a sailor."

"Whatever," she grumbled. "Try being ten thousand months pregnant and confined to a stupid bed."

I laughed. "You know you love every minute of it."

"I do, but I don't have you to share it with," she whined.

The weight of the previous conversation shifted. Thank goodness, no more talk about Lex or me.

"I'll be home soon and come massage your fat feet and keep you company until my nephews come into the world."

"I'll hold you to it. By the way, do me a favor and tell Max that pregnant women can run companies, too."

"Oh no, I am not getting in the middle of that one with a ten-foot pole."

"Well someone needs to keep on top of our company."

I hope she hadn't meant that the way it came out. "I may be here in Italy, but that doesn't mean I'm not doing my share of the work. I did negotiate the extension of the software contract, if you recall."

"I wasn't referring to you, grumpy. I'm talking about my shit."

I wasn't the grumpy one!

"Ari, the R & D department is in great hands. Relax. Jane has it under control. You're lucky Max let her transfer to our ranks. She was the best technology officer Max and Carmen ever had."

"I know. Jane is the only one I'd trust with my research. I'm just ready get out of bed."

"Enjoy it while you can. I've seen the terror my brothers' kids put their mamas through, and I think my sisters-in-law would pray for a day of confinement to a bed. Besides—" Someone banging on the bedroom door interrupted my thought. "Hold on, Ari." I pulled the phone away from my face and shouted toward the door, "I'll be right there."

"As I was saying, my sister-in—" The banging persisted, even louder. "Uhhh! It's probably my mother, angry with me for some new infraction. Ari, I'll call you back. Let me see what's going on."

"Don't forget to call."

"I promise I won't."

"You always say that. It'll be next week before I get to talk to you again."

She had me there. I was notorious for forgetting to call. "Love you, *bella*."

"You too."

I hung up the phone, marched to the door, and pulled it open. My very annoyed and windblown sister-in-law, Leena, glared at me.

"Took you long enough to answer the door."

I scowled back at her. "What the hell is going on? Is there a fire that you tried to break my door down?"

"Milla, you have to be ready." Leena rubbed her temples and tried to steady her breath. "I ran up here as soon as I found out."

This probably had something to do with Mama. It always had something to do with Mama.

"Okay, you're scaring me. Please tell me what's going on." I glanced at the wall clock behind me. "I'm already late for the gala."

Leena pushed around me and sat on my bed. "He's here."

Okay, that's a bit dramatic. "Who's here?"

She opened her phone and showed me a text message:

Please be informed that I have just arrived in Milan. I will spend a few days here and plan to bring my WIFE back home with me. Make sure she is ready to leave.

"Oh shit."

About the Author

Sienna Snow's love of reading started at a very young age with *Beezus and Ramona*. By the time she entered high school, a girlfriend had introduced her to Bertrice Small and Jude Deveraux, and an avid romance reader was born.

She writes sexy romance, some with a lot of heat and spice, and others with a bit of fantasy. Her characters represent strong women of different cultures and backgrounds who seek love through unique circumstances.

When she is not writing, traveling, or reading, she spends her time with her husband and two children.

You can learn more at:
SiennaSnow.com
Twitter @sienna_snow
Facebook.com/authorsiennasnow